Mr. Smith Who Works The Front Desk
an NPC novel

by Jade Griffin

To family, present or missing, biological or table pals, near or far. Love you.

Special thanks to Beedoo! and Heather Rogerson for their prompt edits and attention to detail, plot, and substance! Invaluable!

WARNING – The following novel contains spoilers having to do with the 1920s *Amor Fati* campaign series of Call of Cthulhu tabletop roleplaying games, written by this author. If you have any intention of playing *Ebon Roots*, *Hound Of Fate*, or *Portion Of Vengeance*, please do so before reading this novel. Or enjoy the spoils. Your choice.

What is an NPC? It stands for non-player character in the tabletop gaming world. My NPC series is dedicated to those characters who help out players in the adventures I write but stay silent once everyone goes home. They deserve their stories told. After all, each person is the main character of their own story.

Italics – The Japanese words used in this novel are all italicized as a style choice, due to what it meant to Mr. Smith to connect with something idolized in his youth. On the word *aoi*, which typically means "blue", it was a very fitting nickname for Mr. Smith from Naonori's perspective.

Suggested Playlist –
A Rose in the Devil's Garden – Melancholic Piano and Cello – Dark Academia Study Music
https://www.youtube.com/watch?v=v4pzLNZAcc8

Mr. Smith Who Works The Front Desk by Jade Griffin

Credits

Cover art by Jade Griffin.

This publication contains some references and portrayals of real places and events reinterpreted within a fictional set of circumstances as part of a grief horror adventure. Some historical and outdated viewpoints are utilized for realism but are not the opinion of the author. No offense to real individuals or locations, past or present, is intended.

The Great Race of Yith and the Yithian people are not my creation but are from H.P. Lovecraft's *Shadow Out Of Time* and are in public domain.

No portion of this or any of the author's works may be used for, at, in, on, under, by, or any other prepositions arriving at being associated with artificial intelligence (AI).

Copyright © 2024 Jade Griffin

All rights reserved.

Mr. Smith Who Works The Front Desk by Jade Griffin

Chapters

1891, NOVEMBER 2	1
1891, NOVEMBER 3	21
1891, NOVEMBER 5	32
1891, NOVEMBER 6	42
1891, DECEMBER 4	46
1892, MARCH 12	52
1892, APRIL 13	56
1892, DECEMBER 20	64
1893, FEBRUARY 8	70
1893, FEBRUARY 9	108
1893, MAY 24	116
1893, MAY 25	128
1893, MAY 29	143
1893, MAY 30	150
1893, JUNE 14	163
1893, AUGUST 26	166
1893, AUGUST 27	175
1893, AUGUST 28	180
1893, AUGUST 29	195
1893, AUGUST 30	211
1893, AUGUST 31	242
1893, SEPTEMBER 3	252
1893, SEPTEMBER 4	255
1893, SEPTEMBER 11-12	267
1893, SEPTEMBER 16	292

Mr. Smith Who Works The Front Desk by Jade Griffin

1891, November 2

An ill feeling slammed his guts hard, and not for being thrust through countless back doors of time and space. That happened to him since just after his sixth birthday. Normally – and it still aggrieved him to feel any of this was normal – he suffered through the brief vertigo and tried to gain his bearings wherever and whenever they shoved him. Certainly not this time, tossed so unceremoniously and naked into a grassy field in what felt like a chilly autumn night. Naked was also normal, unfortunately. But, in their rush, Heebs and Jeebs did not make it a gentle transfer. His body ached stiff and hot, discordant with the chill and the sick feeling. That stomach-churning sensation, despite fleeing from things supposedly worse than them, hit as a hard reminder: that he remained stuck with the two beings which, for the past unknown number of years, used him as bait to lure particularly lucky people near so the damn device on his wrist could suck out their potential.

It always made him feel sick – the twisting gut feeling of a person's potential draining away by that fucking luck-vampiric device they phased onto his left wrist. **They** were the true vampires and he hated them for using him to drain people. He hated himself even more for not being able to break away from the bastards. Tried explaining that people needed to stay away from him, that he was bad luck or that there were monsters inside him. Nearly accurate, and it saved them half the time, kept them away from him. The other half… Those people were drained. Sometimes just a little before they felt it and were smart enough to get away. Others weren't so lucky. Once your luck runs out, you die. So, yeah, his captors were luck vampires.

He felt them, pacing slowly in the device bound to his wrist. That's where they hid right before shoving him out of their pocket dimension where they stored all their "food", a blank nexus he'd **not** called home for his entire captivity, where he never felt real and floated in a semi-corporeal state. He felt nothing except his captors moving about, sometimes close, always alien, and their occasional feeding on the stored potential. Feeling that... He shuddered, and not due to the cold. Nothing else ever happened or changed in all that blankness. Not until those... hound-things... broke into Heebs and Jeebs' hidey-hole. His two formless alien captors radiated actual terror. At first, he felt ecstatic. Maybe the crazy-angled, impossible-looking dog-thing invaders would eat his captors! Maybe he'd be free? Nope. The pack pounced on the carefully stored potentiality from his most recent catch of humans and ravenously drained it. Frantic Heebs and Jeebs stowed themselves snug in the device and shoved him who-knew-when-or-where. Despite their flight, he was just as stuck and just as much their bait as the day they stole him and phased the damn device to him.

No one in the vicinity to drain, the sick feeling abated. Good, but he had no food in his stomach to up-chuck anyway. Heebs and Jeebs hadn't let him stay anywhere long enough to eat in... Well, it felt like forever. He didn't need to eat in their nexus place. It stood outside of time as well as space. That's what it seemed to be, with his limited knowledge and no one to teach him shit. Looking in a mirror any chance he got – usually when sent to lure more people, and delaying as long as he could so he'd feel real again and not have to go back to that fucking nexus where he felt his captors eating what was just stolen from whatever poor bastards he encountered in realtime – that's when he started to realize he didn't age in the nexus. He still looked like the same six-year-old kid those bastards stole from Montana in 1973. So, one might wonder how he kept track of time if he didn't feel its creep in the nexus home of his captors. The answer? He couldn't. To preserve his sanity, he chose to believe all the time stolen from him came out to six or perhaps ten… maybe fifteen?... very long years.

He glared at his captors' device. He glared at them. They could feel it, if they wanted to, but the pair were exuding the sedate aura of rest. He was out here shivering from lack of clothing and they were sleeping?!

He'd had enough of it all.

Leaping to his bare feet, he took in a big lungful and belted out, "I FUCKING HATE YOU BOTH! YOU ALWAYS DO THIS TO ME AND I HATE YOU BOTH FOR RUINING MY LIFE AND EVERYONE AROUND ME!"

Great, sharp breaths measured in misty puffs, small fists clenched in frustration, he could do nothing more than vent his rage.

Reason soon reasserted itself. No way to know how long he'd be stuck out here naked, freezing, and his captors not about to help him. They never had before. Never spoke to him, nor tried to communicate in any way. He decided a while back that they saw him only as a bug. A bug used to attract other bugs with masses of tasty potential. He remembered when they first took him, the first and only time they fed off of him. The memory of it ran deeper shivers than any cold the night threw at him. To feel your very potential

Mr. Smith Who Works The Front Desk by Jade Griffin

being sucked away made you feel empty, worthless, hopeless. He never wanted anyone to feel that, yet time and again he was forced to inflict such on people. Maybe this time, he could figure out a way to starve them. Maybe Heebs and Jeebs were hibernating, or stuck, or hurt. Maybe this time would be different… So, he pulled himself together and examined his surroundings.

Night. Late, cold. Tall, yellow grassy fields all around. He turned about, surveying the rest of the foreign environs, and caught an older man and woman standing on a large dirt path not thirty feet away. They stared at him and whispered to themselves.

He stared back, thinking quickly on what to do. By their clothes, it couldn't be his time but it wasn't Victorian and definitely not ancient. Made him think of his great-grandma's cameo. She lived in the late 1800s so that encircled his guess. The grassy field occupying the area as far as his short stature allowed visibility, and with no visible city lights in any direction, he felt his estimation sound.

As the pair whispered privately, he stood silent and observed them. The moon out and full, it cast enough illumination to take stock of some details. The man owned several decades of later years with combed white hair and a trimmed mustache. Nicely dressed with a coat and trousers and even a shiny pocket watch, so not some bum. The woman, also not young, her dark hair and equally dark satiny dress and hat blotted out the stars above her. Hard to tell her age. Left him feeling more awkward, seeing how nice they were dressed and him in his birthday suit. Hadn't felt that in a while; embarrassment at being naked around people. Happened so many times, he learned to live with it.

Mr. Smith Who Works The Front Desk by Jade Griffin

They approached and he stayed very still. Sometimes best to see what the home team would do before deciding his pitch.

As they drew near, the couple's expressions showed only curiosity, as if trying to sort him in this circumstance. When they stopped less than five feet away, he started counting in his head automatically.

"Hello there," the man said.

"Hello," he replied in kind, wondering as hunger began to twist inside him if he could get a meal out of this couple without any trouble.

"And what is your name, young man?" the woman asked.

Sometimes he lied. His parents weren't born yet if he guessed the era right, so he didn't feel it mattered. His namesake might not even be alive, so the answer came out as the truth. "Clark Ashton Smith."

"Well, Mr. Smith, it is good to meet you," replied the man with a convivial smile. "… although I'm not certain why you would be out here all alone in the late of night without a scrap of clothing on you. Where have you come from?"

Perhaps it was the cold. Perhaps just tired of it all. Whatever the reason, he answered without thinking. "Montana."

The man and woman exchanged looks. No doubt trying to figure out how a naked boy from Montana ended up… wherever here was.

"Uh, never mind." He backed away from them. "Just… go about your business, or whatever."

"Wait just a moment, young Mr. Smith. Are you in some sort of… unusual trouble?"

Mr. Smith Who Works The Front Desk by Jade Griffin

He should have bolted, but his bare feet remained planted in the soil as if rooted to the very grass itself. He looked at the man. Looked that guy over real good. Reading people by expression and mannerism became one of his much-valued skills. Something about this particular guy was definitely not the usual. Could it be, after all this time, he had found someone capable of helping him? And how the hell could he find out without spending too much time around the pair and draining this potential opportunity away?

"And if I am?" he asked, showing more suspicion than what was felt. "Who're you?"

"My name is Mr. Arthur Paisley. This is my wife, Maisey, and we're both very pleased to make your acquaintance." The man removed the coat of fine cloth and held it out to him. "You look in need of a place to stay for the night, or at the very least some sufficient attire."

He eyed the man, looking for any hint of devious intent. The woman, too. Neither seemed the sort so far. He tread forward close enough to take the coat, put it on, and step away once more. They were likely taking his distancing as suspicion. Even better.

"Perhaps you'd be inclined to join us, for the time being? Until you're sorted out?" the woman plied.

He was tempted to play the scared child bit and really lay it on thick, see if they took the bait and tried to take advantage of him, or if they truly meant to help him. Something told him not to. That same something had saved him many times from people who would mean harm even to a child. Especially to a child. He couldn't count on one hand the times he'd had to fend off sickos, but if it weren't for that sort of extra sense, he might not even be alive.

Eyeing the pair again, they waited patiently for his response. No coercion. No nervousness, anticipation, or ill intent detected. And what else would he do anyway?

He pulled the oversized coat further up his chilled thin shoulders and gave a nod.

Mr. Paisley beamed in honest delight. "Splendid! This way, lad." The man pointed ahead and, arm still hooked in the wife's, led the way.

He followed, pretending aloofness but remaining alert.

The wife turned to look back, for he trailed a ways. "You may walk alongside us. We don't bite," she said with a humored smile.

He thought it best not to respond.

She did not ask him again, which he was glad, but the pair were in no great hurry to get home. At one point, Mr. Paisley pointed to the clear night sky and asked, "Do you know your constellations?"

"A few." He did in fact. Remembered the two Dad showed him, long ago… before his captivity. Using them, along with anything else picked up from the myriad of people encountered, he attempted to triangulate his location and the time of year.

"Ah, it is always nice to meet a fellow interested in astronomy. My favorite is there." Mr. Paisley pointed to a very familiar series of stars. "Draco."

Hmph. So he was being tested? Alright. "Sir, that is Orion." That also gave him some bearings. He must be near the east side of the United States in the autumn.

"He is right, dear. That is Orion." Mrs. Paisley seconded cheerily.

"Ah, yes. My eyes must be fooling me in my old age."

He seriously doubted that, not falling for such banter. Time to get his own intel. "How far is it?"

"We're quite close. This entire field is ours. Up this way is the main house." Mr. Paisley pointed.

Yes, he could see a light far up ahead. Some kind of lantern perhaps, barely illuminating the beginning of a large home.

They walked the remainder in silence, wherein the appraisal of his new hosts continued. Still seemed harmless enough and, the closer they got, the bigger the home grew. A literal mansion, complete with a servant awaiting them at set of front double doors. The servant swung the partitions wide for them and didn't give him a second look as he followed after. Inside was another servant, a young woman busy with tidying tasks.

"Danneby, this is young Mr. Smith," Mr. Paisley said to the servant at the front doors. "He seems to have been left without clothes. Can you take him to the guest room and see to that? After, escort him to the dining room, if you please."

"Of course, sir." Danneby, who gave him not the slightest bit of uppity glance nor even one of surprise, opened a white-gloved hand to a large, brightly polished hardwood staircase. "Right this way, Mr. Smith."

Led upstairs and shown a selection of nice clothes for a late 19th Century boy. When the servant pulled the door closed to give him privacy, he peeked out the keyhole. Danneby stood passive with his back near the door.

He dressed hastily, because the scent of cooking food wafted finely about the rich home and it was becoming increasingly difficult to contain his need to get some of it inside him.

Finished, he left the room and Danneby led the way without a word.

Despite the plaguing onset of hunger cramps and a sudden thirst, he continued to take in clues around him. Like the grandfather clock chiming the hour of 2 AM, and some paintings depicting unearthly places which hung on the other side of the upper hall. There were statues of other cultures in cabinets and on pedestals as well as artifacts completely foreign to his eyes: an off-white stone bowl with five stubby legs, a balanced upside-down miniature pyramid, and a tablet made of dark bluish iridescent material marked with symbols he could not identify. At the bottom of the stairs lay a glass case covering a set of ancient stones which he thought had familiar markings carved into them. By the time he sat at a massively elongated table straight out of a movie set, he had a whole row of questions to politely ask his hosts who sat further down from him on the opposite side.

"Isn't that better?" Mrs. Paisley remarked, smiling at his clothed state.

He felt it safe to nod. "Thank you."

Full water goblets sat upon the table in front of each of them. He wasn't certain of decorum and noted his hosts were not touching anything at the table but if he sat any longer without putting something in his mouth, he'd start choking on a dry throat. Picking up the goblet awarded no looks, nor did taking a sip, so he drank his fill. His gulps echoed loudly in the silent dining hall.

"How long were you out in the field?" Mrs. Paisley enquired just as Danneby and a plump woman placed a steaming bowl in front of each seated person.

Instantly distracted by the sight and scent of delicious food inches away, he shrugged.

"Let young Mr. Smith eat before he faints from hunger, my dear," Mr. Paisley advised politely, taking up a spoon.

"Yes. I apologize." She seemed genuinely caught in her gaffe and waved him to it. "Do eat."

His own questions postponed, he wasted no time and attempted some vague semblance of manners while inhaling the amazing meal set in front of him. Some type of creamy soup, then a plate of roasted meat, sauteed vegetables, a sauce, and finally a pudding. He didn't care if his host and hostess stared – and stare they did. What mattered was committing the flavors to memory and eating rapidly. Heebs and Jeebs were bound to be upset that their potentiality sucker wouldn't pull in any foodstuffs. Whenever he avoided people so his captors couldn't drain unwitting citizens, they usually yanked him roughly into a different time and space wherein he'd be found unconscious and unable to keep his attractive nature from working its charm on the new marks. He'd gotten smart enough to let it drain a bit from a lot of different people in order to keep Heebs and Jeebs satisfied without any one person being completely sucked dry and doomed.

"Would you care for more?" Mr. Paisley asked from five seats down.

"I would, yes. Thank you."

And the heavy-set woman who smelled like a steamy, bustling kitchen popped in immediately to give him a second full plate, then refilled his water goblet.

While eating a particularly delectable braised carrot at a much slower pace, his hosts felt it was time to pry.

"It appears you haven't eaten for some time, young man. I am a bit concerned for your welfare. As such, I hope you don't mind a few questions. Is there anyone we should inform that you've been found? Anywhere aside from, eh… Montana, you said?"

He shook his head at Mr. Paisley's query.

"A name then, of a relative in Montana to send a telegram to?"

Another head shake in reply.

"We're curious but we really do mean to help you, if you're in need of any," the wife said. "Can you tell us anything? If you're in some sort of trouble, or danger?"

He sighed, and it sounded so much more grown than what his six-year-old voice should produce. "I really don't think that would be pleasant dinner conversation at this time, Mrs. Paisley."

The worldly tone, the experience etched on the young face, actually made her pull back in surprise. She clearly saw what he usually hid: a little body disguising his true age, but also the vast life experience tucked behind innocent eyes. Time to see what kind of people they really were, so he showed all of himself.

He narrowed his eyes at the pair, flicked his gaze between them, and saw that they, too, were not merely bored rich folks wanting to take in a foundling waif. He suspected they, or at least Mr. Paisley, were aware of his uniqueness upon first sight of him. That was evident by the knowing grin which now lay under his host's white mustache.

When Mr. Paisley nodded once to the left and to the right, he tensed. Danneby and the kitchen woman stood in a corner a piece. It wouldn't be the first, second, or fiftieth time someone sent their lackeys to nab him for various intents and purposes. But Danneby and the kitchen woman made no such threats. They quietly left the dining room; left him and Mr. and Mrs. Paisley to talk in private.

His host folded hands atop the table and said, "Now then, Mr. Smith, I hope you'll feel comfortable enough to ask us anything you like and, in turn, we'd like to do the same."

Huh. Hadn't put two and two together before but now he saw what Mr. Paisley was. Didn't often run into them but they certainly shared enough traits with his host that he should have recognized the clues.

He put down his cutlery and eyed the shrewd man. "The artifacts upstairs and in the hall… You're a collector of oddities."

"I tend to find such things, or they tend to find me." Mr. Paisley nodded across the table, toward him. "It's a knack I have, as is discerning the best course to take with each new discovery."

A knack, hm? Perhaps Mr. Paisley led a charmed life. Perhaps Heebs and Jeebs could sense this man across time and space and threw him here for the opportunity to drain such a prize. Just a theory. He took a brief moment to cast his awareness toward the device attached to him. His captors maintained their odd hibernation feel. How long before they caught on to his slacking. Could there be time for a true scheme?

Focusing back on his host, he asked, "And if I'm seen as one of your new discoveries, what is the best course you're discerning?"

Mr. Smith Who Works The Front Desk by Jade Griffin

"Well now, that depends on what you let us learn about you, starting with whomever you were yelling such obscenities at while standing nude in our field."

He shook his head. "Don't want to talk about them yet. What is your goal with your collection of oddities?"

"**Our** collection," Mrs. Paisley stressed mildly, feeling left out. "is here to be studied and understood while being kept in a safe environment. Much of what is here is vastly **un**known and some we have found aren't meant to be known well."

He blinked, an echo of his surprise. That… was unexpected. First, her reply. Second, that she owned as much of this as her husband.

Mrs. Paisley chuckled. "Such a face! Wherever you're from, Mr. Smith, I do hope you didn't assume that I am a simpleton confined to my husband's hearth just because I am a woman." Far from angry, she seemed amused.

Mr. Paisley patted her hand patiently. "My dear, do not assume his origin is any more nor less progressive than our own times."

She nodded. "Quite right. My dear Mr. Smith, we are still trying to assess which category to place you under: that which should be known, or safer to remain unknown?"

Huh again. Not just collectors of otherworldly knowledge but border-line academics. And they already suspected he was from another time?

Mrs. Paisley stood. "Now then, let's start with something small." She closed the gap of seats and pulled out the one right across from him. There, she sat.

He couldn't help tensing up, nudged into a veritable corner. He started the count in his head.

"Are you human?" she asked.

That was starting small? Whatever. "Yes. Are you?"

She grinned. "We are simply odd human beings ourselves."

Mr. Paisley gave a humored snort from five seats down.

"You speak and act well beyond your years," she started again. "Are you in fact a young boy?"

He looked her square in the eyes and replied, "I know I look young but I am a male human of approximate second decade in age and, unless this is 1973, you are correct in assuming I am neither from this time or place."

She didn't bat an eye. "That had been our suspicion, given your state, your more adult mannerisms, and that curious watch you wear which was the only thing on you when we found you in our field." She pointed to his left hand.

Mr. Paisley got up and ambled over to Mrs. Paisley while she spoke, placing a hand on her shoulder just as she finished talking. "You're acting the shark again, love," the husband said to the wife. Then, to him, "Clark, I do apologize if you're not used to people such as ourselves having found and outed you. Even amongst our peers, we are unusual and understand your reluctance."

"It's just that…" Mrs. Paisley cast a look up at her husband before continuing. "We're aware that some things we find have a time frame. Tomes of mythos, for example, should be learned slowly and in small sections. Most magical rites and rituals require proper alignment of the stars and ley lines and need to be completed within a specified hour or day or year. Certain events in history occurred or were prevented with mere moments to spare, because little was known in preventing disasters foretold in ancient texts. We're trying to learn about you in the event you also fall under this category.

Mr. Smith Who Works The Front Desk by Jade Griffin

Will you simply vanish away, in control of whatever means you arrived here? Do you keep your distance due to some past torture? Were you fleeing someone or something and need to be further hidden away before such individuals discover you?" Suddenly, her mouth quirked to the side in an irritated manner and she leaned near. "Is it cultists? Are cultists after you?"

"Not that I'm aware of…" They didn't consider themselves cultists? In his experience, most collectors turned out to be cultists or desired to be such.

"Nasty, power-hungry vermin…" She folded her arms over her chest and fumed quite heatedly.

"It is apparent, Clark, that you are reluctant to talk about yourself and your circumstances, and we can take our time, gain your trust, if you have time to spare, but it would be a great kindness on your part if you would mention anything of note about your nature or situation which requires immediate guarding, warding, or caution. So, what can we do for you?"

Never in all this crazy life had the opportunity arose to explain anything to receptive listeners. No way was he giving this up! But they were out of time.

He sighed, scooted the chair back, and stood, placing plenty of distance between them. He stopped counting in his head. "A kindness? To tell you about my personal timeframes? The kindness would be in telling you to stay away from me. I have no control over where or when I go. Those who are in control are here with me but lay dormant, for now. I don't know when they'll wake or when I'll be forced to leave." He thrust his left arm into the air, the sleeve of his garment sliding down enough to reveal the watch-like device fused to him.

His host and hostess backed quickly to a far wall, expecting his ticking timebomb to go off. Their caution told him they'd encountered other things of heinous effect, yet they appeared unscathed to his keen eye. No missing limbs or burns. Interesting. However, he did not wish to disillusion them and continued with chilled words. "They aren't human, they can't be seen or touched, and they eat the potential metaphysical energy intelligent creatures possess which allows them to affect their time and space. However, I am **done** being their lure. So, tell me, Mr. and Mrs. Paisley, is this really something you can help me with? And am I really something you want in your house?"

Just an ounce of hesitation stalled them, but it wasn't fear. He saw only caution in their movements as they untensed. Mr. Paisley replied, "Yes, Mr. Smith. And with more information, I do believe we can."

"These things holding you," Mrs. Paisley pressed. "Do they kill people?"

"I'm sure they would, but people move around too much. They're out of phase with most things in our reality and we're all in shift too much for them to feed off us as individuals. At least, that's what I think. They phased this device to me. I can't remove it. Can't even touch it. It draws the potential out of thinking creatures. It's why I stay back. The thing has a range of ten feet and starts draining people after ten minutes."

"But we haven't felt any different. Are you certain it hasn't been disabled? Our home has many kinds of wards in place," Mrs. Paisley offered.

Mr. Smith Who Works The Front Desk by Jade Griffin

He brought his hand down slowly and stared at the damn device. "I feel it, just like I feel them. The prey doesn't. Not at first, but I do. It uses my own potential to draw people closer, get them to linger. Stick around it long enough and you lose too much. Your luck sucked away, nothing goes right for you ever. And if your luck runs out entirely? Fate takes anyone with zero potential and hits them with a train, or runs them over with a cart, drowns them in the city well, they die of sudden heart failure…" That shuttered empathy and humanity he always told to wait patiently started banging at his mind. Tears, so foreign to him for so long, welled up. He scrubbed them away as quick as they came. He ground his jaw, eyes glittering with anger and determination. "That's my story. I don't have a planned next move and no idea how much time I have. You got any ideas?"

There was barely a pause, wherein Mrs. Paisley replied, "Some, but most are not pleasant. Exorcism, warding tattoos…"

Mr. Paisley turned to her and suggested, "Try a summoning ritual to draw them out."

He shook his head. "Exorcism won't work. They're not demons. It's a faith-based spell that's been tried on me before. Trust me, it's pointless. And without pushing or pulling them from whatever reality they're native to and linger in, I don't know… Can summoning magic work like that?"

The couple exchanged looks and had no answer.

Mrs. Paisley told him, "I'll gather my things and we'll try tomorrow, hm? Unfortunately, it is quite late, or very early, depending on how you view your day. You aren't tired?"

Mr. Smith Who Works The Front Desk by Jade Griffin

Another head shake. "Time doesn't work in the nexus where they come from and where they'd put me when I wasn't being cast like a lure to attract food for them. It's why I look a lot younger than I really am. I've spent a lot of time in their nexus where I don't really have a physical form, don't feel hungry or tired or anything."

"It sounds positively boring but I'm afraid we must retire," Mr. Paisley said, covering a mighty yawn with the back of a hand. "We are a pair of night owls but even we have our limits."

The couple went to the dining room double doors and opened them. Danneby, who appeared to be the head servant, came up to them right away.

"Danneby, please see that Mr. Smith has a comfortable room." Without waiting for confirmation, the pair went upstairs.

He looked up at Danneby, daring to stand less than five feet away to examine the servant better. Danneby was a man of average height with thinning hair and did not look like a typical butler but that expressionless demeanor fit the bill perfectly.

"Do you know what Mr. and Mrs. Paisley do with their free time?" Perhaps a bold question but he was curious what the servant would say.

"Yes, sir. We are all aware of their activities," Danneby answered, deadpan.

All of the servants, hm? "Do you enjoy working for them?"

"If you are concerned for your well-being, sir, I have not known a couple to be more devoted to altruism. You are in good hands here, sir."

"That's good to know. How long have you worked here?"

"All under the employ of Mr. and Mrs. Paisley must serve for five years with the option to continue employment. None of us have been with them less than seven and I have been in their employ for twenty-one."

"And did you hear any of what we said in there?" He pointed to the dining room.

"It is my duty to anticipate the needs of my employers, sir. Clara and I left to make you feel more at ease but I will inform her of your necessity of limited contact. Our employers do not keep secrets from us."

"So you heard what happens if you are close to me for too long?"

"Yes, sir. I believe it is time to move along. This way."

Definitely not the average butler. He followed the intriguing man up to the same room as before.

Once he was inside, Danneby took two steps back. "If you require anything, sir, please use the bell there." He pointed to a wall with a long cord attached to it.

"What about you and the other servants? Don't you need food and sleep, too?"

A bit of a smile turned the corners of Danneby's mouth. "Yes, sir, but this is our job. Sleep well." The servant did not shut the bedroom door before turning a swift 90 degrees and walking downstairs.

After watching Danneby go, he closed the door and flopped onto the soft bed. A brief yawn fled from him. If he went to sleep, would he wake here? He tried sensing his captors again. Still there. Still not in any rush. As he lay still and lax, fully clothed, couldn't help dwelling on what tomorrow would bring. Not with fear but cautious optimism.

Mr. Smith Who Works The Front Desk by Jade Griffin

For the first time in a long time, he felt warm and safe and full. The lull was a very nice change. Sleep encroached, unavoidable and wonderful.

He woke with a jolt, momentarily perplexed, only to realize he had not been whisked away to the nexus, or to anywhere else other than where he placed his head hours before. Slowly, he sank back to the pillow and comforting blankets.

The quiet. He reveled in it. Not that the house lay silent and still. No, he could hear some industry going on downstairs. Not much, but some. Such a luxury to be here, now, in such safe confines.

He turned away from the bright sunlight hidden mostly behind thick curtains, pulled the covers over his head, and closed his eyes.

1891, November 3

A light knocking roused him from his doze. At once alert, he pulled the covers slowly away and inquired, "Yes?"

"Mr. Smith? It's Mrs. Paisley. Breakfast is past but dinner will be served in the next hour... if you're joining us?"

At that moment, his stomach abandoned all the years of learning to go without and groaned audibly of its emptiness.

The bed lost its appeal. He sat up and told her, "I'll be down shortly."

Yes, food. How lucky he felt, being taken in by these rich, academic, anti-cultist socialites. Not sure how long his luck would last, he readied and descended with haste.

Danneby stood at the bottom of the stairs, but only to motion toward the dining room and open the double doors for him. Within, Mr. and Mrs. Paisley sat at the far end and greeted him with pleasant faces. They wore nicely pressed clothes. Not that they weren't well-dressed last night, but their manner seemed... different, business-like.

When he sat – seven seats down from them – Mr. Paisley spoke up. "We will be going into town shortly but will return before supper. Business to attend to."

Mrs. Paisley added, "I can research the rituals upon my return, or perhaps even the tattoo. Imprints on the flesh tend to be very effective... if you're feeling up to it."

He nodded absently at her talking, eager to get to the meal. The smells from the kitchen set his mouth watering.

"Do stay inside while we're away," Mr. Paisley advised.

Mrs. Paisley explained further, "I've placed magical wards around the estate which have proved effective in the past. It is possible the creatures holding you captive might be waiting for you to step out so they can whisk you away again."

Good to know. It also explained why he was still here. But then the kitchen woman entered and his focus fell entirely on food: a plate with a roast bird of some kind in the center of roasted potatoes and braised vegetables. A little bird for each of them on their plates. He stared at it, then flicked a glance at his hosts.

Both observing his reaction, Mrs. Paisley asked, "If it isn't to your liking, let us know what you might prefer and we'll tell Clara, the cook. Is there something in particular you're missing, from before?"

He studied the way she cut dainty pieces of the bird and spoke only after she'd nothing in her mouth, as well how she avoided eye contact and made the comment a passing one and not another attempt at fishing information of the future from him. Honestly, he didn't know quite what to tell them. Was ice cream even invented yet? Bicycles? Surely not the movie theater or popcorn. Things he remembered... from before. Things remembered just after being taken... His mood sank, as did his appetite.

"We'll have Clara make you something else right away," Mrs. Paisley said. She put her silverware down and snapped her fingers.

"No. It's fine..."

"The look on your face says otherwise," Mr. Paisley remarked. The host stopped eating as well and both of them stared at him with concern.

The small, plump woman came from the kitchen wearing an apron with some stains upon it. She looked puzzled and surprised to be summoned, or perhaps anxious. He couldn't tell for sure.

"Clara, the dove is not to Mr. Smith's liking—"

"I said it's fine." And he hunched over the plate and began carving into the fowl, reminiscent of how Mrs. Paisley worked on it but with no gusto and much darkness.

His gaze flicking between his hosts and the food, he did not miss Mrs. Paisley waving Clara back into the kitchen, nor the fact that they did not return to eating but observed him at his own.

"Mr. Smith, if there is anything—"

"It's just…" he started, and tapered off, because did it really matter? Just eat the damn food! But even putting more food in his mouth and not tasting any of it, a bad mood engulfed him. He sighed, sat back, stared at the meal growing cold. He eyed his patient host and hostess. And he managed to mumble, "The last time I ate one of these, I stole it half-cooked from a blind man."

"Mr. Smith," Mr. Paisley started with genuine compassion. "it is very rare, the person who does not regret things done in their past, even if those things were done to survive. But if things like this are quick to disturb you, perhaps you'll let us know if there are items which we should not put upon the table – both for food and for conversation – hm?"

He nodded, remained silent, and went back to eating. Wouldn't do to let this delicious meal go to waste. What a damn terrible time for guilt to ruin his enjoyment of it. And what a miserable creature he was being. Earlier, it felt as if all the luck pointed him toward finding these generous, knowledgeable people. Now, his very company brought dark clouds. He ate quickly and retreated back up to the guest room.

The sound of carriage wheels and hooves over gravel signaled the departure of the Paisleys. When they'd gone, he snuck a look out his keyhole. No one around, he entered onto an empty hall. Downstairs appeared to be without a soul. Cautiously, he tiptoed to the first floor, saw under the stairs a room with an open door. Danneby, just inside, sat polishing a pair of Mr. Paisley's shoes. The butler glanced briefly at him, then set eyes and attention on the footwear and the job.

Being left alone was new, and yet not. The quiet. That is what set it apart. He grew more and more on edge because, instinctively, he knew it'd be ripped away. Just like always.

"Let us know if you require anything, sir."

The butler's utterance startled him into jumping, which pulled the servant's eyes away from polishing.

Danneby said, "Sir, if I may, Mrs. Paisley's wards make the Paisley Estate one of the safest places there is. You may feel at ease here."

But he didn't, and it must be clear as day. Especially to an observant butler. So, keeping his required distance, he decided to engage the servant. "We'll know soon enough. Heebs and Jeebs don't let me stay anywhere longer than a day if I'm not collecting any food for them."

Danneby nodded, as if agreeing on weather and not the mode of operation of cosmic entities.

"I take it that the Paisleys encounter strange things often."

"They do indeed, sir." Nothing so far surprised the butler, including that question.

"And have you?"

"Only rarely, sir. Mr. and Mrs. Paisley don't often bring active oddities into the estate proper. However, on occasion, that rules shifts on their own." The butler glanced at him, indicating he was considered an active oddity.

He watched Danneby for a time, the calming scratch of bristles against polished leather making a nice rhythm around his thoughts.

Rules move on their own… A comment about fate? Danneby must believe in fate. Personally, he could not. Believe his path destined and unchangeable? No. If he did, then nothing he ever tried or accomplished mattered, that everything stayed predetermined and he was made to be whisked away by unfeeling aliens, that everything that had ever happened to him amounted to pure bad luck. Did he believe he had a destiny? Not especially, but he could not believe in no point at all. He chose to believe in a purpose, the potential to change. There had to be.

Mr. and Mrs. Paisley returned some hours later, just as promised. He saw them arrive while staring out from the bedroom window of the second floor. Cracking the bedroom door open, he heard Mr. Paisley enquire on the state of the house.

"Everything as you left it, sir. Any changes to supper I shall tell Clara about?"

"No, Danneby. Proceed as usual," Mrs. Paisley replied.

"Very good, madam."

"Is he upstairs?" Mr. Paisley.

"Yes, sir."

Footsteps grew louder on the stairs.

He backed quickly away and stood staring at Mr. Paisley when the man pushed the door open.

Mr. Smith Who Works The Front Desk by Jade Griffin

"Good evening, Mr. Smith. Would you be free to join Maisey and myself in the workroom?" Not waiting for a reply, Mr. Paisley turned about and headed down the steps.

He followed and was led to a room further in the estate on the first floor. Undecorated, it had shelves and cabinets as well as a metal table in the center along with a single chair beside it. Mrs. Paisley rummaged through the cabinets, collecting things to place on the table. A small lectern held an open book she glanced at every now and then. The contents handwritten, it was not old. A journal?

Mrs. Paisley told him during her rummaging, "I've researched my collection for some methods of at least keeping you on this plane, if that is what you wish, but the process is long and not pleasant." She paused, facing him with sudden concern. "I... I don't mean to pry but when you turned to run in the field last night, I did see what looked like quite long scars?"

He couldn't help squirming a little, due to her enquiring gaze and also the memory of how he got them. Some transfers left him with more permanent mementos.

"We can well imagine how you came to receive them. Looked to be from some sort of whip," Mr. Paisley commented from the doorway, allowing him as much distance in the room as possible.

"I only bring it up because I want to know if you have a trauma against people touching you. The method I will use requires that."

He shrugged. "Not exactly. You're right. People have hurt me. They just don't generally get to do it for very long. So, no matter the benefits, I don't think it'd be worth it to try whatever you have planned. Don't kill yourself over me."

She smiled that bright smile again. "I wouldn't be at your side for too long. It is a tattoo which takes several days to complete over the course of multiple sessions per day with chantings and readings. I would stand back for most of the casting and only come near for the actual needlework, if you're willing."

A tattoo… She'd mentioned it before.

"Maisey doesn't know if it will keep those you're chained to in place or draw them out or not affect them at all," Mr. Paisley explained. "Not even certain if the process will be noticed and they'll try to make off with you, but it will quite likely bind your physical form to this time and place."

She added, "I can't determine a way to get you back to when you came from, and I don't think it wise for you to simply travel to Montana without anyone willing to receive you or your peculiar circumstances, so Arthur and I discussed it and we'd like you to stay with us. There is plenty of room for you here, and we know all about you, so there's no inconvenience or true danger if we remain vigilant as we work toward removing you from the possession of… of whatever they are."

It wasn't unusual for good people to offer him a place to stay, nor for bad people to do the same, but he felt these people were trustworthy enough to tell them more of his captors. "I call them Heebs and Jeebs, because they give me the heebie-jeebies."

Mr. and Mrs. consulted one another with a look. Mrs. asked, "Is that African, Arthur?"

"I don't honestly know." To him Mr. Paisley turned. "And what is the definition of 'heebie-jeebies'?"

"It's like... the creeps, the shudders, the jitters. A sort of skin-crawling sensation experienced just by feeling them."

"Ah. And there are two of them? What do they look like?"

He shrugged at Mr. Paisley's question. "I don't know if they have a physical form. I just... feel them. I don't know if they can sense me in that way. They don't seem to care if I get hurt and never helped me in the past or yanked me away just because someone was hurting me." He tried to pass it off nonchalantly but swallowed hard at other memories he'd care not to recall.

They noticed. The pause in conversation told him that. But the pair were very practical and she asked, "If you're not amiable to trying the tattoo, I have a sigil on a necklace. Merely wearing it binds a person to a place. You would not be able to leave the home but no one is required to be near you. I don't believe it offers the same type of permanent protection as a ward tattooed on flesh."

"I wouldn't mind all the protection I can get, so long as they don't negate each other. Although it sounds like the tattoo works best, I am concerned that you will be near me too long. The more times a person is around me, the longer they need to stay away, especially if it has started to drain them on a prior occasion. Can you describe each of your methods?"

Her face blossomed into a smile and she did, in detail. He had a hard time understanding the mechanics of what she spoke on but he didn't want to let on that he wasn't grasping it.

At one point in her explanation, she paused, sighed, and smiled. "I see... Well, in time, Mr. Smith, I will be sure to teach you more. I can tell the face of someone not able to keep up intellectually, and I shan't have that face upon our guest again, rest assured. Let's start with the basics of practicum, eh? If you're ready to begin, please remove your shirt and lay there."

Without hesitation, he did as she said, using the chair to climb onto the table due to his small stature. Keeping his head facing her workstation and arms under his chin, he eyed the items set out. A bottle of black ink, a needle, fine crystals or sand, some bits of plants, a cloth embroidered with more of the paisley pattern he'd seen around the doorframe.

"A magical ward is used to prevent something," she began, turning his way. "Keeps a thing out, or in. Barriers. Very versatile. It's what I will be applying with first a drawing and then the more permanent application. You are not to move or interrupt. Arthur will keep a watch on the time. Won't you, dear?"

He craned his head that way and saw Mr. Paisley holding up the pocket watch.

"Ready?" Mrs. asked Mr.

The master of the house nodded once, eyes locked on the watch.

Mrs. Paisley surged toward him. He automatically started counting and tensed up, but relaxed when all he felt were paintbrush bristles applying a cool, wet substance to his bare skin. He reached only six minutes and four seconds before she hurried away to her workstation, out of range. There, she grabbed the needle and bottle of ink. He wrapped his hands around the table edge, bracing himself. She started speaking strange words in clear rhythm and came near once more. The first jabbing sting made him twitch, despite himself, but the words and rhythm of needle jabs soon became a background cadence to his own internal clock ticking away her time. He just passed eight minutes thirty-one seconds, tensing more with each passing one, when Mr. Paisley interrupted her.

"Break, love."

Mrs. Paisley moved away from him without interrupting her chanting, though the words changed. After a period of several more minutes, she repeated the previous chant and her needlework renewed. This carried on for over two hours, each time near him growing increasingly less, per his prior advice. Not once did the device activate.

A long, weary sigh broke the endless chanting. Mrs. Paisley deposited her things at her workstation counter and leaned heavily against it. "That will be all for this evening, Mr. Smith. How does it feel?"

He sat up, moved his shoulders about, tried to twist his gaze to look at the tattoo, but could not see. "Stings a bit. I don't feel any different. Am I supposed to?"

"Not necessarily. We will repeat this again tomorrow three times, and likewise over the next few days, until it is finished. I smell supper and am famished. Replace your shirt and join us when you are available, if you would." Too tired to wait for a response, Mrs. Paisley exited the workroom.

He stared after her, concerned over her state.

Mr. Paisley caught his observation. "She'll be fine. Some spells are more taxing to cast than others. A good meal is what we all need right now."

Couldn't argue with that.

The master of the house left the workroom doorway, presumably to join the wife.

Easing down from the table, the act of grabbing his shirt and pulling it over his small frame caused brand new pinpricks of pain. Small discomforts. They would pass. This could work. He had to believe in that. It had been so long since he believed in anything – truly believed – and this hope held actual promise. Just like the inviting smells from the dining area making him salivate.

    Mrs. Paisley did indeed seem more refreshed by the time he took his seat. She sipped some type of light pink liquid from a fancy glass and laughed over something Mr. Paisley said. The pair were smiling even before he entered, and it was pleasant to see the smiles renewed upon his arrival. Very different from the usual greetings received. It felt so strange to take a seat and be welcomed by people completely at ease around him. He couldn't help staring at them. Over and over, this pair continued to surprise him. He could neither predict what they would do or say next, nor could he fault their character. It hit him again, that feeling of just how lucky he'd gotten. Hit him hard. Made him quiet, thankful, and not willing to do or say anything to disturb such luck.

Mr. Smith Who Works The Front Desk by Jade Griffin

1891, November 5

Day four. Such calm here. He could not help but remain engrossed in the luxury, especially as they were seated near the large sitting room hearth. The fire crackled as snow flit down outside a serenely frozen nightscape.

A knock at the study door broke the calm.

"Enter," Mr. Paisley replied, not bothering to look up from his newspaper.

Danneby did so and placed a bowl of fruit on a stand, then exited without a word.

He eyed the mixed offering and smiled at the three bright orange spheres positioned on the top. "Oranges."

Mrs. Paisley looked up from her reading. "Oranges?"

"Yes. You asked what things I liked, from before. I love oranges, and cherries."

Mrs. Paisley smiled brightly and her brows crested in a neat arc; which told him these were not so common here and now.

Mr. Paisley offered, "I presume the fruits and vegetables you enjoyed were not local, unless the climate shifts drastically, or your family enjoyed wealth."

"No. Neither of those." He snagged one from the bowl and peeled it with his hands.

Host and hostess eyed the act with interest.

Mrs. Paisley said, "They must've been a frequent favorite you enjoyed to be so skilled in attacking them. Let me show you the more civilized way to go about it, if you are to eat them around more prominent company."

He stood back and watched her demonstrate a fancy way of cutting and peeling an orange. Almost how Mom used to do it, when he was little. He nodded politely at her instruction, then copied a fair semblance of her method on the third orange as she watched.

"You're from nearly eighty years in the future. We want to know all about it. What is technology like? Has science surpassed religious dogma? Is magic known to the populace? Have other races become known to humans?"

He hesitated, his expression guarded. "You know I was only six when they took me, so I don't recall much history. A few transfers ago, others found out when I'm from and asked me similar questions but I'm not sure it does any good letting people know what happens later on. Most of the time it probably causes problems, because if you prevent or speed up events, doesn't it mess with the future?"

Mr. Paisley, seated in an armchair, chuckled. "I told you, love."

Mrs. Paisley pouted. "Can't you reveal anything?"

He considered it, debated if the handful of days with them had rooted out any souring of character, and decided they were exactly as they seemed to be in the beginning. Besides, Heebs and Jeebs hadn't forced him away yet. He might as well tell them some things, because it could prompt them to find even more answers for getting him away from his captors.

He looked about, saw the daily newspaper, and took a full sheet. Folded it in half, then into a shape all boys his age could do blindfolded. He then took it up between thumb and forefinger, aimed it toward Mrs. Paisley, and let fly his little paper plane.

With wonder, the pair watched it glide easily to her; and with a delighted cry she caught it.

"Aeroplanes! So common a boy effortlessly designs one from mere paper!" She turned the simple model around in her hands, unfolded and refolded it, marveling all the while.

Mr. Paisley also examined the paper toy. "We've read about flight theories and the designs of Leonardo DaVinci and those in the Orient but for you to fashion this so quickly... I presume we have achieved flight as a common practice in the near future?"

"I think people are close right now," he offered. "Two brothers work out the problem and make history."

His hosts turned their gaze to him. Mr. Paisley said, "I'm sure they will. As I see the great desire to know certain things before they transpire, from my dear wife. I see very well where this could lead. Such machines can be used for good, or for war."

He felt it safe to nod, given that Mr. Paisley guessed that far, but realized it had been a bit of a trap and he just admitted there was war in the future. He frowned and stared at his feet, trying to come up with something else to turn the conversation.

"Don't worry, Mr. Smith," Mrs. Paisley said. "Wars happen throughout history. I'm sure whatever is to come will continue that history. We humans are warlike and irrational as a group. This is why it is so imperative to learn about an individual. Yourself, for example. Can you tell us more about you?"

He blinked in surprise, for no one had ever really asked about him. He then shrugged because his interests were things from the future which he shouldn't mention –

television, toy cars, baseball and the movies, bicycles. That all seemed so trivial and far away. He had no real interest in such things anymore. He had no real interests at all.

"Maisey, that isn't a fair question. Who knows what wonders a boy fancies in the future, or plays with as commonplace? It is much better to use our own imaginations than to prod him further." Mr. Paisley took the newspaper airplane, crumpled it up, and tossed it into the fire, amid a brief whimper of protest from the wife who watched it burn away. "Let's discuss instead your education. No matter the time period, I assume you received some form of schooling or education?"

"Yes."

"Then it is time you get back into that. No matter how long you are here for, you should not neglect your studies."

His shoulders sagged visibly. School? He hadn't thought of that in ages!

"Don't care for the idea, do you? Would it help to know we can hire the very best of tutors this side of the United States of America? Which subjects presented the most trouble?"

He let a half-grin show. "I was only in first grade but the hardest were history – of which I lived through many brief chapters – and math… arithmetic," he corrected, having encountered the difference in lexicon before.

"Interesting. Those are my favorites," Mrs. Paisley told him. "Those, and theology and thaumaturgy."

"The study of religion and the study of magic," Mr. Paisley clarified.

He frowned. "Isn't magic just natural phenomena explained by science?"

The lady of the house turned fully toward him, her brows cresting high. "Whatever do they teach you in future schools, assuming you were old enough to attend?"

"Just barely, though I was adept at reading before starting school. Magic remains in the realm of myth where I am from."

"Here and now, magic is very much real if you know where and how to look, but not as easy to find or learn properly," Mr. Paisley explained.

Mrs. Paisley nodded at her husband's words. "I, myself, have studied magic and religion for decades. The spells I cast do not consult directly with deities. It is an art form in which mistakes are deadly. That is why science *and* theology are key to using thaumaturgy."

He passed her a look of skepticism. "Are you considered a witch?"

A delighted laugh sprang from her mouth. "Not at all. Too much of an academic for that, and too prudent to do any sort of dancing under the moon and the like. No, Mr. Smith, I consider myself a student of the mystic and theological arts, just as I am an artisan of the social arts of grace, speech, and diplomacy – when I wish to be."

He shuffled his socked feet, feeling a chill that had nothing to do with the winter draft or being farther back from the fireplace than his host and hostess. "I was in Salem a few transfers ago. Not for long, but long enough."

"Was it as bad as they say in the history books?"

"I was too young to be taught such things, but I don't think you can read about what I saw." He fell silent and blinked to blot the images from his mind. "At least I wasn't the cause of all that. It started before I got there. And... I didn't feel all that bad about those people being drained for all the bad stuff they were doing, just because they were scared and angry or power-hungry and wanted to blame someone."

"I can only imagine the things you've seen, the places you've been. And at such a young age. However did you manage, existing in a place with nothing to do while your captors lurked freely?"

There went Mrs. Paisley's shark-mode again. Fishing for more information while appearing genuinely concerned. Perhaps she was. Perhaps not. She did raise a question he'd pondered many times. "As near as I can guess, things move without notice in the nexus, and slower than here. I'd do a lot of thinking, remembering. I hated the nexus because I couldn't do anything, but at least I wasn't hurting people or being hurt or cold or hungry. I hated being transferred to a new time and place to do their dirty work, but I was solid and real and craved that more than anything, so I tried to make the most of it."

"As in the way you eat," Mrs. Paisley remarked.

He smirked. "Yeah. Food is a luxury to me. So is being here." He looked at the device on his wrist, concentrated to feel his captors. Still sedate in their mood and he hadn't been near enough to drain anyone of any potential in four days.

"Are you wondering when they might rip you away again?" Mr. Paisley asked.

"Yeah." He shook his head at the unknown. "I don't know if the tattoo is helping or if they just got so scared from being attacked that they don't want to go anywhere for a while. Here, there's food around and no predators so maybe that's it? Even if I'm not actively collect their food?"

"A fair guess," Mrs. Paisley replied, which led in to, "If you're not to talk of the future, what can you tell us of your experiences in the past, or... anywhere else? Have you been to places without human people?"

He debated what should and shouldn't be said and glanced at Mr. Paisley. The man usually offered prudent advice in that area, usually by offering pieces of their own experiences.

Mr. Paisley stretched lazily and didn't disappoint. "We are aware of civilizations of people who are not human – some from the future, some of the past, and some from completely alternate existences to our own – much like your captors. One group we discovered appears to have conquered time and space; again, like your captors. This is why these concepts are not new to us."

"Tell me about that last one and I'll let you know if I've seen them." His turn to play at the info-gathering game.

It garnered a smile of delight from Mrs. Paisley as she recognized his entry into the game.

Mr. Paisley replied, "There are beings some call the Great Race which have been here millions of years ago and will be here again millions of years in the future, or so we've read. In more recent times, they are here now."

"They're hidden among humans?"

"Oh yes. In a very devious way. They appear able to swap their consciousness with that of another intelligent being from any time or place of their choosing. They seem to value knowledge above all things and enact these swaps to gather first-hand accounts of notable events."

"And how did you learn all this?"

Mr. Paisley nodded toward the foyer. "The odd bluish metallic artifact? It's a journal of one of them. Seems his study is the concept of good and evil so he chases after such chaos here."

He frowned at his host, confused. "You can read it? I looked at the cover and it has weird symbols on it."

Mr. Paisley nodded. "Yithian language."

Mrs. Paisley grinned, adding, "I know a spell that allows me to read any language; any at all. Although the chap's name is hardly translatable, he did put it in his journal. Taken me quite a while to read it, as the content is very… alien… and should not be devoured in a single sitting. Still, I've only found the one book, but I know they love to store their collections. We only need to find where. Think of all of the knowledge they've hoarded!"

Husband patted wife's hand. "They're well and good hid, love. However…" Mr. Paisley got up, walked to the desk, and scribbled something down.

He craned his neck to watch but couldn't make out details.

"If you've encountered these beings on their world, lad, or one here who has swapped minds with one of us, we're very curious what you learned about them." The man then took it over and held it out.

He took the paper so Mr. Paisley could move away from him. On it was a sketch of a pyramid-like body, two arms with crab claws for hands, and coming from the… head?... were eye stalks. Next to that sketch lay another, simpler. It looked like a beetle of some kind. He looked at Mr. Paisley. "There are two different ones?"

"Two different forms of the same being, from two different times. Seems they escaped some kind of cataclysm by managing it. I presume they swapped minds with a whole race of lesser beings and survived while the poor creatures left in their old bodies were destroyed. That is what our sources imply. This isn't found in the journal here but in other resources, of which we have many. As I said, they're a bit devious in their existence."

He studied the sketch during Mr. Paisley's explanation. "I don't think I've encountered anything like this, and no one who I thought wasn't human who looked the part. How do you tell who is and who isn't?"

"You can't and it's all quite rude." Mrs. Paisley got very huffy over the matter and crossed her arms. "That is what is incredibly frustrating about them. That, and the fact that we don't know how to stop them from taking over another person. They seem to do as they please and carry on without any regard for whomever's life they're ruining in their pursuit of knowledge. I'd like to catch one and see if they can get past some of the wards and spells about the house." She turned to her husband. "Honestly, Arthur, aren't we attractive enough in our endeavors to entice one of the Great Race of Yith to check up on our dealings and attempt one of their miniature takeovers? I've theories to put to the test!"

"Perhaps what we've accomplished so far is just in its infancy compared to what the future holds, my dear."

He shifted his gaze between his two hosts, marveling at their intellect, enterprise, and outright brazen attitude. How had he gotten lucky enough to fall into their laps? And could they come up with a solution for his particular pair of hijackers?

"On to further things then." Mrs. Paisley sighed, stood, and fluffed out her dressing gown. "Come, Mr. Smith. Remove your shirt, turn about, and let me see the progress."

He did as instructed and started counting automatically when he heard her step very near. Flinched slightly when she touched his freshly-tattooed flesh but it was brief. She stepped away and he put his shirt back on.

"I apologize that this technique must be done in stages, Mr. Smith, but it will afford the most protection I can offer. It is healing nicely and I'll begin the final work tomorrow."

He wondered about testing it when complete but held off asking as her yawn ended the evening for all.

Mr. Smith Who Works The Front Desk by Jade Griffin

1891, November 6

The next afternoon, just as he counted to four minutes and twenty-nine seconds, Mrs. Paisley stepped away from her work. A sigh filled with the ring of accomplishment met his ears.

"It is done."

Slowly, he sat up, rolling his shoulders as always at the end of their magical tattoo application sessions.

A clatter from behind had him jerking that way, and wincing at the elicited pain.

Mrs. Paisley was grabbing the countertop of her work station and had knocked something over.

Mr. Paisley hurried to her. "Rest, love."

She shook her head. "I'm fine. This must be promptly put away."

He watched Mr. Paisley tenderly take the various accoutrement from the wife and place them where they needed to go, then escort her out.

He waited, listened, heard nothing further, and hopped down from the table for a look.

Mrs. Paisley sat by herself in the velvet seat positioned in the foyer, her head resting in the cradle of spread thumb and forefinger.

"Do you have a headache?" he asked, for that is exactly what his mom did when she was so afflicted.

Mrs. Paisley's head came up as soon as he spoke. She smiled at his concern. "No, Mr. Smith. And I'll be fine. Arthur went to fetch something for me to drink. Would you like to know more about the process of spells?"

She was hiding whatever ailed her, but it didn't feel right calling her out on it. Perhaps she wanted to use him as a distraction? If so, he wouldn't deny her and nodded.

She dove in with an eager smile. "On magic itself, it pulls from one or several sources, some willing and some not, which is why one must know what one is doing in order to wield it properly. I tend to follow the disciplines and sources of natural magic, so as not to upset any sentient things, unlike from where other arcane users generally draw their power. They pull from a source and care nothing about it until it is too late."

"What sort of natural source do you draw from?"

"Ley lines. Invisible lines of energy which exist in bands about the entire earth, in various locations. This home sits directly aligned with one. We're in it right now."

He'd heard some of those words mentioned, in passing, several transitions ago. Hadn't paid much attention. Unlike his time in the nexus, in which he felt nothing but the mental equivalent to goosebumps, this didn't feel like standing in the middle of magical energy. Felt normal.

Mrs. Paisley stated, "By making such a permanent change to your flesh, embedding it with this abundant energy source, you shall theoretically be protected, but you may be required to stay near ley lines. We can't quite be certain yet."

"How soon until it can be tested?"

"This time right now is to allow your flesh to heal and the saturation to sink in. Tomorrow you may attempt stepping out of the house, unless you are eager to push boundaries?" She grinned at him.

"Eager to confirm that they can't take me anymore."

"While I am confident in my abilities, I would stress that patience is due. Try tomorrow."

And so he waited patiently and was up the next morning fairly early. His hosts were not. He found himself lingering near the front doors.

Danneby, who actually lived on the property with the Paisleys, emerged from around the foyer hall which bent to the right.

"Anything I can assist with, sir?" the butler asked, mindful of keeping a solid four paces away from him.

"No. Just wanting to go out."

Danneby walked past to fetch a hat and coat from the foyer closet. The butler handed them to him, moved back, and said, "Mr. and Mrs. Paisley should wake in the next hour or so. I can rouse them if need be."

"No." He set the coat and hat aside. Must be patient. Just needed something to occupy himself, so he wandered about the large home, studying many of the curiosities under glass.

Still at it when host and hostess finally descended over two hours later. At least they were fully dressed in nice clothes, as if they meant to go out again.

"Ah, Mr. Smith!" Mrs. Paisley greeted him with a smile. "Up for a bit?"

"Yeah. I mean, yes."

"And anxious to try out your ward, no doubt," Mr. Paisley mentioned with a smile.

"I agree that he's waited long enough. Well, Mr. Smith? Are you ready?"

He couldn't help a grin at his hostess's confidence and nodded.

Mr. Smith Who Works The Front Desk by Jade Griffin

"Go on then." She motioned toward the front double doors, as they kept ten feet between themselves and he.

Grasping the handle and swinging them wide, he ran out into mud and slush and fresh air and sunshine and… and… Breath held, he concentrated to the depth of his ability and found Heebs and Jeebs wriggling and muttering unintelligibly to themselves. He held still, tense, waited longer, relaxed his shoulders, his whole bearing. The feel of his captors waned as his concentration melted beneath sun and sky and wind and mud and freedom. Actual freedom! He ran about in a circle, splashed in the mud, mucking up his clothes and racing about the courtyard gravel as fast as he could and just for the sheer joy of it, all while Mrs. Paisley laughed in delight and Mr. Paisley chuckled.

Just to make sure this wasn't a fluke or time-dependent, he spent the entire afternoon outside and away from the house's magical wards. Danneby brought him a meal, which he ate among the once-tall yellow grasses about the home, now laid low by wind and weather. Nothing at all happened beyond a pleasant time in the winter air.

1891, December 4

One week. Ten days. Two weeks. One month passed and he remained fed, clothed, warm, and safe. He began to feel very comfortable and less anxious, smiling more readily and not afraid that Heebs and Jeebs would whip him away, off to their next whim.

There had never been a span where he lingered in any time so long. Not even when those scientists studied him. That had been a long and awkward week until Heebs and Jeebs decided they were done with the taste of what the scientists had him collecting and whisked him off to Salem during the witch trials and loitered him there for three solid days. So many people were drained completely, it sometimes made him sick to think of it, but he remembered what those people did to their neighbors and relatives after his arrival. A weary sigh escaped him at the memory.

"Something weighing on you, Mr. Smith?" Mrs. Paisley enquired from her end of the table, her head tilted down to catch his lowered eyes and distant gaze.

Seated closest to the doors at the dining room table, he glanced up from his half-full plate, realizing he'd paused in eating. "Mindful that I have much to be thankful for."

She cocked a brow at him and delicately forked a small raspberry into her mouth. "Are you certain you are only two decades old?"

"Only a guess. I'd wager vastly incorrect, but my experiences have made me worldly, wearied, and beyond my age. Honestly, I tried to track time by how many transfers I was put through. I lost count after five-hundred fifteen. Didn't seem much point in it, as neither my body nor my circumstances changed."

Mr. Paisley smiled pleasantly. "Your speech is coming along splendidly. I rarely hear a hint of your prior accent."

"We're quite proud of your excellent progress." Mrs. Paisley beamed.

The husband's sudden throat clearing came through as a clear warning over her comment.

The wife quickly amended, "I mean pleased. We are pleased with your progress."

The exchange intrigued him. So much so that he excused himself, pretending to still be bogged down by his past, and left the dining room. Once out of sight, he caught that Danneby only took note of him standing forlorn and didn't equate it to actual spying, so he was left alone. Alone to stand sullen with his back to the dining room doors and listen in to his heart's content.

"You're too attached, my dear," he heard Mr. Paisley's muffled voice with a worry the husband rarely displayed in front of him.

"I know, Arthur. It's just that… He's so… so…"

"I know, love. Just be cautious. He can't be viewed as a child. It is dangerous." Again, the master of the house stated this with concern only and not as a demand nor even a stern warning.

"But he **is** a child, Arthur. In his heart, if not his mind. He hasn't anyone else, so why not us?" And in a rare display of fervor and heatedness, Mrs. Paisley told her husband, "He can't be our son. We can't be his parents. But **don't** tell me I can't pretend."

"Maisey…"

He moved away, grateful for the dwindling voices. He dashed upstairs, away from all eyes. Didn't want to be seen in his increasingly anxious state.

In his room, he paced as frantically as his thoughts. He'd listened in to see if they'd a devious plan for him. He hadn't known they were starting to think of him as... as... family.

He hadn't thought of his family in a while but, after hearing the Paisleys, it exploded in his face – that cavernous feeling of knowing he would never see them again, knowing they'd never see him or know what happened to him. They weren't even born yet, his parents, but it felt like they were dead. Out of reach, elsewhere and elsewhen.

The tears started, turned to uncontrollable sobs. Not since the beginning of his captors' torment had he waterfalled such grief.

The barest of scuffs outside in the hall alerted him. He silenced immediately, breath held, snot gobbing down his throat. The floorboard creaked. The shadow of feet peeked under the bottom crack in the door. Not far enough away, he scooted along the floor to the bed, quiet, breathing as silently as possible.

"Mr. Smith?" came Mrs. Paisley's voice.

Wiping his face and nose on the underside of the bedspread, he said nothing.

"I'm sorry if we've upset you. Clara has prepared a wonderful dessert called a souffle, if you'd care to join us."

He didn't know that treat but couldn't be tempted. He didn't want anyone to know he was crying, or the real reason why. They could not help him get home, and they told him that, but knowing they felt him part of the family prodded the onslaught of emotion. He shouldn't be near

anyone's family! He **was** dangerous! And it was so unfair, because there hadn't been anything like this in so very long… Not for him. It hurt that he could not get close to them. Of course, not physically, but he had been attempting to keep his distance emotionally as well. In this, he was failing. He liked the Paisleys. Very much so. It wasn't fair to continue to be around them and place them in danger. Yet, they knew of the danger and knew how stuck it made him and were trying to be subtle in the fact that they wanted him to be stuck with them.

The next morning found him undisturbed, having fallen asleep propped against the mattress and bedframe. Dried snot from his crying stuck to the bedspread. He scrubbed at it, not wanting the reminder of last night, nor anyone to find his shed grief.

Dressed in fresh clothes, he took his time wandering downstairs. No sign of the Paisleys. He spotted Sarah first. From across the room, she eyed him warily, paused in her activity of transporting laundry to wash.

"Yes, sir?" she queried with her anxious voice cloaked in an Irish accent.

He couldn't tell if she was always like that or if it were him that made her nervous. Fairly certain he made her uncomfortable, he did not approach and asked, "Do you know where Mr. And Mrs. Paisley are?"

"Out, sir. They're off tendin' to other matters."

He knew they left occasionally and sometimes without telling him. The last time was a week ago, to the day. Perhaps they had a weekly engagement of some kind in town.

"If ye're hungry, sir, I'll have Clara fetch ye somethin'," she offered.

As he had never been encouraged to fend for himself, nor did he even know where they kept food here – having not been allowed in the kitchen yet – he nodded. Like last time, he waited in the dining room until a bowl of porridge, berries, and a glass of water were brought out by Clara, the cook.

After his meal, he felt restless. Went to the large closet by the front doors and meant to grab his coat, boots, and hat, but could not reach the hat on its peg. With a sigh, he procured the stool from a further closet but then there was Danneby holding his hat and waiting for him at the entryway.

He sighed again, at the butler. "I was going to get it."

"I know, sir."

He put the stool back and marched forward to claim his headgear. "I'm not sure if I like being waited on all the time. After living so long either doing everything myself or not being able to do anything at all, having a servant around feels very out of place to me."

"We all must get used to changes on occasion, sir. Enjoy your time outside."

He smirked at the cheeky butler and threw open the doors.

Out into the snow he raced. Didn't matter the direction. The whole manor was surrounded by grassy fields pressed low by snow. Some fresh and not littered with his footprints nor those of the carriage that likely transported the Paisleys away this morning, he dashed through the fresh air. No limitations of space or time or presence held him still. So much glee and freedom filled him that he got up the gumption to push up his sleeve and smirk at the device attached to his wrist.

"How do you like where you picked to send me, you bastards? Ha! I bet you're starving. Haven't had even a drop from someone in over three weeks! But you must be stuck. You gotta be. Otherwise you'd have tossed me somewhere else by now, or left me be. Well, I hope you both starve and feel miserable!" His words in the end turned seething and bitter and he pushed every ounce of hate into them. Testing it. Pressing them. He knew they heard him. Could feel them stirring slightly. Perhaps their rest was even agitated by his emotional taunting. Good!

He waited, felt no further stirrings, no tingling which preceded the discorporation prior to a transfer.

Takin in a deep breath, he exhaled a grand sigh, the air puffing out warm and visible in the cold all around. Cold and quiet. It was so lovely here. He didn't want to leave, so he had to pester Heebs and Jeebs, just to make damn sure they weren't going to take him away from this; that they **couldn't** take him away. They must want to, but they couldn't. He felt surer of it by the day.

1892, March 12

It was a rare occasion in which Mr. Paisley left to do some kind of business and Mrs. Paisley stayed at home. The pair seemed inseparable, which suited him fine, because Mrs. Paisley had a very keen habit of asking him anything and everything if left to her own devices. Mr. Paisley called it "playing the shark" and he couldn't agree more.

As Mrs. Paisley had fallen ill yesterday – a minor fever with sniffles and cough – she remained home in bed. He thought this would lessen her insatiable appetite for knowledge when it came to the subject of him, however she seemed more intent than ever on calling him to her side with all manner of queries. Most of them, he did not entertain, but the whole thing grew tiresome.

Returning from a brisk March walk around the estate's grassy fields where no one bothered him at all, Danneby met him at the front doors.

"Mrs. Paisley would like to speak with you."

His young shoulders sagged. "Very well." Better get it over with...

It wasn't that he didn't like Mrs. Paisley. Far from it. Out of all of the people he'd been thrust around for however many years, in and out of every span of human and alien civilization since Heebs and Jeebs kidnapped him, the Paisleys were by far the most pleasant, knowledgeable, and trustworthy. He really did like it here, and that was a problem. He shouldn't get too comfortable. Not with any of this. It wasn't safe, and it never would be.

Mr. Smith Who Works The Front Desk by Jade Griffin

He took the steps two at a time on his way to the second floor, then knocked at the entryway of the bedroom his hosts shared.

"Come in, Mr. Smith," he heard from the other side.

He did, and shut the door behind him.

Mrs. Paisley sat upright in the large bed with big fluffy pillows behind her. She wore a fur-lined robe embroidered with paisley patterns and held a handkerchief to her mouth. The fireplace crackled to the left, embers glowing brightly in the hearth.

"Ah, good morning, Mr. Smith. Have you slept well?"

"I have. And yourself?" He kept against the door, for that was the only way to keep ten feet away from the woman and her central location in the room.

Before she spoke again, a brief coughing fit paused the conversation. A moment to catch her breath, and she replied, "Not very well, I'm afraid. But I'm much improved! However, Mr. Smith, I did not ask you in to discuss myself."

He braced himself for whatever new query his hostess fancied today and prepared a few quick excuses why he could not answer. Not good to tell people of the past what would come in the future.

"My husband and I share the same birthday of April the thirteenth, which is fast approaching. We hold a yearly soiree, which we will not subject you to. Boring, required affair with the wealthy and influential. But it did occur to me that we don't know your birthday."

He stared. He blinked. He did not reply, because it was the last thing he expected her to bring up.

She smiled that smile which was all kind but also half shark. "Now, now, Mr. Smith. No need to be shy. It isn't as

Mr. Smith Who Works The Front Desk by Jade Griffin

if I'm asking on details of the future. I simply wish to know the date of the occasion."

He refrained from growling out yet another sigh. "I… I don't know."

"You—" A coughing fit seized her briefly. "You don't know?" she squeaked out before more coughing.

His fingers slid over the door handle at his back. "Do you need some water? Or Danneby?"

She shook her head. After a few deep breaths, she continued. "How… How is it that you do not know?"

He squirmed a bit, playing into the role of the six-year-old body he inhabited. "I think it was in the summer? Heebs and Jeebs captured me a short time after my birthday had passed. I don't even know how long they had me for." A bothersome point he tried not to dwell on. More bothersome than an inability to recall the exact day of his birth.

"I see…"

He caught the narrowing of her sharp eyes. Jaw set in a tight line, he replied with a defensive, "I'm not lying, if that's what you're thinking."

Her brows shot up. "I would hope you'd find no reason to lie to us, Mr. Smith. I was thinking nothing of the sort. Rather, I have an idea. It could be that you may never learn how long you were held against your choosing. But, as you won't be born for another, oh, seventy-seven years, shall we then pick a day in the summertime? Which do you fancy? June, July, or August?"

"I'd… prefer not to celebrate my birthday." Mom, Dad, and his brother all worked to throw the best birthday parties; or, the two he could recall. Didn't want the reminder of things long lost.

She offered a little shrug as if it were nothing. "So be it, Mr. Smith. I won't speak of it again. Do be a dear and ask Danneby to bring me some wine."

He nodded while turning the handle and exiting, intent on doing just that. Relief settled him back in his room after. He'd only been here a few months – and what contentment he had in noting real passages of time again! – but it felt much shorter. He was getting too comfortable. Need to watch that.

He stared out from the second story window and sighed, watching the start of snowfall cradling to the ground below. He hoped Mr. Paisley would return soon. Though both Mr. and Mrs. studied, when they could, any avenue which might free him from the device on his wrist, of which no one could touch – free him from that chain to the incorporeal Heebs and Jeebs – Mr. Paisley was the one who often delivered any news of progress, of which he received scant little. Another sigh from him fogged up the glass.

Mr. Smith Who Works The Front Desk by Jade Griffin

1892, April 13

Mrs. Paisley was very correct in her summary of the shared birthday gathering – boring. At least, to a normal young person. He, however, was not normal. Tucked away in his room upstairs, the pleasant burble of pleasantries filtering up to him and through the door made quite the pleasing atmosphere. Not audible enough to catch any gossip or topic of conversation, which was unfortunate. It would have made the whole thing that much more interesting.

Having cracked his window a bit to listen in while guests arrived, he caught several names of attendees – some of which were either already historical or would make history. No young people, but all presumably noteworthy.

The house staff never once mounted the steps, having already seen to his needs with a bountiful tray of the evening's goodies positioned on a table in his room. He enjoyed the party food immensely, but that created an issue he found harder and harder to ignore.

He'd been warned not to let anyone see him, for there would most assuredly be questions and did he want them to be asked? No? Then it was best not to be seen. He agreed completely. However, after three hours and no sign that the calm party would diminish or end anytime soon, he reasoned that he'd enough skill acquired over the unknown years to sneak down to the toilet and return just as stealthy. He cracked the door open, succeeding in avoiding the groan of creaking wood, and listened.

Guests – approximately fifteen of them – lingered in one of two areas, separated by gender. Female voices chatted with Mrs. Paisley's louder and distinct lilt in the dining room, while the deeper tone of quieter gents lay behind the door to the study.

After a gut-twisting eternity of listening, he made his move and darted downstairs, snuck up to the toilet door, strained his ear but heard no one. Completed his business, opened the toilet door a crack, peeked out. Voices coming! He froze, but watched two women wander over to the study door and enter without knocking. The aperture closed thereafter.

He didn't think. He bolted, rounded the corner, dashed up the stairs.

The study door opened.

A woman screamed!

He didn't stop or turn around but dropped to the ground after reaching the second floor. Breath held, body froze to the floor in the hall between his room and the Paisley's bedroom, his ears strained for clues to his next move.

"Genevieve, whatever is the matter?" Mrs. Paisley's voice carried high.

"There's someone up there! A boy! I'd swear it!" The shrill voice of Genevieve resounded loudly in the home.

The study door opened simultaneous to more women clucking below. Then the low mutterings of men. Shit…

"Now, now, everyone, I'm certain the ladies will sort it. Won't you, my dear?" Mr. Paisley's confidence led the thicker shuffle of men's shoes back to the study.

"Of course. Come along." Mrs. Paisley tried the same in a well-practiced manner, and most of the quieting gaggle milled back to the dining room.

"But I **saw** someone!" Genevieve insisted.

Mrs. Paisley sighed, a loud sound in the otherwise vacated hall. "I know. I've seen him, too, on occasion." Her footsteps brought her closer to the distraught guest.

"Who is it?" The whisper barely made it up to his ears.

"Lucius Kinvale; a boy who, for a time, stayed with us. He passed many years ago but, at times, briefly, I've seen or head him wandering the halls."

"A ghost??" Genevieve exclaimed, attempting to keep her voice down.

"Yes. Such knowledge tends to upset guests, and the spirit appears unaware of the living, so Arthur and I ignore him. We see him so rarely as it is. I suppose eventually someone else was bound to see him, but I can count on your discretion, can't I?"

"... Of course. Imagine! Who'd believe me?"

Even he could tell the woman was lying, betrayed by her voice.

"You are a dear. Shall we return to the others?"

"Yes, but... What **shall** we tell them?"

"Nothing at all. Let them enjoy the excitement of a mystery. But it is so very nice to finally have someone else see the poor soul, aside from Arthur. I dare say they'd call us all mad if they thought we believed we'd actually seen a ghost! Best not to say a thing."

"Eh... Yes. Quite."

An uncomfortable and purposeful silence followed.

"Shall we then?" Mrs. Paisley asked, very comfortable with the situation and its outcome.

Soft steps departed. The opening of the dining room doors, brief muted female banter, and then they closed once more.

Relative silence settled, wherein he marveled at Mrs. Paisley's adept handling of the difficult social play. She could easily have threatened Mrs. McAllister, but she did not and made it all the more difficult for the guest to mention seeing him.

Jetting up, he went right for his door, opened it with care, closed it the same, and proceeded to tidy the bedroom to hide any indication that anyone lived in it – on the chance someone wanted to be nosy.

He'd just finished when Genevieve's voice grew from downstairs, bringing justification to his paranoia. Rolling quickly under the primly-made bed, he stilled just in time to beat the footsteps mounting the stairs.

"I only wish you'd believe me," came the voice of Genevieve from the other side of his door.

The aperture opened, creaking its groan. He spied a pair of red bejeweled women's shoes and a pair of men's dress shoes beside her.

"Don't you think this is all a bit much?" her male companion asked, clearly uncomfortable. "I don't believe we should even be up here."

"Nonsense. If they've nothing to hide, there will be nothing to find." She entered his room, went to the closet, opened it.

He tensed, fearing she'd look under the bed next. They were too close already. He started the count in his head.

More footsteps approached, stilling the invading feet which swirled about toward the oncomer.

He knew Mrs. Paisley's shoes very well, having polished them a time or two himself. Relief filled him as those shoes came into view in his doorway.

"I didn't take you both for snoops," Mrs. Paisley said, a note of accusation in her otherwise playful tone.

"Not sure what's gotten into Genevieve, Mrs. Paisley. My apologies," the man said.

He could tell the man hooked Genevieve's arm in his and gave her a tug, for the men's shoes moved toward the door and the women's were pulled off balance with a startled yelp.

"It's perfectly alright, Mr. McAllister. If you wouldn't mind, I'd like a moment of Genevieve's time before you depart."

"If you insist."

The man stomped downstairs, leaving the women alone.

He tried his very best to stay still and absolutely silent, but both women in the room were still too close!

"Genevieve, dear, knowledge of the world beyond is not for everyone. Some cannot even see ghosts. Or did you think I was lying?"

The guest did not respond.

Mrs. Paisley let out a sigh. "I see. However, there is no proof of a living boy here, is there? Then why is it so hard to believe it really was a spirit?"

"I suppose that is true. I'm sorry, Maisey, and it being your birthday as well." Genevieve started away.

Mrs. Paisley followed and both left the zone of influence of the device on his wrist, thank goodness!

"It really doesn't bother you, knowing a ghost dwells here?"

"Not at all. I find it a comfort that there is more beyond than anyone can see." Mrs. Paisley closed the bedroom door.

Their voices dwindled and his shoulders sagged on a hefty sigh. Under the bed he remained, waiting, just in case anyone else tried to explore. The evening's quiet lulled him into nodding off.

He jerked awake at the sudden crack of a horseman's whip and a hearty "Hya!" preceding the grind of carriage wheels on wet gravel. The doors to the estate closed. He yawned.

Footsteps once more took to the stairs but he believed it to be only Mrs. Paisley's cat-like approach.

The door opened. He saw her shoes which confirmed his guess.

"Mr. Smith?" she called softly.

He rolled out from under the bed and rubbed at tired eyes. "Sorry."

"You've nothing to be sorry for. You did admirably. I apologize that the party dragged for so long."

He sat on the bed, looked over at the closet, remembered the young clothes which were there even before he arrived at the Paisley estate. "Is what you told her true?"

"Yes. All but the ghost part. I've never seen Lucius's ghost and I don't expect to."

"Ghosts aren't real?"

She smiled on him and stepped into the room. "Ghosts are very real, Mr. Smith, but none reside here. I've checked."

"Who was he? Why was he here?"

Mrs. Paisley sighed. A sad one. "Like you, he hadn't anyone else. Just a boy in need of a place, a home." She did not add "family" but it was as if he heard it anyway.

"How did he die?"

A pause. More sadness. "The black spiders around the house which we warned you of?"

He nodded. Black widows. Had them where he came from and he'd seen them many other places. A common enough danger.

"He was catching them, for me. I study them, you see. He knew the dangers but did not know that their bite would cause him to have such a terrible and swift reaction…"

As her eyes and words trailed away, so did his desire to know. "Sorry. I shouldn't have asked."

Her eyes found him and her smile returned. "No, it was many years ago. You've nothing to feel badly over."

"It upsets you still."

"It does, but you were obviously curious." Mrs. Paisley entered further, shortening the distance between them by too much. "It is very hard not to blame myself over the loss of someone I'd begun to see as family…"

He was already counting in his head when she boldly sat at the end of the bed and added, "Just as I'd feel if something were to happen to you."

He needed to move away but didn't want to offend her or make her more miserable. Perhaps a few more seconds. She looked so sad.

"We won't let anything happen to you, Mr. Smith. Don't fret over the matter, nor over what Mr. and Mrs. McAllister might say."

She sent a hand over to pat his – a very warm reassurance which left him desiring to reply in kind. Only untold years of caution kept him in check.

The clear and confident step of Mr. Paisley ascended the stairs, prompting the wife to a quick stand and glide to the doorframe, out of range of the draining device. With a final smile, she said, "Good night, Mr. Smith."

Mr. Smith Who Works The Front Desk by Jade Griffin

She moved past her husband and on to their bedroom.

Mr. Paisley looked into his room, cast a glance his way.

He gave a nod to the old man's questioning gaze, assuring Mr. Paisley that nothing was amiss.

The master of the house returned the gesture with a content smile before shutting the door, footsteps moving on to join the wife.

He contemplated the whole of it after the pair closed their own bedroom door. Another person they'd taken in before him. Ghosts were real. Mrs. Paisley got too close for longer than normal.

He monitored her behavior over the next few days and into the next week but Mrs. Paisley neither approached him without cause nor did she linger any longer than necessary, so he let it pass.

Mr. Smith Who Works The Front Desk by Jade Griffin

1892, December 20

Though the wind buffeted them both and constantly threatened to throw him to the ground, he channeled his fury and sorrow to plant his feet and stand as unbudging and silent as Mr. Paisley during the funeral.

A kind of horror not experienced since being abducted had greeted him three days ago when he awoke to find Mrs. Maisey Paisley draped across his bed like a wilted flower. His screams summoned Danneby, the other servants, and Mr. Paisley, who ordered the staff out. His screams choked off to silent terror, for Mr. Arthur Paisley entered his room and loomed over the scene, expressionless. His panic grew as his host continued to stand too near for too long and the device on his wrist began to drain the master of the house as well. Was Mr. Paisley trying to die? Or would the man try to kill him?

He took in a breath to speak, to yell, ready to talk his host down or to bolt if it came to that.

Mr. Paisley bent with swift tenderness and collected the wife's body. Arthur only looked at Maisey. Never at him. The man turned toward the door, steps heavy but not from the effort of transporting the lifeless wife. It was just too much. The sorrow of this pair's parting broke him to tears.

At the threshold, Mr. Paisley paused. Without turning, the broken man said, "She always wanted children." And the gentleman swept out with haste, the expired lady's wispy gown waving their departure.

The thunder of Mr. Paisley's fading steps, the lightning of the servants' wails, the silence of his room pattering against his brain… He ran to his door and slammed it shut. That did not stop the rain of his tears.

Why? **Why** did they let her die?? He **hated** them more than ever before, but also himself. How could he have let this happen? Why hadn't he felt her in the room, or the device doing its heinous task? Why couldn't he stop this? If someone were to die, why did it have to be someone he cared about?

The only conclusion was that his time with Heebs and Jeebs had changed him irrevocably. He remained a danger to everyone and shouldn't be around people. Not living people. Not anymore!

His fury and sorrow boiled over, he ran outside and spewed all of his hate into the damn device on his wrist. "C'mon, you bastards! You drained someone completely! Get me **outta** here! You always yank me away after, **so do it**! I don't wanna be here anymore! **Take me away!**"

He yelled at them for what seemed hours but the most he received from his captors was an overall contentedness and the impression that they didn't plan on going anywhere at all. That, and a hoarse throat.

Out of exhaustion and indecision, he returned to the guest room. No one came to check on him. If he could have locked his door, he'd have shut out the whole world. He didn't deserve to have anyone look after him! The Paisleys didn't deserve this…

He did not know when he slept but knew it was late when he rose the next day. The high sun crept well into the room and brought an instant scowl to his face. Still in the Paisley's mansion. He had to use the toilet, calm his ravenous stomach. That meant facing everyone in the house.

Mr. Smith Who Works The Front Desk by Jade Griffin

Creeping to his door, he opened it a crack. Tried to miss the creaky bit and miscalculated, its abysmal groan a shriek in the pure silence. Thankfully, no one dwelled upstairs. Hurrying down, he saw the maid, Sarah, step well away from him before he reached the bottom. She looked afraid.

After using the toilet, he made straight for the dining room but skidded to a halt as its doors opened. There stood a sad version of Danneby. Dark, droopy eyes, an actual crease in the normally pressed slacks, and a decrease in the attention to well-combed hair betrayed any attempt on the butler's part to make things look business as usual. It wasn't business as usual.

"The afternoon meal is long past, Mr. Smith. If you'd like—"

"Can you bring it to my room?"

"Of course, sir. Anything in partic—"

"No, Danneby," and he went back upstairs.

A small tray of meats, cheese, fruit, and a pitcher of water arrived outside on the floor a short time later. He collected it and consumed it without ever tasting a bite. He paused mid-gulp at the sound of horse hooves on the gravel of the courtyard. Meal abandoned, the window became his next pursuit and he gazed down through the rippled glass to see Mr. Paisley exiting the carriage. How long had Mr. Paisley been gone? Where had his host come from? Making funeral preparations or eviction arrangements for the live-in who killed the lady of the house? Only fair. Mr. Paisley clearly loved her and now she was gone. Because of him. **He** brought this into their home. He—

The trod of heavy boots ascended the steps, and then a knock at his door.

Mr. Smith Who Works The Front Desk by Jade Griffin

He didn't answer. He didn't want to talk to Mr. Paisley. He didn't—

The door opened. Mr. Paisley entered. Sleepless rings crowded sad eyes and too much weighing on that mustached face to ever pull a smile up again. The master of the house slouched and looked as if the world placed boulders on the poor man in his room's entryway.

That sight clinched it for him. If Heebs and Jeebs would not take him away, he'd do it himself. He told Mr. Paisley, "I will leave within the hour."

Mr. Paisley shut the door. "No, you will not."

The master of the house approached him, but he took a step back for every one and found himself against the wall. Mr. Paisley went right up to him. The man was too close and smelled of not washing and of preservation chemicals. The thought that Mr. Paisley had spent the whole day personally embalming Mrs. Paisley, or even attempted thaumaturgy to bring her back, made him sick. He ducked under the man's arm and fled to his bed before he lost his meal.

Mr. Paisley followed but did not crowd him as before. "You will not be leaving. You will not be harmed by myself or yourself. I won't allow it. We've lost too much already and I will **not** stand for more!"

Never had Mr. Paisley's voice raised above talking volume. Now, it shuddered the very window at his back. The man wasn't bearing down on him but remained too close. He started the count.

"I understand the blame, but you will not leave me alone in my grief. Is that understood?"

He considered it, considered a lot of things, but in the end he nodded.

Mr. Smith Who Works The Front Desk by Jade Griffin

"The funeral's tomorrow. I need you there, son—"

"**Don't** call me that," he seethed with sudden ire. "My name is Mr. Smith. It's what she always called me…"

The past tense reminder deflated Mr. Paisley even more. With a quavering voice, the widower said, "That she did, Mr. Smith. That she did." The distance between them was closed as the man sat upon the bed and leaned against his small form. Sobs began to shake Mr. Paisley.

He didn't know what to do except put an arm around the man and ignore the smell of body odor and whatever chemicals lingered on the wrinkled, rich clothing.

Mr. Paisley grabbed him in a hug much tighter than his loose hold.

Time ticked by loudly in his head. Too much time. He let the man go but Mr. Paisley held on. "Mr. Paisley, you need to let go. Mr. Paisley! Arthur, your time's up! **Let go!**" He struggled but still the man held firm. He felt the device on his wrist activate.

Just as he was about to yell for Danneby, the butler entered to address the fussing. Danneby caught a brief look at the master of the house crying on their ward before Mr. Paisley pushed up from the bed and staggered toward the butler. Danneby looked warily back before escorting the master out.

He moved to the entryway, saw that the butler still looked after Mr. Paisley, and said, "Don't let him up here for at least five hours, Danneby." And he slammed the door shut.

Damn it! What was Mr. Paisley thinking?? And the five hours was more of a guess on the reset of the device. During one particular transfer, some scientists in the future thought they learned what happened around him and did experiments with sending people in to sit with him for different periods of time. It seemed to take four or five hours for the device to reset and not just start draining the same person immediately, but Mr. Paisley had accidentally done so a time or two – lingered too long in its range. He tried to be diligent but, to be honest, everyone in the house had at least once stayed too long near him and activated the device. Did the reset time away from him need to be longer and longer after each activation? He couldn't be sure, so he must **not** be lax. He **couldn't** let it happen again!

It became a litany, a rule, during the funeral and after, even up in his room where he stayed as long as possible. A reminder. Don't let it happen. Don't let anyone near. Never again. The gray stillness of the house consumed everyone in it, visible in the eyes of the staff seen briefly at mealtime and by his forced solitude. Mr. Paisley he saw only on occasion. The master of the house spent more time out and away by carriage than he spent inside for the first week or so. Fine. He wanted to be ignored. He deserved no less.

1893, February 8

There came a knock one gray, cold afternoon. Mr. Paisley entered, despite not getting an invite in. He looked well enough, wearing fresh clothes, but tired lines remained permanently etched on the worn face. No, not tired. More resolute.

"I know you feel responsible. You and I both. There isn't anything to be done about it in this case but to move forward. I know you don't care to go out and you have no interest in meeting new people, but I feel it's time I shared what pushes me through the day."

Mr. Paisley, standing in the bedroom doorway, was correct. He didn't feel like doing any of those things. Didn't feel like getting off the bed he sat in all day. And his guilt certainly kept him from wanting to seek any relief.

"I can tell you're going to try and fight me on this, but know that Maisey was just as to blame. She was not some naïve girl. The woman acted positively reckless at times. Always pushing the boundaries of knowledge, danger, and patience. I love her and I miss her but my grieving is spent and we have work to do."

He cast a suspicious glance up at the man. "Work?" Learning many things living with the Paisleys over the last year, he never once was asked to do work before.

"Those creatures that chained you to them. Wouldn't it be better to work toward learning more about them so that they may be extracted and then dissected in order to prevent any future persons from being harmed by them, or others like them?"

Mr. Smith Who Works The Front Desk by Jade Griffin

His brows rose. By work, Mr. Paisley meant to put his anger to productive use. Honestly, he'd love to rip them out of the device and torture them himself for all the misery they caused. He also had no idea if Heebs and Jeebs could be extracted without breaking the tattoo Mrs. Paisley needled into his back. If there were a chance Mr. Paisley could help with that, and maybe get revenge for having taken Mrs. Paisley's life, it'd be stupid not to try and very much worth the effort. He did not, however, desire to jump into whatever it entailed. So he asked, "What did you have in mind?"

A bit of the man's old smile popped up. "Get dressed, eat, and join me in the study."

He did all three of those quickly, for he dared to hope that whatever his benefactor had planned would work.

The study was quite large and filled predominantly with books and a few artifacts. The large tortoiseshell globe in the corner by the window had always captured his interest. It happened to be where Mr. Paisley chose to stand.

"You've been allowed to read and learn about whatever struck your fancy in this room whenever your tutoring concluded. It is time you received a different sort of structure to your education."

Wary, he stayed at the doorway. "Not another tutor, I hope. The one I have now keeps getting too close; and too suspicious. Asks a lot of inappropriate questions. She thinks you rape me and that's why I don't want anyone near me."

Mr. Paisley cocked a brow at him. "How crude. No, Mr. Smith, I am referring to my own areas of expertise: the occult, science, business, and politics. Maisey was the resident expert on theology, societal etiquette, and thaumaturgy but I know she's taught you bits of each and that will be sufficient for now. I have also invited a different sort of person to instruct you in an area I was never inclined to pursue: the art of the sword."

More surprises. "You're having someone teach me fencing?"

"No. In my younger years, I traveled extensively and stumbled upon the more cultured styles of the Orient. You will gain instruction from a swordmaster of Japan. He is due to arrive in a month or so. You appear to treat everyone with due respect, which I believe is a sign of brighter future times, and by your grin I suspect a foreign person will not be an issue to learn from."

Far from it. Japanese culture and fighting skills were something exotic and exciting in his time, seen predominantly on film. Whoever it would be, they'd instantly have his respect. "Will he speak this language?"

"Some, likely. He will be made aware of the limits of your closeness but lied to about why, as we've discussed for prior instances. I've seen him work and you will be pressed for endurance."

His grin spread wider, eager. What kid wouldn't love this opportunity?

"Today, you will begin learning the others I've mentioned. We'll start with business."

Not his preference but he decided to humor Mr. Paisley. This did, after all, start him out of his depression and would hopefully lead to ending Heebs and Jeebs' imprisonment of him.

Mr. Paisley strode past him and into the foyer, expecting him to follow. He did, with reservation, because he heard the front doors open and the clatter of hooves and carriage wheels on the snowy gravel of the front courtyard.

He stopped twenty feet away from Mr. Paisley, who stood at the doors with Danneby holding a small hat, coat, and gloves for him.

"Come along, Mr. Smith," his benefactor coaxed, exiting and climbing into the carriage.

Get in the carriage? He wasn't sure if Mr. Paisley wanted to die along with the driver or what mad scheme cooked in the man's head but chose to give a little trust. He snagged the coat from Danneby and crammed his arms in while edging to the entryway. There, he saw the coachman atop Mr. Paisley's carriage which had the door closed, and a second horse awaiting behind it, saddled and ready.

Mr. Paisley leaned out the carriage window into the light snowfall. "You haven't much practice, I'd suspect, but there is no time like the present, Mr. Smith. Mount that horse and we'll be off. Follow us, if you please."

It was true. He had very little experience with horses, but only due to his age prior to Heebs and Jeebs interfering with his life. His parents, he recalled, owned a few horses so at least he wasn't going in with blinders on.

Buttoning his coat, he wandered up to the bay mare, gave her a pat, and hauled his small form up into the saddle. When the front coachman snapped a whip at the horse pulling Mr. Paisley's carriage, he did his best tapping his steed with the heels of little boots. The horse jerked forward, starting their journey.

At least, he thought to himself, they weren't going too fast. He could barely see Mr. Paisley's carriage, so much snow hit his face with biting cruelty half the way and the wind buffeting him the other half once that ceased. The trip was not short, either. They traveled over an hour before he realized they were headed to the city proper.

Mr. Paisley's carriage pulled to a stop at a street corner in bustling east central Chicago. He followed suit and waited, pulling his coat closer about him as the wind picked up to a howling pace once more. It threw snow as if spitting vilely at his efforts to do something with his life again. Given everything so far, the blustery weather proved easy to ignore. Not so easy to ignore Mr. Paisley when the man stood beside his horse and waved him down.

He handed the reins to the waiting coachman and joined his benefactor reluctantly, on edge now that he occupied a sidewalk in a busy city. Too many people. Too many opportunities to get too close. He looked about, saw not many near, and forced himself to relax a little.

"This way, Mr. Smith," Mr. Paisley coaxed, holding open one of two glass double doors.

He skittered in quickly and fully, placing as much distance between he and... Wow, the place was huge! He stopped just inside, marveling at the sheer size and simple elegance, the massive, open floor plan and vaulted ceiling. Seven small couches, five coffee tables, a twelve-foot-wide walkway leading to the other end of the room, and so much space in between all the furniture. And no one at all around. And were those wards concealed as decoratives on the doorframe?

"What is this place?" he queried, cautious in his curiosity.

"Don't fret," Mr. Paisley said, observing him taking it all in. "There isn't anyone on the first floor at the moment aside from you and I."

Mr. Paisley strode past him and made for the far end. There, his patron sat at a single desk positioned beside a filing cabinet.

Still puzzled, he wandered up close enough to look the desk over. Pens, paper, a filing basket, and a candlestick-style telephone on the desk. Everything nice and clean and uncluttered.

Mr. Paisley picked up the receiver, dialed two numbers, and spoke into it. "We shall be up momentarily."

He cast a look of surprise toward Mr. Paisley. No audible reply came back, so he asked, "Who was on the other end?"

"Mr. Vince Young, President of the Paisley Foundation." Mr. Paisley reclined in the seat.

"The Paisley Foundation?"

"Yes. No one here has been told anything about you aside from you are a boy I have taken in, and that you like your space. I meant what I said. It is time to let some others in on your circumstances and perhaps together we can sort you out. This is, after all, my foundation – a collection of trusted people to look for, and look after, the curious knowledge that's out there." Mr. Paisley pointed out toward the snow-covered street. "What you've seen at the house is a very small measure of what's been found, Mr. Smith. Come. I'll introduce you to the others and then you'll have a proper tour."

Mr. Paisley got up and started for what he now saw was an elevator door.

He did not follow. "Mr. Paisley…"

Arthur Paisley spun and pinned him with a stern look. "I did not bring you here to remain on the first floor. Come along."

He took a breath to settle himself and not look as anxious as he felt before following his benefactor into the close confines of the old-fashioned elevator. Old-fashioned to him. Looked new outside and in. He pressed himself to the farthest end he could while Mr. Paisley personally operated the elevator switch, but it wasn't far enough away. He silently willed the elevator to proceed quickly so the damn device would not start draining Mr. Paisley.

The elevator made no stops other than the one Mr. Paisley commanded, making the trip very short. The number on the top of the switch read as Floor 5. The lift opened and he stepped out quickly into sudden clatters of repetitive sound. Didn't matter what would be there. He had to get further away from Mr. Paisley. Up here it was, at least, almost as open as the lobby floor.

The clattering sounds came from a bank of four typewriters, each with a seated typist studiously typing away and mostly succeeding in not staring at him. Just a few glances every now and then. Aside from that set-up in the very center of the huge room, he saw what looked like four corner offices with closed doors and nothing else but glass windows going all the way around the square building.

"This is where the four Corners do the bulk of their work," Mr. Paisley said, pointing out each corner office. "President, vice president, secretary, and treasurer. The Corners and myself run the Paisley Foundation."

The president's office door opened. Out strode a tall, blond man who smiled at first sight of them. Strode right on up to them, which made him step several paces back. The man was intelligent enough to go no further than Mr. Paisley.

"I see what you mean about him liking space. A bit young, though, don't you think?" the man asked Mr. Paisley.

"Do not be fooled by Mr. Smith's size or visible age. He is more than capable of understanding the true nature of our business and may well become the most valuable of assets, if utilized with care." To him, Mr. Paisley said, "This is Mr. Vince Young. While most decisions affecting the motion of things are decided by the four Corners and myself, nearly all immediate items are brought directly to Mr. Young."

He gave a nod of understanding.

Mr. Young did not take Arthur Paisley's words to heart, for the man strode right up to him and knelt before extending a hand. "Just Mr. Smith? Surely there's more."

One brow raising in warning, he folded his arms across his chest, unaffected by the man's charming airs. "There is always more to a person than anyone can see with a simple look but, in my case, Mr. Smith will do and I require no pandering. No need to kneel before me like a smitten knight, Sir Young." And he waved the man up like he imagined a bored king would do before backing himself away.

The room stilled at his words. Even the typists' keystrokes slowed, hovering above their station at his unapologetic response. One typist coughed, likely to cover an outburst of a laugh.

Mr. Young glanced at a smirking Mr. Paisley before rising once more. Then the tall man flicked an impatient gaze at the typists, who dove busily back to their clacking.

A smile wreathed the president's face as he again turned to Mr. Paisley's guest. "An aficionado of the Arthurian lore, eh? You and our vice president, Sergei, will have much to talk about." President Young pointed out the office across and on the far side of the room.

"Another time," Mr. Paisley interrupted and went to the closest office door. "First, the others."

Not bothering to knock – but then the place belonged to the man – Mr. Paisley opened the door and waved someone out. It happened to be a woman with chestnut-colored hair who put her hand to her mouth in surprise at first sight of their guest.

"Oh my..." she uttered, unable to stop staring.

Mr. Paisley told her, "Treasurer Tricia White, this is Mr. Smith. There will be a meeting in ten minutes in Conference Room 2."

Treasurer White gave a nod and went back into her office, her eyes only leaving him then.

By this time, the door to their left opened and a sandy-haired head poked out, followed by the rest of the man. This one was taller even than President Young, had a mustache and goatee, and stared openly and curiously at him from beside Mr. Young.

"Secretary Harold Midsommer, this is Mr. Smith. Meeting in ten minutes, Conference Room 2."

Mr. Midsommer looked at Mr. Paisley. "...Right. We're to be briefed on Mr. Smith then?"

"And the other matters. I suggest you bring your notes."

Mr. Midsommer wasted not a moment and turned toward the office just vacated.

In the meantime, Mr. Young was trying not to stare, and failing, while Mr. Paisley wandered to the far office across from Mr. Young's. Knocking enticed a burly gentleman with a bushy beard out and to follow Mr. Paisley. When the two came near, Mr. Young spoke up to introduce him.

"Mr. Smith, this is Sergei Grummond, the Paisley Foundation's vice president."

When Mr. Grummond moved forward to offer a hand for a proper handshake, Mr. Paisley moved quickly in the way.

"Mr. Smith and I will descend now and await you all in Conference Room 2. Five minutes," the patron told the two Corners.

Into the elevator Mr. Paisley went and he followed quickly.

When the mechanical entry closed, his mouth quirked at Mr. Paisley in distaste. "Do you think this is at all a good idea?"

"I do. And the conference room is large enough. There shouldn't be any problem keeping sufficient distance." Mr. Paisley turned to the elevator control, opened a hidden compartment on the round portion which indicated access to other floors, and set it to the fourth floor. Once the elevator carriage was in motion, Mr. Paisley regarded his skepticism with a cocked brow. "They're quite reasonable people who have often been put up against unreasonable situations."

He shrugged, animating his arms comically to display exaggerated resignation.

"Enough of that. We both needed a kick in the trousers, and don't think for one second Maisey wouldn't do it herself if she were here."

That reminder cooled a growing anxiety and tempered a souring mood. Mrs. Paisley would indeed have spearheaded this whole introduction with absolute glee.

The elevator opened onto the fourth floor which contained a very long, wide hallway with doors on both sides. Passing them, he noted those on the left had no window but a number in the sequence of one through five set into a brass plate beside each of the quintet of entryways. The two on the right had a very large window a piece along with a brass plate. They entered the closer one labeled CONFERENCE ROOM 2, where a long table and many chairs took up much of the space.

  He immediately took the farthest chair and pulled it to the furthest corner of the room. Yes, it would be enough space, but barely just, by his estimation. Better to overestimate than under in his experience.

  He sat and asked, "Their curiosity is going to get the better of them, so I'd like to know: What are you planning on telling them?"

  Mr. Paisley did not answer, for the ding of the elevator heralded the arrival of persons entering the hall. No chatter or hushed voices preceded the four Corners as they filed into the conference room and took their seats on either side near the head of the table, where Mr. Paisley finally sat. They kept looking between Mr. Paisley and him, but he certainly wasn't going to start this off, so he turned his gaze to the founder.

  Mr. Paisley dove right in. "I appreciate you keeping me appraised during my period of mourning, but my absent ends today. Business shall resume as normal."

  "Sir, we want you to take all the time you need," Secretary Midsommer said, expressing true sympathy.

  "I have taken all that I require, Mr. Midsommer. Mr. Smith will be a casual observer today but is likely to take a more pronounced presence in the future. We will carry on as usual, however please respect his necessity for space. And, Mr.

Midsommer, Mr. Smith's arrival at the Paisley Foundation does not change my previously stated wishes. There will be no file on Mr. Smith in the Repository. Ever."

He watched their expressions carefully and saw that this decree came as a surprise. So much so that they looked unsure of their leader's decision. Must be a highly unusual order.

"But, Sir," Mr. Grummond spoke up, revealing a thick Russian accent. "Everyone has file who encounters Paisley Foundation, or whom we have interest in."

"This is true, and not even myself nor my wife have been exempt, but Mr. Smith is a most unusual case. Know that it is for the best, that information will come when it is deemed prudent, and that Mr. Smith should not be treated in any way like a child."

"How…" Ms. White, Treasurer, trailed off before starting again with, "How are we to treat him, sir, if he is to be a frequent guest?"

"As a peer of equal standing in matters of the Paisley Foundation."

That went over even worse. The room fell silent as they mulled the sentence over. He felt it a bit much, as well. Seen as a peer to these people? That would be hard for anyone to accept.

Mr. Midsommer asked, "Sir, if we are to proceed, and treat him as a fellow Corner, may we know as much about this equal in the room as we do of each other?"

Mr. Paisley's mustache pulled down in mild irritation. "Seems we can't get on with any current business until you've all got this sorted, eh?"

Mr. Smith Who Works The Front Desk by Jade Griffin

Mr. Grummond, vice president, smiled convivially. "Sir, with respect, you say very little about boy you allow to live in house with you for a year. And way he look at us is not like boy. As you say, do not treat him like child. He is what then? Age reversal spell? Or Yithian?"

He harumphed in dismissal and slipped out of his chair, drawing everyone's eyes. "Definitely not Yithian." He paused, gave them a moment to digest that his seven-year-old-looking self not only knew what Yithians were but was now keen to answer in a straightforward manner. Well, if Mr. Paisley really wanted them to treat him like an equal, he'd best show them he was up for it. "I am familiar with many unusual subjects, some of which were taught to me by Mr. and Mrs. Paisley. For example, I noted the wards about the building's entrance. Those likely keep most out, but they weren't done in the same style as Mrs. Paisley. One of you must've applied practical thaumaturgy. You have many questions, but so do I. And, although I have been stuck like this for some time, Mr. Paisley feels I might find answers here. That is what the Paisley Foundation does, does it not?"

While President Young and Vice President Grummond exchanged looks, Secretary Midsommer answered him.

"Er... Yes. That is correct, Mr. Smith. Would you be amiable to telling us more about yourself if we went 'round and did so first?"

He considered it, then nodded.

"I was the one; who put up the wards, I mean. I was told I had a talent for practicing the arcane and made it my specialty." Midsommer's voice thinned. The next words revealed why. "Mrs. Paisley was very encouraging and taught me much."

So she must have worked extensively here. They did seem well-acquainted with her. He wondered briefly why the couple never mentioned this place before today but, given what they did here, it was most likely for his and their protection. And Mr. and Mrs. probably still assessing him at the time.

President Young, seated beside Secretary Midsommer, took the next turn. "My parents work hard for all the wrong reasons and tried to raise me with their ideology. Mr. Paisley has seen more promise in me than they ever could. He granted me opportunities on my merit, not on my bank account. I strive to be more than I am and feel great honor to have been nominated into the office of president following Mr. Paisley's move to acting Emeritus."

Rich boy wanting to please everyone. No surprise there.

"My turn," Vice President Grummond grinned mightily. "I was Russian Empire spy. My name was Sergei Grumm but officials added the 'mond' to be more American." Grin still in place, the man's voice shifted to a clear American style. "Although I can speak more fluently with less accent, I prefer to keep my native appearance in practice, because it often fools all the right people." The thick Russian accent flooded back again. "Was part of spy training, and very handy here."

"I don't have as colorful a story," Treasurer Tricia White told him. "…but my family name, de Lorraine, is deeply entrenched in the occult. Not all, but most have done terrible things, to others and to themselves, and I did not escape their machinations. When I did fight against them, they retaliated with a vengeance. I would not have escaped without the assistance of the Paisleys. Though I cannot be compared to

Mr. Smith Who Works The Front Desk by Jade Griffin

Mrs. Paisley, I do follow in her path and choose to use my knowledge, resources, and skills for the good of mankind and work to undo the subjugation imposed by my forebearers."

Impressive. Pulled herself from terrible circumstances.

All eyes on him once more, he knew exactly what he wanted to say. Displaying an appropriately restrained amount of fury and sorrow, he stated simply, "I have a bad luck aura which killed Maisey Paisley."

Mr. Paisley slammed both palms onto the table and shot to a stand, voice thundering. "MR. SMITH! WE HAVE BEEN OVER THIS!"

Everyone froze at the bellowed words. He wondered if the Corners had ever seen Mr. Paisley so upset. He hadn't. Even if they had, the exchange between benefactor and ward looked unsettling to the assembled people.

Taking in a deep breath, Mr. Paisley calmly stated, "Maisey acted carelessly and **we** are left to regret it." Mr. Paisley's eyes went to Secretary Midsommer. "Please amend Maisey's file. Cause of death: proximity to calamitous individual."

'Calamitous individual'. He would have barked a laugh… if it didn't fit him to a tee. Calamity seemed destined to follow him.

"Are you dangerous?" President Young asked in the silence, heaps of caution ladled on.

"Anyone can be dangerous, but it isn't something I control. Don't spend too much time around me and you will be fine."

This did not seem to settle their minds. Many anxious glances flicked about the table. Only Mr. Paisley and Mr.

Mr. Smith Who Works The Front Desk by Jade Griffin

Grummond met his gaze. At least it stopped their immediate interest.

A light knock at the closed conference room door broke through the quiet. No one responded but it opened anyway. An older woman – bony arms, curly grey hair, and a cheery smile – carried in a large tray of snacks.

"Good morning, Corners, Mr. Paisley, and Mr. Smith."

Mr. Paisley settled back into the head seat with a sigh of resignation at the interruption. "Good morning, Dolores."

No one said anything while the serving woman set out a stack of plates and a smaller tray of fruits, cheese, slices of toast, and two pots. He assumed they were coffee and tea, given that cream, honey, and sugar were also on the tray. He paid close attention to Mr. Paisley's expression, because he wanted to know what sort of person this Dolores might be and how she fit in with the Paisley Foundation hierarchy. Was she not in the know and just a basic serving person? Or more like Danneby and the house staff at Mr. Paisley's mansion, or something more like the Corners?

When Mr. Paisley appeared to be waiting patiently for Dolores to finish her task and gave over nothing else, he looked to the Corners but could not tell whether they were cowed by the previous outburst or just silent because the serving lady was in the room.

Once all had been placed on the table, she held her tray against her chest with a smile and a sigh. "There now. Have at it and perhaps your day will continue without any more shouting."

Ah. Wondered how she knew his name. He remained the only new name and face, and his was the only name Mr. Paisley bellowed.

Mr. Smith Who Works The Front Desk by Jade Griffin

The benefactor turned a sheepish face to the serving woman. "Apologies for yelling."

Dolores stood in the doorway, fingers laced together in front of her, the tray hooked into the crook of her bony arm. She looked on each face in the room. "I should say so. I'd be surprised if the typists didn't hear you yelling at Mr. Smith." And then she looked at him. "I took the liberty of guessing your preference, young man. If there's anything special you'd like…?"

He looked over the assembled foodstuffs and then, to her, replied, "An orange, if you have it, if you please."

A bright smile smooshed more wrinkles upon her face. "It **would** please me. So polite! Anyone else?" The serving woman's focus turned to each of the Corners, who mumbled negatives or started in on what was already brought.

"I expect each of you to eat, and I'll know if you don't. Food improves the mood, I say, and the mood is quite dour. Wouldn't you agree, Mr. Smith?"

He grinned, immediately taken with the woman and her plucky attitude. "I would, Ms. Dolores."

The serving woman chuckled. "So polite! Dolores is just fine, young man. I'll return with your orange."

When the delightful person left, he expected the room to darken once more and for them to prod him for more information. No one said a thing aside from asking to be passed this or that and did what the lady told them to do – eat. How odd. Was she secretly in charge? A charm on her or her food? Was she someone's relative and they all obeyed her wishes to make life easier around the office?

The serving woman returned moments later. She handed him his orange and a paring knife with another cheery smile

Mr. Smith Who Works The Front Desk by Jade Griffin

before breezing out, leaving him not even time to start his usual proximity count.

Smirking and inspired by her cheeky nature, he said to the room, "She was a delight."

Around a mouthful of toast piled with cantaloupe and butter, Vice President Grummond said, "Is bad, veeery bad, to get Dolores mad."

Treasurer White leaned his way, despite the great distance between them. "You aren't the first to come here who requires certain precautions."

"And what happens when she gets mad?" he queried while peeling his orange.

"Volatile destabilization. Literally, not figuratively." President Young spread a dollop of jam on a slice of toast.

His paring paused while regarding Mr. Young after such a statement. "She literally blows up?"

Secretary Midsommer swallowed a bite of apple. "Not her. Objects. When angry or startled, she projects bursts of psychokinetic energy."

Sergei Grummond chuckled heartily around a mouthful of food. "Boom! Lamp burst into little bits. It make exciting show, but one who cause boom must clean up mess."

Pondering that interesting tidbit while eating his orange, he admitted that this Paisley Foundation certainly held a collection of interesting folk. Not unlike himself. Was it really a possibility that an answer could be found here to remove Heebs and Jeebs? Not in any immediate timeframe but perhaps in the future, when they were more used to him and could offer their expert opinion and help.

He walked over to the main portion of table with small plates, browsed the offering of comestibles, and selected some things to eat. As he reached for each item, they tensed but did not move away.

"This bad luck aura you mentioned..." Mr. Midsommer queried. "Do you know its range?"

"Approximately ten feet." He did not go back to his seat. He started counting and looked each one of them in the eye to confirm they were paying attention. "And ten minutes before it starts."

That statement set off a wave of relaxed shoulders.

"Is good to know," Vice President Grummond said. "If we are to work together, yes? Less conflict when such parameters are known." The big man eyed Mr. Paisley expectantly.

Arthur Paisley glanced at each of the Corners before the founder's gaze fell to a barely-touched plate. As if considering the recourse if Dolores should return and be upset, Mr. Paisley pulled off three grapes and munched them quickly before saying, "I suppose it was a bit much to ask, ignoring the white elephant in the room. Just know, despite what he said, he is not to blame for what happened to Maisey and none of you should think ill of him for it. Given the circumstances, Mr. Smith being welcomed into the Paisley Foundation's fold was part of Maisey's plan and is officially part of business as usual. Are there any other concerns to address pertaining to him before we move on to usual matters?"

Secretary Midsommer's throat-clearing called for recognition. "Is it a curse? Was it something Mrs. Paisley couldn't undo?"

Mr. Paisley answered. "It is not a curse, and Maisey helped him as much as she could. I will be conducting my own

Mr. Smith Who Works The Front Desk by Jade Griffin

research into the nature of his situation, but I warn you again that this is a path to tread lightly. As you all are familiar with the policies of the Paisley Foundation, you know some information is not for everyone and Mr. Smith's circumstances fall under that category. We will say what we can, if we can, and the rest must be as it is."

"Exactly how old are you?" queried President Young.

"Old enough. Yourself?"

Despite the non-answer, Young smiled and replied, "I'm thirty-seven. Should've made you guess that."

"Are you human?" Treasurer White asked.

Those three words made him pause. A little smile started at his mouth but his thoughts went far away because... "That was the first thing Mrs. Paisley asked me." He sighed, set his shoulders confidently to plow ahead, and answered, "Yes. I am simply an average person in non-average circumstances."

"And, if I may," Harold Midsommer's face turned a bit flush, cluing him in that this would be an awkward question. "What is your relationship with the Paisleys? What was your relationship with Mrs. Paisley in particular?" When it looked like Mr. Paisley prepared to rebuke that query, Midsommer added, "Forgive me, sir, but Mr. Smith wasn't at the funeral."

He frowned, tossed a glance his benefactor's way. He did attend Mrs. Paisley's funeral. In fact, they were the only ones who did, and he thought that odd, given how well-known she appeared to be here. Clearly, Mr. Midsommer was fond of the woman.

"He attended one with me and no one else. Given his circumstances, I decided the necessity of two funerals: one in the morning and one in the afternoon."

Mr. Smith Who Works The Front Desk by Jade Griffin

Yes, that was smart. Beyond smart. It was valorous. Despite tremendous grief, Mr. Paisley thought of the needs and feelings of others. His respect for the man grew even more.

"I… I apologize, Mr. Smith." Midsommer did indeed look full of regret. "I should not presume any callousness or malintent on your part. The Paisleys have done more for each of us than anyone can repay and we're only trying to look out for him in kind; especially after what's been learned of Mrs. Paisley's death."

He nodded. "I understand. I consider the Paisleys very close friends. Mrs. Paisley in particular and, in retrospect, too close a friend."

Not wishing to hide it any longer, he showed the room his grief through a lack of appetite and no further conversation.

"Eh, I have question. A not-sad question," Sergei posed in the grave quiet. "Mr. Smith, your mode of speaking is unique. From where do you come?"

Hm. Mrs. Paisley's lexicon lessons must have slipped. Need to try harder. "Far, and I cannot go back, so I remain here."

"You are… old enough, as you say, and stuck in young body?" Sergei persisted.

"Yes, and very patient with questions so far when what I'd like to see is what the Paisley Foundation actually does, specifically for people in mysterious and uncertain conditions, such as I find myself. It is my intent to reveal more to the appropriate people – those who can help me get out of the condition I am in, and to stay away from those who simply wish to have answers only for themselves. I am sure each of you, Mr. Paisley included, want to know if my condition can be turned into something useful but I am equal parts cautious of others and wishing to be rid of it. And if that doesn't sum up my state of affairs to the satisfaction of those in this room, for the time being, I see no possibility of us working together." He looked pointedly at Mr. Paisley.

It was a character check and he made that very clear. Were each of them desiring answers for themselves, or to help him?

"That is our cue to move on to current matters," Mr. Paisley said without missing a beat. "Mr. Midsommer?"

"Er, yes, sir." The man in question opened a ledger and checked it. "President Harrison's wife is ill, making it difficult for him to pursue a high-profile re-election campaign. Per your previous advice, we sent a representative to lend assistance as needed, in an effort to ease him out of the running."

They had influence over the presidency, did they? Interesting.

"Professor Leopold Schwartz has died – natural causes, near as any can tell – and his most accomplished pupil was offered the position. Mr. Terrance Cooper has since turned down the offer and taken residence elsewhere so the board is asking for our opinion on who should fill the office of Miskatonic University's vice presidency."

"My vote is for Professor Cedric Vandercott," President Vince Young offered, selecting a handful of grapes to munch on. "Decent family, worthy background, solid morals."

"Disagree." Vice President Sergei Grummond folded big hands atop an ample belly and grinned at Mr. Young. "Why have solid morals, knowing what they do there? He will be crushed by what he learns."

"Molded. I've seen his character first-hand. I believe he is worthy." Mr. Young stood by his selection.

Mr. Grummond raised a hands high in concession. "I cast my vote for Dr. Thomas Travask. Sturdy, older gentleman already on staff as Head of Medicine. A true scientist. Morals not so solid, given type of work he does. Would be more useful to our purposes."

"Any other nominees?" Mr. Paisley asked. When no one answered, he said, "Let us then cast votes. All those for Professor Cedric Vandercott?"

President Young raised a hand. So did Ms. White.

"And those in favor of Dr. Thomas Travask?"

Mr. Midsommer and Mr. Grummond raised their hands.

"That leaves it in a tie, and up to me." Mr. Paisley considered it in a long pause, then said, "We will choose Professor Cedric Vandercott. Mr. Midsommer, please inform Miskatonic of our recommendation. It will look more favorably on us, due to the fact that Professor Vandercott is popular with staff and students. Been checking up on his progress lately and it is excellent. And while Professor Vandercott will become Miskatonic's vice president of their board, that will leave his spot open. See if Dr. Thomas Travask would nominate someone for us to fill it, himself included."

"Yes, sir." Midsommer scribbled notes down.

Further more normal business was conducted while he sat quietly and listened. Wondered if the Corners conducted more business than nudging politicians and institution heads. A half hour more of such talk commenced before Mr. Paisley ended the meeting. Mr. Midsommer stacked the meeting papers. Everyone stood and left. Everyone but Mr. Paisley. He similarly stayed put.

When the Corners exited, the building's founder turned all attention to him. "Mr. Smith, as promised, a tour."

He followed the man into the hall and to the elevator.

"You've seen Floor 1, 4, and 5. Now for 3 and 2." Mr. Paisley worked the lever in the elevator carriage and they descended.

The mechanical aperture opened onto Floor 3. He peeked out inquisitively, saw another long hallway like Floor 4, but this one had only two doors – one on either side at the very center of the hall.

"Go on. The entire Paisley Foundation is open to you, Mr. Smith," the old man encouraged, shooing him out.

He entered the long walk and proceeded to the right entryway. Inside was a vast room filled with nothing but filing cabinets. Scores of them! He moved to the opposite door, opened it, and found an identical room, though it had even more filing cabinets. "Records?" he enquired.

"Correct. Third floor is the Repository – of information. Anyone who has anything to do with my foundation, anyone we have an interest in. You will find them all filed inside. It is part of the secretary's position to keep them up to date. Also the vice president's job, but Sergei has terrible handwriting and is an even more deplorable typist."

"The typists don't add entries?"

"Not usually. They perform a different role. You may peruse any file at your leisure, as can any employee, guest, or asset of the Paisley Foundation."

"Anyone? That is unwise, as secreting information seems the Paisley Foundation's credo."

"If you are a guest, it helps us decide what to do with you. If you are an employee or an asset, there is nothing to hide."

"Except me."

"Hence why you have no file. Anything which should not be known by even our own members is not included. Shall we move on to Floor 2?"

He opened a hand toward the elevator and followed when Mr. Paisley went that way.

The elevator partition opened next onto – again – a very similar hallway. This one had five doors on the right and one large door on the left.

"This floor is for Acquisitions. A note of caution here, Mr. Smith. Those furthest two on the right are used as interrogation rooms. The closest three are holding cells for unnatural things. They are highly warded areas which can at any time contain various creatures. The third one is currently occupied."

"And if I want to know what is in there?"

"Make certain you are prepared for anything."

He went to the first ingress – a holding cell – and opened it for a quick look. Small table, chairs on opposite sides. All appeared to be bolted down. The second room identical, he noted the wards in both rooms were different. Likely to contain different creatures or people from casting certain spells.

On to the third room, purportedly occupied. He grasped the handle and paused. Wards decorated even the underside of the grip. Very small. Very hard to spot if you weren't looking carefully.

He looked to Mr. Paisley, out of the elevator but many paces away, and queried, "Is it safe?"

Mr. Smith Who Works The Front Desk by Jade Griffin

"It should be."

"That isn't very comforting."

"We deal in many unknowns, Mr. Smith. Sometimes the only way to find out is to try it out." Mr. Paisley put both hands in coat pockets.

He hesitated for another moment, if only to apply the other aspect of the Paisley Foundation's credo – some things were not to be known. But, he reasoned, there must be a better understanding for him as to what work they actually conducted here, and what they've experienced, and so he opened the door; slowly.

Peeking in, he spied a metal-barred cell. Appeared to be silver, shiny and polished. Behind the bars lay a book. He frowned and stared at the thing for a moment.

Footsteps behind him, he turned briefly to see Mr. Paisley. Didn't like how close the old man got, as if pushing him into the room. It garnered a frown from him in response.

Mr. Paisley ignored it. "Go in if you like; wait and see."

He had no idea what for but eased into the room; mostly because Mr. Paisley wasn't moving away and he needed to put space between the two of them.

He took his time staring at the book behind the bars, scrutinizing its cover and texture. Nothing about it seemed off, although it occurred to him that it might be enchanted. Dull brown cover, no words or symbols on it. Looked incredibly mundane and unappealing. Hm. Perhaps that was the point.

A glance at Mr. Paisley revealed nothing of what he should do, so he waited.

The device on his wrist activated.

Startled, he yanked his left hand up to inspect the thing, then cast a worried look at Mr. Paisley, who stood a good twelve feet away.

"Move farther. It's—"

The book wobbled, then exploded in a burst of arms and legs and eyes and noise. "Hey, hey, HEY! What is that thing?? Get it away!"

Before him, behind the bars, a creature now scrambled to get as far from him as it could, pressing its gambol of elongated arms and legs into the corner of the room's furthest wall.

"Exit the room please," Mr. Paisley stated in a calm manner.

He did, battling with what to ask first while backing into the hallway. As soon as he was far enough away – from Mr. Paisley as well as the creature – the device on his wrist stopped pulling in potential.

As the creature calmed and unbraced itself from the back wall, Mr. Paisley entered the holding room. He traced some symbols onto the door lock with a finger. The mechanism clicked open and fell away. Mr. Paisley opened the partition wide to allow the occupant its freedom.

He backed up farther into the hall. Still kept a solid watch on the thing but made sure to keep a larger space between them.

Egg-shaped eyes in a shaggy-maned face peered around the aperture's edge, regarding him warily. The humanoid creature was all furry or hairy, all a solid brown color, and it stood just under his own short height, which made its staring all the more pointed.

Mr. Smith Who Works The Front Desk by Jade Griffin

Mr. Paisley stepped out of the room entirely and pulled from a pocket a wrapped candy bar which was handed to the creature standing beside the entryway.

It accepted the treat, but it never stopped staring at him. Reminded him of the baleful gaze of his Uncle Jeff's cat.

"This way, Mr. Smith." The founder moved to the opposite side of the hall, opened the single door available, and held it wide.

He stayed where he was. So did the creature. He crossed his arms. "Really? No explanation whatsoever?"

"Do you want me to explain the effect of an asset in front of Hob, or would you care to discuss it in private later?"

Not much to argue there, as he didn't care to mention himself at all to anyone presently, let alone whatever Hob turned out to be, so he made for the other side of the hall. In passing, he noted Hob ate the candy bar – paper wrapper and all – while maintaining a glare his way.

This entryway, he noted upon passing the threshold, was warded with common glyphs meant to repel otherworldly evil. And inside the very large room sat the most organized bazaar he'd ever seen. Acquisitions, Mr. Paisley called this floor? Looked like whatever the Paisley Foundation acquired ended up here. Weapons of all types, artifacts from all over the world, objects he had never seen before which might not even be human in design, and, oddest of all, what looked like a bank vault in the back. And, beside the vault, a single door.

Mr. Paisley stood against the doorframe to Acquisitions while he moved in farther to get a better look at the thousands of objects. Sort of like a museum. Mr. Paisley told him once that the artifacts at the estate were a small measure of what was found. This sure looked like the motherload.

The slap of large bare feet on tile pulled his attention toward the room's entrance. There, Hob stood next to Mr. Paisley, shooting him more eye-daggers.

"What if I want to know?" it asked.

"You know what we do here, Hob. A thing that is not meant to be known shall not be known."

The creature appeared to vanish. He wondered if it shapeshifted into something too small to see, or if it teleported, or both.

Having leaned around a high shelf filled with all manner of bowls, utensils, and pottery for a look at its antics, he asked, "Is it gone?"

His benefactor pulled another candy bar from a different pocket, set it on the ground, and had barely time to straighten back up before the creature appeared, snatching the sweet up and eating it – wrapper and all – just like the previous one.

As it had no issue being inside a warded room, he concluded that the creature was not evil nor meaning harm. Must be no threat. He took a few minutes to stroll about the giant Acquisitions room, circled back, and stood the required distance from both Mr. Paisleys, for now there were two of them. Clearly, the shapeshifting creature could look like whatever and whomever it wished, flawlessly.

"Well, Mr. Smith? Explain yourself," one of the Mr. Paisley's said.

He smirked and flicked a glance at the real Mr. Paisley before turning his attention on the false one. "Your mimicry is excellent, but Mr. Paisley needs no explanation from me." And he took a large step toward them.

Mr. Smith Who Works The Front Desk by Jade Griffin

The one who spoke threw its Mr. Paisley arms up and scurried away, transforming back into the hairy Hob. "No more of that! Unpleasant feeling!"

Altering his expression to a more welcome smile, he replied, "I agree. I apologize for that. It wasn't intentional."

"Perhaps it is best to leave now, just in case," the real Mr. Paisley told the creature.

"One more, for my troubles?" it coaxed, holding up its grabby, absurdly long arms.

Mr. Paisley produced two more candy bars and placed them into the waiting hands.

It accepted the bounty gleefully, giggling to itself and hopping back and forth on two knobby legs. Hob then dashed about the Acquisitions room.

He thought perhaps it was displaying hyperactivity due to the sugar, but it made its way right to the door beside the vault. Transforming into what looked like Mr. Young, it opened the wood partition and left.

"I presume it is gone now?"

"Yes, he's off. Got his treats and a general dislike for being around you."

"Is it safe letting that creature out looking like that?"

"There are far worse things to look like than impersonating Mr. Young until he gets to where he wants to be."

"And that creature was…?"

"Shall we reconvene in the conference room?"

He sighed at the delay and motioned for Mr. Paisley to precede him.

Once seated the appropriate distance away in their respective chairs earlier filled on the fourth floor, he eyed the founder expectantly.

"Hob is a bogle. As you've seen, they can shapeshift into living things or objects. Mischievous – neither good nor evil – and clearly the device on your wrist will pull from more than just humans and aliens."

"And what is Hob considered?"

"A native creature of lore, neither human, monster, nor alien."

"You have some sort of an arrangement with Hob?"

"Yes. I asked him here to test that device, explore its limits on creatures like him."

"I'm not sure if I approve, using him as a test subject, but I understand the caution. Still, bribing him with sugar?"

"Bogles love sweets, or as far as I can tell. Perhaps only that one does. I've only encountered the one, however I find many mythologicals can be swayed by sweets alone."

"Do they come here often?"

"Very infrequent. However, on occasion, some are brought in or find their way in. Sensitive creatures, mythologicals; both in their emotions and their ability to perceive the world around them. He was sleeping when the device started to drain him. Woke him instantly."

He stared hard at Mr. Paisley, for endangering Hob and allowing the device to drain even a little bit of anyone, and for the reminder that Mrs. Paisley failed to wake before it drained her completely and she died. It soured his mood entirely. So much so that he stated in a firm tone, "I want to leave."

"You are free to saddle the horse yourself and return to the estate. It is at the livery, end of the block. I have further matters to attend to here. If you'd care to wait another hour or so, I will be leaving then."

Mr. Smith Who Works The Front Desk by Jade Griffin

He mulled it over, grumbled in his head because Mr. Paisley knew he could not saddle the horse by himself, nor did he wish to stand too close to whomever would offer to do so for him, and decided with a nod.

"Good. Feel free to look about but take care when opening doors. Anything bearing a warning should be taken as a strong one."

Mr. Paisley stood and walked out.

He sat there for a time in the quiet, considering the events of the day. Didn't want to be around any more people, so he wandered back down to the third floor to peruse the Repository's files.

The amount of filing cabinets was daunting, accentuated by their height. However, upon closer inspection, each contained meticulous labels, outside and in. A ladder nearby proved less difficult to wield than anticipated and, within moments, he found the cabinet containing data on Paisley Foundation employees. As the Corners held the most interest, he picked from there, but not alphabetically, despite that being their order. He chose the vice president, just to learn more about the intrusively-curious foreigner.

Everything the big Russian said was exactly what appeared in the file, as well as military history and the fact that the man maintained an unrivaled marksmanship score with any firearm picked up. It also listed a local home address, lack of relatives, an employee performance review, and even Sergei's hobbies. All of this reiterated precisely what Mr. Grummond presented: determined, forward, and smart. Mr. Paisley's first meeting of Sergei happened when the spy caught and interrogated the founder on something called the Paisley Society. After, Mr. Paisley kept tabs on the Russian and, when the Paisley Foundation formed, offered the Russian spy a job as an agent. Within the year, Sergei was put through several psychological tests and performance reviews before being offered the position of vice president. Sergei turned it down at first but, after a week, reconsidered and formally accepted.

Mr. Young, he discovered, disowned a much more famous name: Vincent Cartwright, of the Cartwright steel moguls. The file noted that Mr. Young broke from the Cartwrights and remade a new persona with the name Vince Young. Clarity of direction and tenacity awarded the young man work under Mr. Paisley in the enterprise of exploration for a year or so, proving to be a very capable, driven young man. At Mr. Paisley's urgings, the position of president was offered, accepted, and Mr. Young had so far performed admirably in the role.

Mr. Midsommer discovered the Paisleys and their eclectic pastime over a rather boring dinner – Yes, it really said that in the file, and he wondered if Mrs. Paisley typed these up herself – as a precocious teen whose sensitivity to the arcane led to snoop where one wasn't meant to in the Paisley Estate. Dinner guests none the wiser, Mrs. Paisley rescued the adolescent from being trapped in an unnamed artifact and that began an instant fascination with learning magic, much to Mrs. Paisley's delight – Again, he read it exactly as written, colorful text and all, and hearing Mrs. Paisley's voice in his head rattling off the words. She was clearly taken with Harold Midsommer, however the youngster often kept a distance. The file also contained reports on the youth's progress in magic through teen years, a note on the mastery of something called psychometry, and a note of overcoming a shy nature. Mr. Midsommer sat as an obvious choice for the position of secretary within the Paisley Foundation.

When he finally picked up Ms. White's file, he noted the difference in paper right away. Off-color, the folder watermarked with wards on the exterior of the slightly thicker pulp. It wasn't any kind of ward he recognized, though they did have Mrs. Paisley's floral flourish to them. With one finger, he lightly lifted the edge and flipped it open. Nothing happened, so he began reading.

Tricia was her first name but her original last name – de Lorraine – labeled her as a member of a very dangerous and old family of evil magic-users. She changed her name to Tricia White after the Paisleys saved her from her relatives.

The details of what Tricia fled and how the Paisleys saved her were vague in print, but he was fair at reading between the lines. Use of words like trauma, abuse, and trying to break young Tricia peppered the short summary of her formative years and—

Fast footsteps in the hall.

He turned in time to see Treasurer White round the doorway and slow as soon as she saw him. Clearly, she'd run down here, but he waited for her to approach and speak up.

"… Ah. Hello again," she began, a little out of breath and trying to hide it as she strolled across the long span separating them. She stopped a good fifteen feet away and maintained a slightly tense posture. Her tone, however, remained inquisitive. "Researching more information on the Corners?"

"A bit. I'm not familiar with these wards, however." He held up her file. "What is their purpose?"

Mr. Smith Who Works The Front Desk by Jade Griffin

"Ah…" She took a pause, and a breath. "Mrs. Paisley and I worked on them together. It's to prevent magical eavesdropping. They're anti-scrying wards. I am also made aware if anyone opens the file to read it."

"Why aren't the others protected like this?"

Another pause, her neck craning a bit to try and see what page of her file his eyes lay upon. "No one has quite the devious family that I have, Mr. Smith. Some ways of tracking me are ones which not even Mrs. Paisley could prevent, however there are measures we can take against them."

As the subject of his current attention was literally a few yards away, he closed the file, faced her fully, and asked, "Can you tell me about them?"

"I can, however… I'm a bit concerned. I know I'm not to treat you like a child, but the things my family have done…"

"Are most likely similar to things which have been done to me in my past. Believe me when I say I understand your reservation." He gave a brief nod, acknowledging a shared pain. "I'm more curious about them and who they are, less on what they have done to you."

Her shoulders abandoned their stiff posture and she offered a little smile. "That I can most assuredly relate."

The amount of horrors dispensed by Treasurer White on the depravity of the de Lorraine family stretched back to the Crusades. His mind wandered to a transfer where Heebs and Jeebs put him in the middle of that. Another instance of emotional and physical scars he tried to ignore.

Ms. White trailed off and regarded him with concern. A sliver of caution in her voice, she asked, "May I ask… How old are you?"

His mouth firmed into a thin line as he thought what best to say.

"I apologize if this isn't something we're meant to discuss..."

A sigh blew out of his child mouth and the truth followed. "I don't know. I could be eighteen or a hundred and eighteen. Old enough is the best answer I can give."

"I see. As I explained, the de Lorraines are masters of stealing youth. Clearly, you don't care to be in whatever situation you are in, unlike the deliberate measures my family indulge in, but I will say that, whatever your situation, I hope you never encounter them. They will drain every last bit of value from anyone and anything they target, even beyond death. As you are a person in what seems to be a unique and unnatural situation, you would be snatched up in an instant if they knew about you."

As he had no intention of getting that close to any of her relatives, and no desire to go around the city unescorted, he felt this would be fairly simple to accomplish. "Mr. Paisley seems to have my safety and the safety of others first and foremost in mind, but I'll try to be vigilant. I don't suppose you have any pictures of any of the de Lorraines in question?"

"The few we've managed to find are in their files, and I provided likenesses as best I could." She pointed to the filing cabinet adjacent to the one he was perusing. "They don't generally let their likenesses leave their various estates."

"May I ask what is stopping them from grabbing you off the street on your way to and from work?"

She squirmed at such a query. He almost regretted bringing it up, because she seemed a very nice sort who clawed her way out of terrible circumstances, but the answer would tell him more on the safety precautions employed at the Paisley Foundation.

"Mrs. Paisley was able to find an incantation that prohibits the direct use of their magic against me. Nothing stops the indirect application, nor from hiring thugs to make off with me or spy on me. It is a great worry and I must also remain vigilant."

"They must know you work here."

Her throat bobbed with an uneasy swallow. "They do, and it is a concern, but as I said, I must remain vigilant as well as not allow them to take any further agency from me. I can't live in fear of them. Mr. Smith, where are you from, might I ask?"

"Montana." Only right he should give a little, since she provided so much information about herself.

"I'm not certain how things are in Montana, but Chicago is filled with all manner of treachery. I do hope the Paisley Foundation can help with your situation – whatever it may be – but, in the meanwhile, please keep inquiries on the de Lorraines to myself and Mr. Paisley."

This warning came as a surprise. "Do you feel there are compromised people working here?"

"No, but the de Lorraines are pernicious and patient. They can smell opportunity. Sometimes I fear they have means of listening for any mention of their name." The treasurer's eyes flicked about, wary, before settling to him. "Just... be cautious. As I said, they would find you an irresistible acquisition, no matter what the truth of your situation may be."

Not the first time someone thought to do so, though he'd hoped those days were behind him.

Movement by the entryway had them both looking that direction.

Mr. Midsommer peered in, obviously looking for Ms. White.

"Mr. Young is requesting I bring you and the newest acquisition to his office."

Given Secretary Midsommer's attention never wavered from Treasurer White, he wondered if the man referred to him as an acquisition but, as they left without another look his way, he determined Midsommer meant something from Acquisitions which sat one floor below them.

So much information at his fingertips… He was perusing the relationship between the local mob factions and the mayor of Chicago when a hearty throat-clearing had him swivel bodily toward the doorway. There stood Mr. Paisley.

"I see you found something to fill the time," his benefactor remarked.

He replaced the files where they were meant to go. "Yes. Interesting information." The *thunk* of the closed filing cabinet echoed in the room.

"Indeed. Do you need more time?"

"No."

"Excellent. I also wish to return home. Shall we?" Mr. Paisley waved ahead, allowing him to lead the way.

Mr. Smith Who Works The Front Desk by Jade Griffin

1893, February 9

"You need a job – a specific task – while you are here, Mr. Smith," Mr. Paisley told him the next day while they walked into the immense first floor lobby of the Paisley Foundation. "I will leave you to explore and seek one that may appeal to you. See what you come up with. I have other matters to attend to at present."

Mr. Paisley strode past him quickly and entered the elevator, leaving him to his own devices.

As he'd only just started his second day of knowing this place existed, he couldn't tell if this was typical behavior for the Foundation's namesake and benefactor. Should he also ascend?

When the elevator's arrow arced over to the right side, he hit the button to call it back down. Easy enough to manage the vertical conveyance, he sent it to the fifth floor.

The mechanical partition slid open to the constant clattering of keys from the four typists. All four Corner office doors remained shut. He then took a brief moment to wander about the typists, giving enough time and space between each one not to trigger the device on his wrist. The typists were a man and three women, each flicking a nervous gaze at his approach. Did they know about his "calamitous" nature? Not sure. None jerked away, nor paused in their task when he came by to see what each person typed. Journal notes, each one slightly different but all four on the same subject of some sort of adventure Mr. Paisley had taken. Hm.

Finding nothing for himself to do, he took the elevator down one floor wherein conference rooms and what looked

Mr. Smith Who Works The Front Desk by Jade Griffin

like small hotel rooms took up most of the space. At the end of the hall, however, lay a sixth windowless door. He brazenly opened it. Inside appeared to be a long kitchen but Dolores was not inside. Instead, there stood a big man with thick, black hair wearing a white shirt, pants, and apron.

The big man whirled his way, glared furiously, and stomped near. "What the hell you doin' in my kitchen?!" he bellowed, throwing his arms up in a threatening gesture.

He glanced further in the kitchen, looking for some help if the big man gave chase. The only other occupant was a teen – possibly the man's son given the resemblance – who stared balefully at him amidst the chore of cutting vegetables.

"I said git!" The big man stepped nearly on him, forcing him out. The door slammed shut in his face.

Given no time to recover from the encounter, the elevator opened and Mr. Paisley along with Mr. Young stepped out. He glanced from the kitchen entry to the approaching men.

"Hm," Mr. Paisley eyed him, then the avenue in question. "Ventured into the one place off limits?"

He snorted a laugh. "A warning would have been appreciated."

"Victor Senior and Victor Junior are particular about their kitchen and who goes in there. I don't bother them at their work and they don't lord over mine."

He shook his head at Mr. Paisley's methodology. "This place has the strangest hierarchy."

President Young cocked a brow at him. "I find it refreshing. Everyone has a fair standing and at least some say here. You don't approve?"

"It isn't about approval. I feel… As if all I am doing is blundering where I am not meant to be."

Mr. Smith Who Works The Front Desk by Jade Griffin

Mr. Young turned abruptly and made for the elevator.

Mr. Paisley replied, "This is a place of business with a specific function required of each of its employees, clients, guests, and assets, Mr. Smith. Employees are those like the typists, the Corners, and agents sent out on errands of a more direct nature. Clients are those of the public we do business with and whom do business with us. They do not know what it is we actually do here. Assets are people and things of specific value to the Paisley Foundation. Guests are those who know what it is we do but we have not decided whether they are to be employees, assets, or to be contained. Perhaps you need assistance in determining which category you fall under."

He narrowed his eyes at his benefactor. "You called me an asset yesterday. Twice."

"I did. Time to show those here you are much more." Mr. Paisley glanced toward the elevator.

President Young emerged from the lift, strode down the hall to him, and held out a broom and dustpan procured from somewhere. "Not the most glorious of occupations but this will help you settle into how things run here. Take this around for a week, explore, collect any dirt you can during the Paisley Foundation 'adult' worktime, and report back on your progress." Mr. Young smiled pleasantly.

He did not know how to take that. Usually, looking like a child proved greatly advantageous. Here, not so. The others knew he wasn't a kid. On top of that, lacking an adult body with its strength and height denied certain occupations and it currently irked him. Assuming Mr. Young gave him a task to keep him out of the way, he fumed. That was no way to treat someone meant to be on an equal level!

Mr. Smith Who Works The Front Desk by Jade Griffin

He'd decided to refuse the menial tools when a glance at Mr. Paisley told him everything he was missing. The old benefactor smiled. The kind wherein Mr. Paisley knew he had the potential to figure out the subtext and waited for it to register.

He stared at the dustpan and broom, reviewed the words Mr. Young said, and grinned when it clicked. Collect dirt, eh? President Young wasn't talking about actual dust. Instead, go around and spy while conducting the menial labor task. So be it. He took up the tools and set to work.

He found, however, by the third hour, a large discrepancy: whatever his real age, he wasn't given much opportunity to learn some of the basics even a teen-aged person would know. Cooking even the simplest thing, for example, had been a delightful lesson taught to him by Danneby two months after he arrived. Hadn't used a knife except to defend himself before Mrs. Paisley showed him how to pare fruit. And, despite the delightful banality of it, he had never swept anything in his life until Mr. Young handed him the broom. Eager to perform his best, a small body made the task of sweeping very difficult.

Struggling with both in little hands, still trying to get the hang of it on the fourth floor and not look the total fool, the elevator opened. Vice President Sergei Grummond's bulky form swaggered out, came within steps of him, and loomed with a grin. "Enjoying new task, Mr. Smith?"

He took the required number of steps back to maintain a safe distance and cocked a brow at Mr. Grummond. "It is an acceptable use of my time. I am quite new to learning the business of this establishment."

Mr. Grummond chuckled mightily, hands on hips. "Big words for small body. Tell me, Mr. Smith, what do you fear?"

He cocked a suspicious brow at the vice president. "Mr. Young told me you were interested in Arthurian lore, not dissecting the fears of those around you."

The vice president shrugged unabashedly and stepped closer. "Eh... Both."

Straight-faced, he replied, "I live in constant fear of inadvertently killing anyone who lingers near me." And he looked pointedly at the big man standing too close.

Vice President Grummond chuckled loud, long, and with much gusto.

He waited patiently to see if a point to the interruption appeared.

Humor suddenly abandoned, Mr. Grummond leaned down to eye him like a specimen under a microscope. "Mysterious Mr. Smith... I wish to unravel you. In spare time, of course, and with little pestering. Is like game, even if I am only player of game. Is another big interest, games. Do you like games, Mr. Smith?"

Patience spent, he ground his jaw and stepped even further away, giving the vice president an unbudging, "No." He had, quite literally, lived a type of sick game for a very long time and wanted to forget the rawness of such memories. Being bounced around time and space by Heebs and Jeebs turned him off games completely. Especially as he remained a game piece.

"Oho! Such a face!" Mr. Grummond commented, pointing boldly at him but taking no further steps near.

"Is there some reason for the interruption, Mr. Grummond? If so, please speak it promptly so that I may return to work." He took up the broom in a defensive hold, similar to one of the stances he'd seen fighters use in movies.

Such an act raised Mr. Grummond's brows high. "No need for feeling attacked. Is way to learn. I am always learning. You learn, as well. Learn sweep. Learn ladder of business hierarchy here. Higher up ladder you go, more to be learned. Where is final rung for Mr. Smith, eh?" The Russian took a wide grin back into the elevator.

Mr. Smith stared after. Strange man, Sergei Grummond.

He went to the elevator and watched its arrow swing. Up, stopping on the fifth floor.

Having had enough of feeling out of the loop, he waited approximately ten minutes and also went up to start sweeping.

He ignored his awkward use of the tools, ignored the curious or furtive looks from the four typists who never seemed to break away from their clacking keys, and instead focused on the voices within each of the four Corner offices while passing by with ample time for listening – and of course ample space to not draw any potential from anyone.

"Mrs. Rockefeller, how are you this morning? Ah, thank you. Mrs. Paisley will be dearly missed. I appreciate your concern but we are conducting business as usual. I'm calling to inform you that Mr. Paisley will be regretfully unavailable for John's New Years party. Thank you, yes. You are too kind. Good-bye." That came from Secretary Midsommer's office.

"Mr. William Niven? I'm given to understand you've procured a very interesting rock specimen on your most recent travels. Yes, that's the one. Is there a chance the Paisley Foundation could purchase it from you? Discretely, of course. Yes, that's correct. No, I believe that is a fair amount, Mr. Niven. I will have one of our men personally deliver the funds to you, in exchange for the specimen. Where would you like to meet?" President Young's office.

"Agent Dane, how are things progressing at Ellis Island?"

"Very well, Ms. White. We'll continue to keep an eye out for those refugees on your list when the main building opens up."

"Thank you. Your diligence is ever appreciated. Let me know if your accompaniment is having difficulties and we'll send more agents."

"I will."

He swept quickly away, just in time before the door opened and a dark-haired man exited the treasurer's office. The man halted immediately upon spotting him, stared briefly in surprise, and slowly backed into White's office. He didn't shut the door and could clearly be heard, as well as the treasurer's reply.

"Uh... Did you know there's a kid out here?"

"Yes. That's Mr. Smith."

"... Mr. Smith?"

"Yes. His arrival was announced at yesterday's agent briefing, however you were out on assignment. Mr. Paisley brought him in personally."

"As...?"

"An employee of the Paisley Foundation, just as you and I are."

"...Ah."

The dark-haired man exited her office once more, headed for the elevator, and glanced back only once. Obviously still trying to reason through it.

So, if that Dane person was classified as an agent, that meant another level to the Paisley Foundation's hierarchy. A level which remained unaware of his calamitous nature, and anything else about him, yet completely willing to accept that and move on with his task. Interesting. A look at the busy typists found them keeping their eyes on their work. Was their subtle wariness an indication of knowing the necessity of staying away from him, or merely that of concerned folk not sure how to place him in the hierarchy here? Certainly, Victor the Cook held no qualms about approaching him in a threatening manner. That may mean only the Corners and Mr. Paisley knew. And probably for the best. People changed when they learned he was a walking bomb.

While it would take time getting used to the physical activity of sweeping, he took it upon himself to add emptying trash bins to his list of tasks. So much could be learned from a person's trash, and both tasks allowed the honing of skills he relied on while bouncing around time and space: stealth and spying.

Mr. Smith Who Works The Front Desk by Jade Griffin

1893, May 24

After finishing his actual job of cleaning, tidying, and dusting, he took his usual route down to the Repository. So much information... Also safer to explore than the Acquisitions floor with its small contingent of weird gadgets and magical artifacts – most of which the Repository labeled as items to stay away from, not to mention the holding room across the hall which currently held a feline cryptid Agents Dane and Turner captured a few days ago.

Most of his time at the Paisley Foundation, he swept and caught little bits of news and happenings – like the capture of the feline cryptid, or the funeral he could not attend for an agent he barely knew who died trying to secure the creature. It was a strange occupation, to be sure. Sometimes dangerous. Everyone worked very closely, and yet kept a distance. For him, who did not go out on dangerous missions nor talk to public figures, that distance became more and more tangible. He passed the random agent checking in or sent out. They acknowledged his presence, like everyone else, but ignored him thereafter. It seemed all employees relegated him into the category of not-to-be-bothered-or-questioned. Couldn't say he didn't welcome it – for the most part – and even felt a lack of the usual pesterings from Mr. Grummond. Odd that, because the man bothered him daily his first month. But not this week.

The Repository also remained a place of solitude with only the occasional visit by Ms. White or Mr. Midsommer. That suited him fine most days, but today felt different. Perhaps loneliness started tapping at his brain. Perhaps he just needed more interaction beyond reading about people and their pasts.

Large footsteps heralded someone's entrance. An unmistakable step he'd keyed his brain to recognize.

Looking up from his perusal of an early adventure of Mr. and Mrs. Paisley, the grinning face of Vice President Grummond dropped his mood like a stone. Perhaps lonely, but not enough to tolerate the big Russian. He'd long since tired of such encroaching conversations. Returning the file to its cabinet, he shut it and meant to pass Mr. Grummond.

"You are seeking answers? I can help."

He did not slow while nearing the imposing figure and told the man, "No, thank you," and hurried past.

"But your condition, Mr. Smith. You seek answers, yes?"

He paused, turned around.

Mr. Grummond's grin grew. "Ah, there is face of interest! Yes, answers! But, in order for answers, must ask right questions, yes?"

"... Yes?" Did the man have any news or simply trying a new method of prodding for information? He couldn't tell but started the count in his head.

"So, what is question most wanting answer, Mr. Smith?"

"How to end the circumstances and cause of my condition." Still couldn't tell whether the guy was fishing for information, but the vice president did have a point. Question now was whether he felt like trusting this person with any more knowledge of his circumstances. He didn't completely trust the wily Sergei Grummond, but Mr. Paisley did. Perhaps it would be enough to trust that. So, he related with reluctance, "The nature of my condition is neither magical nor natural. It is alien." He held up his left arm, let the sleeve slide back and expose his skin.

Ever curious, Mr. Grummond hurried near to examine the thing which had been attached to him for untold years. "Oh? What is this?" The vice president touched it – tried to – but of course the man's thick fingers passed right through the thing. He yanked his hand back, then tried again to pluck at the device.

"As I said, it is alien. It was phased to my wrist and drains the potential of anyone who lingers near me longer than ten minutes, if a person is in range. It can't be removed or hindered, not even by wards. Mrs. Paisley tried."

Mr. Grummond's eyes flicked briefly to his at the reminder of the person who had expired due to being too close to him. He didn't like saying it either, but the reminder was needed, for everyone's safety.

"How do you track time near people?"

"I count in my head."

"What time do you have?"

"Three minutes, forty seconds."

"Hmph. I count two minutes, fifty seconds."

"Better safe than sorry."

The Russian's bushy brows crested in an arch of surprise. "What expression! Clever words, Mr. Smith. And how long you have this?" A thick finger pointed to the device.

"Too long."

"Device does not drain you?"

"No, but I feel when it drains people, unless I'm not conscious."

"It does not work based on you." A statement and not a query, the vice president turned his arm this way and that, looking for more details about the device. "What alien did this?"

"I never saw the ones who put it on me, and I don't even know if they made it." Just a theory. And, no, he did not feel like telling the Paisley vice president about Heebs and Jeebs.

"And purpose of collecting potential of people?"

"Food source."

Again, Mr. Grummond's brows hiked skyward. "Are aliens here now? Or collect it at some time? Automatic transfer point somewhere?"

He frowned at the Paisley vice president. "I find it interesting that you're aware so many options exist."

"I use infinite expanse of imagination, Mr. Smith. Six minutes, seventeen seconds."

"Six minutes, thirty-eight seconds."

"You train your brain for this counting?"

"Yes. It helps save people."

"You wish to save people? You do not like draining?"

"I hate it. I want the aliens to starve."

Sergei Grummond's grin renewed. "Ah, so they are a they and they are here."

He ground his jaw, not used to the rapid-fire queries. Hadn't meant to let that slip. "Are you quite finished, Mr. Grummond, or do you have any actual means of helping me?"

"To help, I must experience effect. We stay here and let it affect me."

"No. Absolutely not."

"Will it kill me?"

"Not right away, but it could!" he replied adamantly.

"Is worth testing, yes?"

He glared fiercely at the Paisley vice president. "No! Unless you are trying to die?!"

"I am not. Experiences help feel alive, and help determine limits of condition and device. Eight minutes."

He shook his head. "I already know its limits, and I can't allow it. Eight minutes, fifty-two seconds." He stepped back.

Mr. Grummond matched his retreat with an advancing step.

He moved again.

Mr. Grummond followed, as if a kind of dance.

"Stop it!" he demanded.

"No. I must feel—"

He bolted for the Repository door. Too fast for the big Russian man, he zipped out and down the hall.

Vice President Grummond chased after him.

At the elevator, the clomp of big feet behind him forced a confrontation with the oncoming giant.

"Stop!" he shouted at Mr. Grummond when the Paisley vice president closed in a mere three feet away. Pressing the button to summon the elevator, he threatened, "I'll... I'll tell Mr. Paisley!"

The big man sighed patiently. "Mr. Paisley knows."

"That's a lie. He wouldn't put a Corner in danger like this."

Sergei Grummond's entire demeanor lost all hint of mischief and connivery and stated calmly, "I volunteered. And he would, as would I, to help you. And both trust that you will not let me die."

Why wasn't the elevator door opening? He pressed the button several more times. Why couldn't he get away from the Russian spy?? "Please!" Anxiety twisted his face.

Mr. Smith Who Works The Front Desk by Jade Griffin

"Remain calm, Mr. Smith. What is time?"

"I..." The memory of Mrs. Paisley, dead, draped over him, hit hard. He swallowed through a tight throat. "I... I lost track. And it doesn't work that way. You need to get back, before—"

The device on his wrist activated. His guts twisted with that sick sensation, the feeling of someone's very potential being pulled out of them.

"You are pale, Mr. Smith. Has it begun?"

A tight nod as he tried swallowing again, throat dry with fear.

"But I feel nothing, and you moved away. Does time not reset?"

Thin arms locked tightly at his sides, he begged, "Please get away!"

"No. Not yet. Extended proximity triggers shorter timeframe before drain begins?"

"Yes." Had to calm down, ease away.

Vice President Grummond blinked and looked at both hands. "Feel out of place, and wearied."

"That's enough!" he yelled before bolting while Sergei Grummond remained distracted.

Ran back to the Repository, tucked himself between the tightest filing cabinets available, and breathed in deep angry breaths until calm and quiet settled him once more.

"Mr. Smith?" came the welcome voice of Mr. Paisley a short amount of time later.

Relieved but still angry, he didn't reply.

"Mr. Smith, please come out."

"Did you know?" Yelled it as an accusation, not a question, because he had to be sure.

"We all did."

He emerged from his hiding spot, a glare fiercely in place and aimed at his benefactor. "I told you already about the limits of exposure, and that it doesn't reset completely. You **know** what it feels like. You **know** what it can do to a person! **Why** would you allow this?"

Mr. Paisley let go a sorrowful sigh. "Because... I can't find any other way to help you."

He issued a sigh of his own and wandered near. Not too near, but near enough to be heard without shouting. "Mr. Paisley, you've helped me more than anyone else ever has. But it is hard to live with this if the people around me I am meant to trust start pushing the limits of what can't be controlled. Is Mr. Grummond alright?"

"The others are monitoring him as we speak. We were waiting in the elevator, holding it."

"Mr. Paisley?"

"Yes, Mr. Smith?"

"I hope you understand when I say I don't feel like going back into the hall, or even back to the estate. As long as everyone is leaving, I'd prefer to stay the night here."

"... As you wish." Mr. Paisley left at a solemn plod.

Only after silence followed the elevator's mechanical descending whir did he emerge from the Repository. There, he watched the dial as it lowered to the first floor and remained.

Silence. An absolute void of noise. Not the swallowing nothingness of the nexus but air and space and gravity full of a lack of industry and presence. A grin sprang to his face at the novelty. Rarely – so rarely – had he experienced solitude like this. To him, it was the purest form of freedom. In sheer

Mr. Smith Who Works The Front Desk by Jade Griffin

joy, he ran up and down the hall, into the Repository and out, back into the hall and finally flattening himself up against the wall beside the elevator.

It made a different sound, slapping his left hand on the wall. His right hand smacked a very solid, sturdy impact. His left impacted against a hollow-sounding surface.

Calming his exerted breathing, he turned about and examined the surface. Looked identical to the casual observer but, just there, a slightly wider seam in the pattern of construction.

Reaching his little fingers into the groove, pulling did nothing. He pushed on the flat surface, heard a click, felt the wall push back. He let it and watched the hidden door swing open on its own. Easing in for a cautious look, he noted a staircase leading both up and down.

He left the hidden partition open and, using the elevator, traveled down to the second floor. Pushing on the wall in the same general vicinity as the floor above, an identical outward-swiveling hidden entryway opened. Its stairwell connected to the one above, with more stairs descending.

Entering the dark space, he noted no insect or arachnid residue, nor any rodent droppings. No dust either, nor lighting. He knew the building stood for just under twenty years– constructed shortly after the Great Chicago Fire and paid for by Mr. Paisley – and the Paisley Foundation itself wasn't established until 1888, only four years ago. Was this passage kept secret from him because not even the Corners knew it existed? Or, more likely, finding the access proved yet another test of ability and resolve.

Taking care in the darkness, he let the handrail guide him down the flight of stairs. No creak of floorboards from the solid wood. Didn't smell fresh so it must all have been made along with the building. And, when the railing ended, he sent a foot out to feel forward. A final step and flat concrete greeted such exploration. He took another step. Still flat. Hand out, a smooth wall met his palm, along with a handle. He pushed it open.

Fading late afternoon daylight flooded the hidden stairwell, reflected off of the polished wood surface of the first floor's front desk. He blinked away the glare and ventured out into the lobby.

At the glass double doors, he checked them and found that those who left for the evening locked up. Good thing, too, as he hadn't a key nor could the mechanism be locked by hand from the inside.

Watching the light leave the sky, the shuffle of a handful of people all going wherever they headed in the rising wind and sudden cloudy sky, he moved to a wall not in direct line with the glass front of the Paisley Foundation. Wanted to observe without being seen. Wouldn't do to have a constable come by demanding why a boy was alone at night in the building. Some places even had a curfew. Did Chicago in this era? Not certain, he tucked himself closer against the wall as a lone man walked past right near the front windows. Didn't look in. Just trudged past.

A bit too close for his liking. He used the hidden stairs to retrace his steps back to the second floor, guided by the dim light of the Acquisition's hallway, as the hidden entry remained open.

No one around... What would be best to do in such a novel span of time and space? Without leaving, the best thing to

Mr. Smith Who Works The Front Desk by Jade Griffin

spring to mind was checking the offices of the Corners and try to learn more about them.

He'd done so at the Paisley Estate. First in Mrs. Paisley's workroom when neither were around, he read her journals and learned of her fondness for consuming melted chocolate in cold milk. She also considered it uncouth and would not partake around anyone. Snooping in the desk of Mr. Paisley's study, he learned his benefactor liked to doodle on scraps of paper and found a whole drawer of scribbled drawings of monkeys, elephants, giraffes, strange fish, tattooed people from foreign lands, flowers and fruits, and objects he couldn't identify. Those were all loose. In a bound book, Mr. Paisley inked beautiful cityscapes, ornate artifacts, and labeled them all. Some he now recalled seeing in the Paisley Foundation's Acquisitions while others – like the Yithian journal – rested at the estate.

Curious enough of his fellow Corners to go poking about in their area, he went to Vice President Grummond's office first. Not locked, he similarly found very little beyond poorly-scribbled notes. Mr. Paisley wasn't kidding when commenting on the Russian's atrocious handwriting. Couldn't make out any of it, though he supposed it could be in Russian.

Ms. White's office held only client and artifact information, a calendar of Paisley Foundation business of which her attendance was required, and a total lack of anything personal. Like Mr. Grummond's office, it held no decor nor mementos.

Mr. Young's office held the bounty. No family photos, but it seemed the man put every accomplishment noted on paper upon the walls. Business degree from a well-known university, photos of Mr. Young shaking hands with various leaders of company and nation, and even a photo of a youthful Vince Young and Mr. Paisley standing next to an impossibly large and very dead anaconda. By their feet, someone wrote AMAZON - 1879 - SOMETHING ELSE THE MORGAN EXPEDITION MISSED.

With the typists gone, he poked about their desks next. Each of the four were identical with a basket of hand-written notes to the left and a basket of typed-up notes to the right. A single black Remington typewriter sat neatly in between. He looked at the notes, and at what was typed, and he could not determine why accounts of the weather, politics, and even some jarring nonsense were being typed up – repeatedly in some cases. There must be a reason for four typists hired by the Paisley Foundation to continuously spew out copies. So, he sat in one of the typist chairs and started clacking away out of whimsy, without any skill or agenda.

Pounding away at the keys as if a maestro on piano, he felt unexpectedly worn. Puzzling, for he knew his body well enough to warrant questioning whether something else transpired. Halting the typing lessened the onset of weariness. Resuming renewed the effect.

Looking under the typewriter revealed nothing, but a very close inspection of the spot directly under the keys – exactly where the key point sent the letter up to strike a mark on paper – a tiny rune glowed with each tap. Eyes round with amazement, he watched the miniscule glow fade with inactivity. Fascinating! What purpose could there be in activating these runes? He had no idea and knew the only way to find out involved asking the very people he wanted to be distant from at present.

Mr. Smith Who Works The Front Desk by Jade Griffin

    The last office held little interest – that of Secretary Midsommer. The Paisley secretary was a quiet sort. Used to be shy, according to the file the Paisley Foundation kept. Brilliant and shy. All of it reflected in a rather impersonal office space. A clean, orderly desk, a painting of a beautiful countryside, the type of notes and calendar you'd expect would be in a secretary's office. Only one thing of note: One drawer of the desk remained locked.

    As the evening wore on and there was less to occupy himself, he debated where to take rest. Exploring the fourth floor – while avoiding the door at the end of the hall which led to the kitchen – he found the hotel-like rooms to be identical and unoccupied. Five in all, each contained a bed, night stand, lamp, and hooks to stow hat and coat. He chose the one closest to the kitchen door, as a water closet was found tucked beside it. He settled fully dressed, falling asleep to imagining the cook, Victor, pacing just on the other side and ready to snap at any person who might invade the culinary territory.

1893, May 25

He woke several times in the night, his mind restless. A rustling in the hall woke him immediately. A lifetime of being on constant alert had not dulled due to his domestic life with the Paisleys. He was up and creeping to the room's ingress in a blink.

"Mind that fruit, son."

He jumped back at the unmistakable gruff tone of Victor.

"It's heavy," the teen complained, clear struggle in the voice.

"Build you some muscles is all. You can manage."

He thought of offering to help but knew his minute stature made that a silly gesture. And, of course, the threat of Victor or the son yelling at him again for intruding on their 'space'.

His ears caught the door at the end of the hall open, the pair shuffle in with whatever they carried, and the metal catch clicking shut.

He sat on the bed, didn't feel like lazing about, remade the bed close to how it had been before, and checked the time. Barely 6:00 AM.

With the time apart from the others, was it enough of a statement that he adamantly hated draining people and wanted to avoid it at all costs? Or more a reaffirmation to himself? The Corners would be in around 8. Was he so riled, there remained a need for continued avoidance like some petulant child? Unsure how to answer the first two, he definitely did not want to hide and reviewed himself in the room's mirror. A quick straightening of shirt and hand-combing of hair. A nod at his satisfactory reflection. Time to start the day and move on.

Resolving to face each of the Corners as soon as they arrived, he went to the first floor. And, as the elevator opened, Dolores stood ready to enter. Upon seeing him, she exclaimed, "Oh!"

The glass bulb of the front desk lamp burst with a loud pop.

"Mr. Smith, you gave me a fright!" She patted her chest, either ignoring the broken glass behind her or having not heard it. "You are here rather early. Have you eaten yet?"

"No. Thank you for asking." He stepped from the elevator and moved toward the nearest couch.

"May I bring you down anything?"

"As long as it isn't any trouble."

"So polite!" she beamed. "No trouble at all. Any preference, aside from oranges?"

"No, Dolores. Thank you. Do you by any chance know where spare lightbulbs might be kept?"

She frowned, confused. "Lightbulbs? No, Mr. Smith. Such maintenance falls on the Corners."

"There isn't a maintenance person employed here?"

"No, Mr. Smith. I'd imagine it would be part of the duties of the person at the front desk, or yours if you're still tasked with sweeping and cleaning."

He cast a look at the front desk. Often near, cleaning around it and under it, but having never seen anyone sit there aside from Mr. Paisley or Mr. Young on a few occasions. He made himself familiar with every past and present Paisley employee filed in the Repository and the spot never held an official front desk person. Why even have the furnishing?

"If there is nothing else, Mr. Smith, I'll go up and fetch you that breakfast."

He smiled and gave a nod.

When she left, instead of using the elevator, he took two of the plentiful Paisley brochures and used them as a makeshift broom and dustpan to clean up the shattered, powdery glass. This kept his hands free of the shards and it was cleaned up enough so that he could sit at the desk and enjoy the bowl of oatmeal, glass of milk, and orange Dolores brought him.

After, he used the provided paper napkin and floor one's water closet to clean up the remainder of the glass dust before taking the tray and dirty dishes up to the fourth floor. He left that in one of the conference rooms. Dolores seemed competent enough to come looking for the items, so he left them where it would be easiest to retrieve them. Then back down to await the Corners.

A single clock in the lobby hung high on the back wall, above and behind where the front desk sat. He chose again to sit at the chair of the front desk. Too big, he propped himself up with a book of law found in one of the desk drawers. Wanted the Corners to feel his watch of them the whole walk to the elevator, and the front desk itself was situated a good twenty or so feet from the conveyance, so he'd stare at them all he liked and as uncomfortably as he liked. Make sure they knew precisely how it felt being backed into a corner – pun unintentional. And if any gave him grief? Well, perhaps this wasn't a suitable place to spend his days.

At exactly 7:44 AM, Mr. Young and Mr. Paisley arrived. Not together – as Mr. Young stepped out of a carriage coming from the west and Mr. Paisley from one to the east. Mr. Paisley gave him a nod of greeting and kept walking.

Mr. Young's pace slowed a bit when a look passed between them, but the blond man neither spoke to nor acknowledged him further as both men rode the elevator up. Good to know his unnerving stare made an impact.

At 7:49 AM, Ms. White and Mr. Midsommer exited the same carriage and entered the front doors. They spied him right away and did not dodge the obvious scrutiny he bestowed upon their presence. They walked right up toward the desk, in fact, but politely stayed a solid twelve feet back.

"Good morning, Mr. Smith. How was your evening?" Mr. Midsommer queried. The man's mouth pulled a bit to one side, betraying apprehension.

"Worried about me?" he asked, a brow raised to question the man's sincere tone.

The secretary pulled back, affronted.

The sharp, vibrating ring of the candlestick telephone situated on the right side of the desk interrupted further conversation.

Treasurer White picked up the receiver and listened. Her gaze flicked to him. "Yes, sir." She passed the receiver to him.

The slightly grainy voice of Mr. Paisley issued from the telephone without hesitation. "Mr. Smith, we will be meeting in Conference Room 1 in half an hour if you'd care to join us. After normal business is concluded, we can address anything you'd care to bring up."

"Thank you, Mr. Paisley. I shall." He replaced the receiver and looked up at Mr. Midsommer and Ms. White. "I will wait here until Mr. Grummond arrives."

"He won't be joining us today," Treasurer White told him.

A frown of concern pulled in his young brows. "Is he well?"

"Yes. He will be in tomorrow."

"But is—"

The glass entryway was opened and two of the four typists came in.

"Mr. Smith, you may address such questions at the meeting, which I must still prepare for. Excuse me." Ms. White made her way to the elevator, followed closely by Mr. Midsommer.

The elevator door closed before the two typists could arrive at it, so they had to wait. The man, whom he recalled overhearing named Mark Cunningham, smiled at him while waiting.

"Have you a new position, Mr. Smith?" the cheery man queried.

"Not quite." He smiled back, because the guy did not deserve his wrath, and because he had no idea what the typists knew and didn't know. They must hear at least part of the goings-on, but with all of the clacking and focus put into their work… Hm.

Still unsure about the role of the typists, having not found it in the three months of working here, he asked the friendly Mark Cunningham, "What is the purpose of your typing?"

"The purpose?" Mark looked at the fellow typist, a middle-aged woman who kept her eyes only on the elevator. "Oh, the usual."

"You aren't very good at lying, Mr. Cunningham, but it's good to know you are aware that putting words on paper is not the purpose of your task."

"Er... Yes." The guy gave a sheepish smile. "Sorry, Mr. Smith. We type. We don't talk."

He nodded, respecting the typist's obvious loyalty and desire to leave the conversation thus.

"You shouldn't've spoken to him," Mark's fellow typist muttered in a low, husky voice, but not so quiet that he missed her words. "He is to be kept away from."

Glad to finally confirm they knew, but kept it to himself.

By the time the elevator opened, the third typist arrived. Gave him a pleasant nod of greeting but kept quiet as she awaited the return of the elevator. The fourth hurried in at just after 8:06 AM. Surprised to see him at the front desk but more concerned about reaching her destination, she pressed the elevator button several times in an attempt to hasten its descent.

He slipped from the seat and joined her in the elevator, much to her surprise. Inching away, despite the fact that he kept himself as far from her as possible, the typist queried, "Which, eh, floor, sir?"

"The same. Thank you." He placed his hands neatly in front of him and leaned against the elevator's wall.

The young blond woman paused briefly, eyed him with wariness, but shook her head and opened the side panel next to the lever. She set it to Floor 4.

Never wondered when the typists arrived and just assumed they went right to work like everyone else. Curious, he decided to follow the late typist and see what transpired.

As they sped upward, he kept his inquisitiveness to himself. Let her exit the elevator first, held the mechanical portal open until he saw her enter the further Conference Room 1. Only after did he step out.

"That... That Mr. Smith person came up to Four with me," he heard the late typist say, and not too quiet about it.

Pleasant chatter and the clank of silverware on dishes paused.

Quickly and silently dashing into the nearer Conference Room 2, he pressed himself against the adjoining wall behind the open conference door.

One set of footsteps entered the hallway. "I don't see anyone, Deb."

"He **did** come up, Marilyn," insisted Deb, the late typist.

"Perhaps he continued to Five?" Marilyn's feet carried her back into the other conference room.

"Nothing to get your stockings in a bunch about." That from the middle-aged woman. "We have our jobs and he has his. Sit and eat."

The clank of dishes and silverware resumed.

So, the typists ate breakfast here before going up to their task, eh?

"Will you be taking your children to the World's Columbian Exposition? I've caught glimpses of their construction. It looks magnificent." That was Deb.

"Next month. You?" Marilyn replied.

"In the summer. What about you, Mr. Cunningham? Perfect place to take a special lady."

He heard Mark chuckle. "And who said I have a special lady?"

The three women twittered.

The unnamed older woman added a humored, "Mr. Smith was right. You're a terrible liar."

"He's terribly perceptive," Mark commented without aggrievance. "I didn't know what to say when he asked our purpose in typing. Still can't tell if he knows."

"Next time, don't say hello. Just nod and keep walking," warned the middle-aged typist.

"You spoke to him?" Marilyn's voice spilled out a smile.

"Why not? I hadn't started my shift yet."

"He gives me the willies." Deb.

"You'd best get over that. And don't ask questions. President Young told us Mr. Smith is like the Corners. Just needs more space than them and to keep our distance."

"You're such a stick-in-the-mud, Maude," Marilyn sighed.

Ah, so that was the middle-aged one's name.

"A stick in the mud who still works here. He may be like the Corners but we all have a job to do. People here count on us. We don't get paid to poke around. Longevity is all in how you pace yourself."

"Don't worry about me, Maude." A cup settled to a saucer as Deb continued with, "I don't plan on poking anything, or learning about magic or mysteries. I also don't plan on going anywhere. Where else would pay a gal half this good?"

A pair of footsteps entered the hall.

Panic seized him briefly and he pressed himself tightly behind the conference room door.

The person in the hall knocked three times at a far wooden surface. Chairs began their stutter as people in the next room stood up. A door opened, more footsteps, and Dolores's cheery tone filled the other conference room.

"All finished? Now, Ms. Braum, drink your juice before you leave."

A bit more shuffling about, the noise of dishes being stacked, and from the end of the building closer to him, the elevator opened. Even hidden behind the door, he got a brief view of the secretary, treasurer, and president with Mr. Paisley just as the typists walked past them. Some nods and smiles were exchanged. Once the elevator closed, he slipped out of his hiding spot and caught up to the managerial staff as they entered Conference Room 1.

"Good morning, Mr. Paisley, Corners, Mr. Smith," Dolores paused to greet them all upon exiting Conference Room 1 with dirty dishes stacked on a tray.

"Good morning again," he returned, always happy to smile at the cheery old lady.

She beamed at him while the three Corners and Mr. Paisley all swiveled about, having not heard him behind them.

Moving on from the surprise, the Corners and founder entered the conference room and started in on the breakfast assortment set out upon the large table.

"No Mr. Grummond this morning?" asked the patient old woman.

"Not today, nor for lunch. Thank you, Dolores," Mr. Paisley replied.

He watched where she went, curious. Dolores entered the Victors' door without knocking, humming a pleasant tune to herself. Interesting, but it was also a delay he chastised himself for and hurried to a far seat in the conference room.

Mr. Paisley grabbed a piece of toast, buttered it, and queried, "Mr. Midsommer, what have we today?"

He listened to their current business, none of which was pressing, and patiently waited his turn. When it seemed they'd wrapped that up, without any break in flow, Mr.

Paisley asked, "Mr. Smith, you have some concerns to address from yesterday?"

"Correct. If we are to work together safely and effectively, there cannot be any more of such nonsense."

Mr. Young cocked a brow at him. "Nonsense?"

"Yes. It was nonsensical for Mr. Grummond to be put in danger."

Treasurer White spoke up next. "Mr. Smith, we are very concerned about you, and for you, but concern can only go so far. The Paisley Foundation always has a reason for the things we do, even if the reason is not readily available to all involved."

Anger bubbling just below the surface, he contained it neatly and replied, "How very political of you, Ms. White. You of everyone here should have realized – given that you know our pasts bear similarities – that neither of us like having choice removed. I was given no choice, nor was my opinion and expertise sought. You simply **allowed** the doing of a thing you knew I would be opposed to. Perhaps you have all become disillusioned due to my appearance, but I wish to make this very clear: Because my condition causes harm, and I do not wish to cause any harm, I will not tolerate my absence in further decision-making when it comes to my particulars."

"We were trying to—"

"Help me? By hurting someone else?" He leaned forward to press his resentful glare on all of them. "Others experimented on me before, left me in a small room with people none the wiser, only to see how long they may last. Again and again this was done. I had no say, treated like a thing instead of a person. How can I trust that **you** won't?"

Oh, their faces showed the weight of his words. Revealing something about himself was worth it, seeing their guilt and the realization of what they'd done. But he emphasized anyway with, "I know what I know of my condition… because people did what they did without regard for others. If I truly have a say here, I refuse to allow that sort of behavior regarding myself."

The room remained silent and his.

"Now, as it is a great concern of mine, can one of you tell me why Mr. Grummond is not here today?"

Mr. Young answered, "Agent Turner is keeping an eye on him. I stopped by Sergei's house before arriving this morning. He was sleeping soundly. Snoring, in fact. Yesterday, he reported feeling very tired due to extended proximity near you, but plans to venture out and see if there are any residual effects of having some of his potential drained away. He mentioned playing some games, but I believe he means to try his luck at gambling."

He thought over this information, and his next words, carefully. The hard part was schooling his anxiety over hearing the Paisley vice president intended on going out when – after a quick estimation in his head – twenty percent of the man's potential had been sucked out. "It isn't wise. He needs to stay where he is and allow his potential to naturally realign or refill or whatever it does to stabilize. Otherwise, accidents befall those who have been drained."

They contemplated his explanation, shared a look between them, and it was Mr. Young who again spoke up.

"I'm sorry for how you were treated in the past, but everyone who works here understands there is a certain level of hazard to it. Perhaps it was not mentioned to you. Perhaps it doesn't seem so, given your own experiences. The situations and entities encountered here are not only stressful but usually dangerous. And, as you are still very much an unknown quantity to us, please forgive that our current procedures have not gone over favorably. We may trust you, Mr. Smith, but we know nothing about your condition aside from what you told us on your first day here. I'm also sorry to inform you that our caution was and is felt as warranted. The danger of your condition needs mitigation. Without being told more about it, we were forced to seek answers elsewhere."

His accusatory stare latched onto Mr. Young. "If you trust me, why not trust that I can keep my distance? You must not trust me very much at all. Or perhaps you didn't believe me and felt I made the entire thing up? After all, what proof do you have that my condition even exists unless you test my boundaries? Do you wish to continue to test my boundaries, Mr. Young? If so, come sit next to me and feel for yourself."

Mr. Young shifted but did not get up, nor did anyone move any closer.

Mr. Paisley, offering no part in either side of the argument, let a little smile show.

"What?" he demanded.

"Everyone here has a great lot of experience dealing with all manner of people and situations, Mr. Smith. What Sergei volunteered for was my idea, but everyone needed to see how you handle yourself around people who feel they know what is best. Good to see you stand up for yourself, and that you are comfortable enough with people who are meant to be trusted to speak up and believe you'll be heard."

Given how the others looked at the founder – a mix of surprise and humor – they hadn't been privy to Mr. Paisley's hidden purpose.

"That doesn't make it any more valid," he argued.

"I beg to differ. I won't be around forever, and this shows you have teeth and not just a condition which you have no control over." To the others, the founder said, "If there is nothing else, this meeting is concluded."

No one offered anything further and retreated to go about their tasks.

He hadn't thought about his benefactor's mortality aside from keeping the old man away from him. But that remained a truth. Mr. Paisley was old. Where would he live when his host passed? Was his stable life here an illusion?

He and the founder shared a look.

Mr. Paisley stood slowly and stretched, looking more unsteady than usual. No loss of balance, or the good mood. "This concerns you, but I will have you know your welfare has always been my chief concern, Mr. Smith. Even when I did not specifically state such to my employees. They needed to see you speaking up for yourself just as much as you needed to see that you could. Know that I have seen to your future. You will always have a place here – if you choose to remain at this profession – and today proves you have a say in this place and your future, even when I am not in it."

"Why is it always secrets and subterfuge? Why can't you just tell me things? Or them? And what of the typists?"

Mr. Paisley looked surprised that he brought them up and asked, "What of them?"

"Are they aware of their true purpose here?"

"Figured it out yet?"

"The typewriters are enchanted. I haven't learned the reason yet, but I worry you keep too much from your employees."

Mr. Paisley sighed and started out. "The typist pool is aware of their very necessary purpose, as they are very much aware that knowing more than that is not what they are valued for."

"And what **are** they being valued for?" he pressed, following the founder out into the hall at an appropriate distance.

"Certain folks possess an abundance of magical energy that they do not use or require. The extensive wards about this entire building work because they are constantly being supplied with a surplus granted by the willing few we have hired for that purpose. Each day they leave a bit drained but return replenished after a night's rest. They are so diligent that their services are not required on the weekends, nor after hours."

"Why then the subterfuge with the Corners?"

"Some need to be reminded in a particular way of one of our chief tenets here; that no one should know everything, Mr. Smith. Not I. Not them. Not even you."

"It would make things more pleasant," he grumbled.

Mr. Paisley whirled on him. "Perhaps I introduced you to the Paisley Foundation prematurely. Perhaps you needed more time, after Maisey. For that, I apologize. Tomorrow begins a new lesson, Mr. Smith. One you have been looking forward to, and one which will keep you busy at my estate for several weeks, away from this place and people. It should give you more perspective on how you would like to continue spending your time – whether with the Paisley Foundation or in some other endeavor."

Mr. Paisley's decree rang with irritation and finality. That, coupled with the announcement of his absence from the Paisley Foundation tomorrow and in the foreseeable future, produced mixed feelings in him. Probably for the best. Why then did he feel the need to apologize, or be grateful, or provide comfort to the old man? Yes, he cared about Mr. Paisley, but it still felt right to tell them off. They were in the wrong. The Corners and benefactor should not have pressed him as they had. Yet… that feeling lingered. Trust betrayed, not sure where he sat with any of them, but still wanting to believe his relationship with the old man remained intact. Complicated feelings. It made his horseback ride to the Paisley Estate very long.

Mr. Smith Who Works The Front Desk by Jade Griffin

1893, May 29

Last week marked the start of his absence from the Paisley Foundation. Today was the start of something new entirely.

Anxious, he waited on the estate porch during a bout of blustery sleet and wind. Such cold sent exhilarating chills down his arms. They matched the waves of anticipation coursing through him as the carriage pulled to a halt in the slushy gravel courtyard. Had to remain polite and formal to greet Mr. Paisley and their new guest. Hands clutched to fists in his coat pockets, he stood with proper posture and an eager smile while the coachman hopped down and opened the door.

Mr. Paisley emerged first, and then their guest. It was not an old samurai as expected but a man half Mr. Paisley's age with short, black hair and narrow eyes gazing calm and far. Robed in black and gray clothing from an Asian region of origin, the guest exited the carriage with grace of movement. The man pulled from the carriage a long, thin package wrapped in brown paper – bigger than a normal sword.

He tried very hard to contain himself but immediately bowed low as the pair entered the home. As always, he maintained proper distance, closed the double doors, and dashed to the study's open entryway.

Mr. Paisley told him, "Mr. Smith? Tell Danneby to bring in the green tea. Then you may join us."

Giddy, he raced to the kitchen, startling the butler into nearly dropping the prepared tray.

"Sorry, Danneby. We're ready for tea."

"Yes, sir."

He hurried away and on to the study where their guest sat very proper. Only after taking his own seat eleven feet away and they all stayed quiet that he took note of Mr. Paisley's mood. If their guest was finally here after such a long wait, why did his host look mildly perturbed? Living with Mr. Paisley for over a year, he knew when the old man wasn't happy about something.

Danneby came, poured the tea, and left.

Mr. Paisley took a cup, as did their guest, so he came forward and got his, taking it back to his seat. He copied the other two, sipping in the lull and enjoying the environment. Tried and failed to keep wandering eyes from lingering on the long, wrapped package poised against the wall behind their guest.

When their cups were placed back on the tray, Mr. Paisley's throat-clearing precluded conversation. "Mr. Smith, may I present Egawa Naonori."

He stood quickly, bowed low and formal, or as much as he remembered from movies, and forced a straight face so he wouldn't look the grinning fool. "Very pleased to meet you, Egawa Naonori, sir. Shall I refer to you as *sensei*?"

Naonori stood, an effortless movement. The swordmaster finally spoke, using fair English with a pleasant Japanese accent. "No, as I am not permitted to formally train you."

His querulous gaze flicked between Naonori and Mr. Paisley. "What?"

"Mr. Egawa has informed me on the ride here that he is a swordsman – *kenshi* – but not a swordmaster, and that his uncle, whom I requested, has been dead a number of years. Also, given the state of things in Japan and China, *bushido* and *kendo* are not quite what I recall, nor are they as accessible as I believed. However, he has agreed to come and fulfill my request."

Naonori bowed in full respect for Mr. Paisley. "I cannot replace my uncle, nor is teaching outsiders permitted in our practice of *kenjutsu*, but a debt is owed and I will teach you what I know." Naonori picked up the packaged belongings, placed them on the floor.

As the swordsman went about unwrapping the package, he craned his neck for a better look. Noticed Naonori was barefoot and wondered if his footwear should be absent also, despite the cold. Ah. Mr. Paisley still wore shoes, so he refrained from doing anything unless instructed. On the edge of his seat, he blinked in surprise at the long, curved object Naonori lifted from the brown paper.

The wooden sword held reverently in both hands, Naonori locked eyes with him. "*Bokken*. Training sword."

He nodded dismissively, eager to behold the glint of steel and braid work known on all proper Japanese swords. That had to be what Naonori reached in for after putting aside the *bokken*.

Naonori pulled a second item from the wrapper. It was a long bamboo sword but split in four pieces and rebound at the guard. Confusion furled his brow, as did mild disappointment.

"*Shinai*. Teaching sword." Naonori turned to their host. "Where shall practice be held?"

Rising with a grunt, their host said, "Follow me."

They were led to Mrs. Paisley's old workroom, long cleared of her materials and notes.

Naonori held a weapon in each hand and used the *shinai* to point into the room. "Remove shoes and coat at the door. Stand there."

"I'll leave you to it," Mr. Paisley said, exiting in the same move.

He hurried to comply, standing where directed. Finally alone with the swordsman, it occurred to him that something important had not been addressed. "Did Mr. Paisley tell you to keep your distance from me?"

"Yes. I have been told this, but it may be tested. We begin with standing. Like this."

He mimicked Naonori's straight back, far-apart stance, and pretended he also held a *shinai* with two hands in front of him.

Naonori approached very close, made a circle around him, stood beside him.

"Toes like this. Feet this way. Knees here," Naonori instructed.

He corrected his stance again.

Naonori continued to stand beside him. Close. Made him nervous. His stance wavered.

The *shinai* came down hard against the back of his right leg. *Wacka!*

Startled him, but also showed the weakness of his stance as he lost his balance and fell.

"Try again."

He stood, rubbed the back of his leg, saw no real damage done, and eyed Naonori warily.

"If you fear teaching sword, you will never be ready for training sword," the *kenshi* warned.

Mr. Smith Who Works The Front Desk by Jade Griffin

Very true. And, honestly, he'd been through so many worse things. For the next few weeks, this was a chance to focus only on learning true skill in defense and perhaps offense. So, he planted his feet and did as instructed, however he did not lose track of time and, after eight minutes, bowed to Naonori.

"We must take a break." Without further explanation, he jogged out of the room. Jogged out favoring his right leg, as it was the favored limb to receive the teachings of the *shinai*, as well as his back. Sure to have bruises, but he couldn't help grinning to himself. It felt good, this training, and something to keep with him and practice whenever he wanted. Another thing to do alone.

The rest of the day proceeded thus, with several haltings due to Naonori's proximity to him as the swordsman corrected his stance, posture, or how he pretend-held his sword. Due to the continual closeness, the device would often shorten the timeframe of an individual so frequently near him. The disruptions became often and longer as the day wore on, something Naonori did not make mention of. At least, not to him.

In the evening, he snuck over to where the *kenshi* and Mr. Paisley were having tea in the study to listen in on their conversation.

"Determined, dutiful student, but too many breaks."

"He is mindful of space, Naonori. You'd do best to follow my advice."

"I endeavor to train fighters, not boys who cannot stay on a battlefield."

"It is a different kind of battlefield he fights on. By keeping his distance, he is winning. I suggest incorporating the distance in his lesson. Push him to create more space between himself and his opponent."

"It does not make sense. *Kendo* is for close combat."

"Some things are not made to make sense. He is one of them. Your uncle told you what I do?"

"Yes."

"Then heed me and keep your distance."

"As long as you pay your debt, this I will do."

He backed away, silent, ignoring the aches and pains in favor of ruminating over lessons learned. Mr. Paisley owed Naonori a debt and not the other way around? What did the swordsman want? No idea. It plagued him as he attempted to sleep, found himself unable to – and not only for the revelation of the situation between host and guest. Rest remaining elusive, he wandered downstairs.

Passing the study, he caught Mr. Paisley watching him and paused.

"Sore?" asked his host.

"A bit."

"Did the hot bath help?"

"Some. I haven't been through anything this physical in a long while. Just need to get used to it. Thank you, for this." He entered and took a far seat.

"A change of direction and focus often sets one right. Liking it so far, I take it?"

"Very much. Although… I'm a bit confused."

"Oh?"

"Naonori. What is it you owe him?"

"He is not seen as a master in his own country and cannot teach in the way taught by his uncle. He wants a place in America to do so."

"I see," he got out through a sudden yawn. "Sorry."

Mr. Paisley waved him on to bed. "Goodnight, Mr. Smith."

As he left the study, he caught the peeking gaze of Naonori through the crack of the guest room door across and down the hall. Hopefully, the Japanese man's curiosity would not be a problem.

Mr. Smith Who Works The Front Desk by Jade Griffin

1893, May 30

He woke with bruises and aches but a renewed eagerness. Dressed but foregoing any meal, he hurried to the workshop and found Naonori seated on the floor awaiting his arrival.

"Less breaks today, *Aoi*."

He did not respond, mainly due to the fact that he couldn't comply with the request, but also because he wasn't sure what "aoi" meant, or if it meant anything beyond a familiarity with the student. Hopefully not a derogatory, he ignored it and followed instruction. Only one *wacka*! from the *shinai* on his back to correct his posture before he had to call a break at just under eight minutes.

Jogging from the center of the workroom, he made for the exit.

Naonori cut him off and shut the door in one effortless move, left hand holding the *shinai* pointed at him, the other resting on the hilt of the *bokken* tucked under settling robes.

"There is no learning if you are not here to learn," the *kenshi* said, taking a step toward him.

He backed up three paces, tense. Was this part of a lesson or just a stupid move on the part of his new mentor? Not sure. Not until he spied something new in the workroom. A broom.

Dashing for the improvised weapon, he snatched it up and pivoted Naonori's direction, falling into the stance learned yesterday. The broom's bristled end pushed more weight that direction, but he managed to fend people off with less effective things in the past.

The *kenshi* stayed at the exit until the improvised weapon lay in hand, then the swordsman flowed effortlessly toward him and brandished the *shinai*. Not menacing nor meaning to strike. Testing.

He did his best to maintain his stance while circling away and toward the door.

"Why?" Naonori asked, following, never making contact with his broom though their weapons remained inches apart.

What could he say that might satisfy the man and keep the required distance? "I apologize, but it is a thing I must not say until I have learned what I can from you."

Naonori maintained the adopted position.

He knew time ticked away but held himself firm. If this didn't work…

The *kenshi* straightened out of the fighting stance and lowered the *shinai*. Uttering an acquiescing, "*Hai*," Naonori issued one nod.

He ran to the exit and hurried out, broom in hand, breath quickening. Curiosity? Ego? Testing boundaries? Whichever, his bait of offering an explanation at the end of training seemed to work.

After twelve minutes of time, he re-entered, broom in hand, showing no reluctance but obviously prepared for antagonistic closeness.

Naonori stood exactly where the two of them had left off, so he returned to the center of the room and bowed. Just had to be ready if the man—

Naonori dropped into the stance taught yesterday, *shinai* held out in front.

He did the same, copying the move with his broom.

The distance between them just shy of ten feet, Naonori stepped to the left in a gliding motion, feet barely rising above the floor.

He duplicated the move, finally achieving enough space between them.

Naonori did the same but moved to the right, and he in turn recreated each step as near as he could gauge, mirror-opposite. The gliding foot thing was only tricky with his leading foot, but repeating this moving dance of martial arts about twenty times with slight variations forward and back cemented the motion. Less breaks, yes, but it didn't feel much like learning aside from the footwork. No practical application.

The next day, two more stances were taught, less distance granted while the *shinai* was used to train him on how not to stand, and more bruises and blisters than the first day despite how short his training turned out to be. They worked for only two hours before Naonori called a halt to the training.

He didn't feel like discussing his frustration with Mr. Paisley but listened to host and guest in the evening, if only to learn what was on Naonori's mind. The *kenshi* rarely spoke, even during lessons.

"How is he progressing?"

"*Aoi* is eager, but his need for space is a challenge."

"A challenge, but not a hindrance?"

"No. If I can teach a one-armed man *kenjutsu*, so I can with *Aoi*."

When he entered the workroom on the third day, a crudely-constructed humanish figure stood waiting for him beside Naonori. Just a chair with a stuffed shirt and a mop stuck in horizontally to simulate arms, but easily recognizable as a training dummy.

"This is a suitable partner to practice with?" the *kenshi* asked.

He smiled. "Yes."

And lessons resumed, but this time he was told to use the stances and broom on the dummy. Naonori stepped in several times with the *shinai* to teach him the error in how he did it, but then his instructor moved away in less than a minute each time. The day existed in short bursts of proximity and long moments of studiously held stances away from his mentor, but the only breaks required were for biological necessities.

The fourth and fifth day continued this instruction, with more variety in the lessons. He felt his own performance improving – proved by less *wacka*s from the *shinai*, callouses forming on his hands, and confirmed in the evening where he would seek out a spot to listen to instructor and host chat before bed. Sometimes they would talk about Asian politics, which intrigued him. He didn't learn until the seventh day that Naonori was aware of otherworldly things. A brief mention but it held great relevance, both in revealing more about Naonori and about Mr. Paisley.

"The book there which you said not to read. It is the same as the painting in the hall?"

"It is."

"Did you read it?"

"… Yes. Long ago. Once." The weighted reply held reluctance.

"And you do not believe me worthy?"

"It is not a question of worth, Naonori. It is in one's ability to maintain a sense of self and willpower when confronted with the demonized creature bound to the tome. In all reflection, it is not about personal worthiness but that it is simply not worth the risk. The risk is that, should you fail, I would be left to destroy your possessed body. I would care not to lose any more people to the damnable thing, nor tempt Jiim. Please do not touch it."

"*Hai*," came Naonori's quiet affirmative.

He knew the book of which they spoke. Mr. Paisley told him all about it in his first week in the home and made sure he knew to avoid it.

On the tenth day of training, he entered and found the battered dummy up against the back wall. Naonori sat in the center of the room, the *shinai* resting across the *kenshi*'s legs.

He hesitated.

"Come. Sit."

He did, and started the count in his head.

Naonori picked the *shinai* up with two flat palms and held it out toward him.

Unexpected, but he accepted the training weapon.

Naonori stood, and so did he. In the same move, his instructor pulled the *bokken* from where it had always been tucked in robes and held it in both hands while dropping into a fighting stance.

He backed up two paces, *shinai* held firm.

Naonori came at him on the left.

He tried to block with the *shinai*, but the *kenshi* used completely different moves while holding the wooden training sword. Ended up dodging out of the way, breaking his stance, and fumbling to place his feet once more and be ready.

"*Shinai* is for hitting. *Bokken*, like the *katana*, is for slicing. Both are good to learn."

Holding a sigh, he wished Naonori explained first and then showed the lesson. So be it. *Shinai* gripped tight, stance light, he awaited Naonori's next lesson.

New, deep bruises had him groaning the next morning. The one that really made him ache came at the last hour, when Naonori brought the *bokken* down on his right arm. Didn't block in time, and thankful the *kenshi* could pull the strike and not break his arm. They were hard lessons, but he learned them quick. In the evening, he gained more insight, reflected in the nightly report given by Naonori to Mr. Paisley, who was often gone during the day.

"Has a place been selected for my *dojo*?" he heard Naonori ask over evening tea in the study.

"Anxious to leave?"

"I will stay the month, *Peizuri-san*. However, I ask if *Aoi* will be a student at my *dojo*."

"Yes, a place has been selected, purchased, and the promotion has already begun. As for whether he shall be a student there, I do not know."

He tucked himself tight in the hall inlet when Naonori retired to a guest room. With the click of the downstairs guest door, he trotted over to the study.

"Ah, Mr. Smith. Sorry to have missed supper."

"I understand. Paisley Foundation business?"

"Yes. The Corners asked about you again. Dolores as well. I assured them you are doing well. They did ask if you'd be returning anytime at the present."

He thought on it while taking his usual far seat. It was something he found himself considering more and more each evening as he lay in bed to the subtle throb of bruises. "Yes. After sword training has concluded."

"Happy with your progress so far with Naonori?"

"Yes. I've been meaning to ask… Why does he call me *Aoi*?"

Mr. Paisley chuckled. "You no doubt heard his own version of my name while listening in? The name 'Mr. Smith' is also difficult with his accent, and confusing to give you a title when you look so young, so it appears he has chosen a name for you. *Aoi*, according to Naonori, is a word for the color blue-green, but it also means unripe or new, so it is an accurate description of you with your green eyes and novice ways."

"*Hai*," he replied with a grin.

Concluding his second week, Naonori greeted him with a second *bokken* – something he must have missed from the *kenshi*'s first unpacking – and they spent most of the morning clashing wooden swords.

The next day, his fifteenth lesson, Naonori was different, agitated. He couldn't reason a cause at first. Perhaps unhappy with the progress? Distracted, he contemplated it while blocking his mentor's second strike.

Naonori pushed through the strike and grabbed his left wrist.

Uttering a startled gasp, he tried twisting away.

The *kenshi* held him fast, staring at fingers passing through the device phased on his wrist.

"Let go!" he demanded, relaxing his body, attempting to command Naonori by strength of person alone.

"What is this?"

"The reason why people should stay away from me."

"Magic?"

He did not reply, but tried one final yank, thinking Naonori's attention divided. It was not and the *kenshi*'s grip held like iron.

"If you do not get away from me, it will kill you," he warned, his voice an ice flow.

Naonori's gaze flicked briefly to him.

"How?"

"It doesn't matter how. Let. Me. Go." He tried again to get the man off with sheer willpower.

Naonori, immune to his wishes, tried to grab, touch, or make contact in any way with the damn device.

Anger filled him. Why didn't anyone listen?! He replanted his feet and jabbed forward one-handed with his *bokken*.

Naonori dodged, expertly twisting his wrist and flipping him hard onto his back. Harder than any blow from *shinai* or *bokken*. Knocked the wind out of him and stars swam in his vision.

"Tell me **how**." Naonori bit out the words, revealing a hatred never seen on the *kenshi* before.

The device on his wrist activated.

Still reeling from landing on the hard stone floor, that all-too-familiar, gut-twisting sensation spurred him to frantic action. He curled, twisted, wrapped his arm and legs around Naonori, and bit the man's grabbing hand hard. Got a solid punch to the face that sent him tumbling to the floor.

Couldn't help a grin at his success. Hard to keep it at the cursing of the Japanese man. Presumed cursing. It was all foreign words. Looked really pissed.

Anticipating more confrontation, he stood, *bokken* still in hand, and slid closer to the open workroom door.

Naonori charged.

He bolted, yelling, "DANNEBY!"

The butler, sweeping debris out the entryway, assessed the situation in a heartbeat. Hard not to, what with him frantic and their foreign guest plowing after him shouting whatever in very heated tones.

Danneby, that excellent butler, slid that stately form right between he and the enraged *kenshi*.

Affording the scene a quick glance back, he barreled past, threw open the front doors, and flew out barefoot across snow, gravel, and slushy yellow grass.

Gasping for breath some minutes later, far past the house, pressing himself into the snow-leveled grassy field, he paused for a listen. Nothing.

Damnit... The only explanation he could come up with – both for the early triggering of the device and the *kenshi*'s crazed behavior – was that the Japanese man had to have seen it some time earlier and snuck into his bedroom to examine it while he slept, lingered too long, and gotten at least partially drained. If that were the case, the best thing was to get away. Hard to do at present, given his lack of winter clothes and snow starting. His teeth chattered after only a minute. Hadn't been so exposed to the elements in a while. Grown accustomed to halfway normal life. Was it worth it being around normal people? Look at how he disrupted the Japanese man's usual nature.

Footsteps crunching through slush and gravel drew near.

Very few places to hide with the grass pressed low by so much recent weather...

Bokken still in hand, he curled himself into a tight frog pose, ready to spring at Naonori.

But his eyes latched onto only Danneby and he sank down to the wet ground in relief.

"Come, sir. The situation has been handled." The butler held out one of Mr. Paisley's long coats.

He stumbled up and into the warm clothing, unafraid of what may be found inside. More curious than anything.

At the doorway lay a prone Naonori with Clara glaring down, a large pan held ready to strike again. She clutched the handle of the cooking implement like how people hold swords. Handled, indeed.

"He's not gettin' up anytime soon, sir," she told him, the fumes of anger in her words directed clearly toward their foreign guest. "What nerve!"

Hurrying past the fallen *kenshi*, he went straight to his room to change. By the time he came down, Naonori was nowhere to be seen.

"We have placed him somewhere for safe-keeping, sir," Danneby answered his peeking around.

By mid-afternoon, banging on the walls revealed the location of their misappropriating guest. They went ignored by staff so he chose to ignore them, too. It wasn't long after when the skid of carriage wheels on gravel and slush heralded the arrival of Mr. Paisley.

He let Danneby explain the situation but stood by and watched his host's face shadow over and jaw tighten with concealed rage. One look at his young face, bruise forming from the delivered punch, and Mr. Paisley quietly headed down the hall and to the left toward the source of the wall-pounding.

He didn't hear anything from the room after Mr. Paisley unlocked the far door and went in. Couldn't have been more than a handful of minutes and his host exited. The entryway held open, Mr. Paisley let Naonori out. Clothes disheveled, hair mussed, and eyes always on the floor as the *kenshi* went to the guest room.

Mr. Paisley sighed and walked over to him. "Are you hurt?"

"No. At least he's calmed down."

"He will be leaving presently. Danneby? Ready the horse for Mr. Egawa."

"Yes, sir." The butler hurried outside.

That left he and Mr. Paisley standing in the hall.

A certain awkwardness filled the distance between them – one he didn't feel but Mr. Paisley certainly did.

Made him feel obligated to explain. "It isn't an excuse but... I don't think he could help it. I've seen it before. Rare, but sometimes people can't comprehend the sensation of being drained and linger longer, like they're missing that instinct of self-preservation. I didn't want to hurt him but I bit him to get away from him."

"There is no need to justify your actions, Mr. Smith. Naonori was told certain rules to abide in my house and he has not followed them. That is on him."

Couldn't argue there, nor could he help feeling both relief and regret at seeing the *kenshi* leave on horseback in silent disgrace.

Mr. Paisley did not eat supper that night and spent the rest of the evening in the master bedroom.

He felt bad and wondered if reminding his host of his willingness to return to the Paisley Foundation might brighten things.

No opportunity came in the morning. Mr. Paisley was already gone, so he ate alone. Didn't see the man all day or night and enquired with Danneby.

"Handling foreign matters, sir. He will return tomorrow."

So he waited. In the morning, breakfast lay ready upon the dining room table. Alone, he started in on the meal.

Just after the first bite, he heard the double doors open, shut, a bit of clothing shuffled, and then Mr. Paisley graced into the dining room, taking the head table seat.

"Sleep well?" his host enquired.

He swallowed a gulp of milk before replying, "I did, thank you."

"I have something in the back for you, after breakfast."

Intrigued, he ate at a faster pace.

Upon following Mr. Paisley out and around the side of the house, he noted a post had been planted into the ground, wrapped with thick rope. It looked like…

"Is this a target post?"

"It is. And something else as well." Mr. Paisley went to the back wall of the estate where a small, wrapped package lay. Retrieved, it was held out to him.

The shape long, thin, and slightly curved, a grin sprang instantly to his face. He tore into the wrapping and beheld a beautifully dark green-braided and decorated scabbard. Tucked inside, a *katana* wound with green and ivory braiding about the hilt. He slowly slid the blade from the scabbard and delighted in the shiny metal of a real sword.

"It may seem a bit big, but my theory is that you'll grow into it. I saw the way your eyes lit up at the implements he brought and assumed nothing less than the real thing would delight you." His host's smile fell under great emotional weight. "They are also an apology. The sword and target post are for you to practice with at your leisure so you may retain the lessons learned, but I apologize for introducing you to someone with such hidden ambitions. Naonori is not the man his uncle was. At least with the target post you may practice in safety and not be antagonized."

He regarded his host, saw regret on the old man's face, and said, "I'm not upset over him. I grew complacent as well, because learning swordsmanship was something I desired before being taken. It… it was something to grab hold of from my past. But Naonori taught me valuable skills. One is a lesson hard-learned this past month, from not just him: Even with special skills or abilities, people will be people. Curious, dangerous, stupid, kind. It is a reminder that people make mistakes. If I am going to stay here, I must accept that and… and forgive. It is a reminder that I am also just a person. If it is alright with you, Mr. Paisley, I will join you at the Paisley Foundation tomorrow."

His host smiled with great pride. "It would please everyone to have you there once more."

Mr. Smith Who Works The Front Desk by Jade Griffin

1893, June 14

He greeted the morning with apprehension. Many began like this in the past, waking with the uncertainty of what would transpire each day, each hour. Hadn't had a day like this since the end of his first week with the Paisleys, but this was new territory – going back to a place where he told people off for how they treated him. Never had the chance. Kept telling himself he was within his rights to do so, that Mr. Paisley supported him and, according to his host, the others remained eager to see him back. When he finally arrived at the livery stable sharing the same block as the Paisley Foundation and passed the horse to the waiting stableman, he took two deep breaths before continuing to the foundation's glass doors.

Arriving later than intended, there was no sign of Mr. Paisley or anyone else in the lobby. No matter. He started work straightaway.

Taking the garbage from all five floors, he kept eyes and ears open for news as well as the current mood. Seemed business as usual on the trash-bin run, except the Corners kept more to themselves. He caught Mr. Midsommer glancing at him a few times. He tried to break any tension by offering a smile to the quiet Paisley secretary who rewarded him with a similar if slightly awkward expression. What became apparent to him was the lack of vice president Grummond. It bothered him. Not just a passing bother but enough that he decided to inquire of the Corners when he went up to dust, right after emptying the garbage in the large concrete garbage box outside.

Because the communal trash bin stood a bit tall, he'd taken to bringing his broom to not only tote the sack of collected trash but push the bin's lid open. Just after tossing the garbage in, there came a scuff of large feet directly behind him!

He didn't think. Tightening his grip, he planted himself in a fighting stance and swiveled about, launching the broom handle forward, right into the gut of the person who startled him.

Vice President Grummond doubled over with a loud "Oof!"

Immediately, he straightened his posture, but did not apologize. What was the big man thinking, coming up behind him outside?

"You are upset," the Paisley vice president acknowledged on a wheeze. Taking a moment to collect a whole breath, Mr. Grummond nodded toward the Paisley building beside them. "Inside. We talk."

Not certain if he should allow it but there seemed no trickery or ulterior motives in the big Russian's demeanor. Just a bit of poor execution in attempting a conversation.

"Did not mean to startle you," Mr. Grummond opened, completely serious. "but must address events of last month."

"I don't particularly feel like addressing them any further, if it's all the same to you."

The Paisley vice president's head shook adamantly. "Is not same. Mr. Smith, many things shape lives. Many bad things shape mine. Wanting to feel threat of death – to feel alive – is part of motive, alongside learn more about your condition. I have no family, no legacy. For piece of me to be taken by you... That is piece of immortality."

They locked eyes. He wanted the man to understand, but Mr. Grummond similarly desired him to see the other motives as valid. Perhaps it was part of the Paisley vice president's religion or personal beliefs – this talk of desiring immortality due to a lack of familial legacy. Something he understood, yes, but did not agree with such thinking. Sure, if you believed energy could neither be created or destroyed, only changed, as in theories he'd heard on one of his transfers, then, yes, everyone held immortality. He definitely didn't see it that way. Perhaps having a drawn-out and harsh life made him too cynical. Perhaps something to work on now that he had what appeared to be a more stable life? The first step of that was to forgive the big Russian man.

So, he sighed and said, "Please don't do it again."

"I will not. You have my word."

His eyes followed as the man departed for the elevator. Sergei Grummond dropped the thick Russian accent to deliver that solemn promise. It was the first time the Paisley vice president said anything he believed without question.

Mr. Smith Who Works The Front Desk by Jade Griffin

1893, August 26

It stood out in a strange way, fluffing up directly under his chin. Not the regal or happy look he was going for. Cursing under his breath, he glared at the tie and more importantly at himself. The world-wearied, seven-year-old face forever familiar stared back, furious in concentration and frustration. Didn't want to mess it up, even if it were merely a dress rehearsal, but that wasn't the only thing bothering him. Space. Space bothered him. He felt honored to be asked to Ms. White's wedding, but quite nervous. Would there be enough room and time to make certain the device on his wrist took no opportunities, potential, or luck from any of the gathered? Yes, most would know of his spatial limitations. What of any guests who did not? What of them? He did not want to be responsible for ruining Ms. White's special day, nor ruining the lives of anyone in attendance. Why did he even accept the offer?

Because no one had ever asked, nor did he think anyone ever would.

Selfish. Yes, selfish of him... But this was a time of celebration. Could he not celebrate a little as well and trust that he, if no one else, could keep those attending safe from his forced condition? At the very least --

"You are stuck with that thing?"

He whirled at that thick Russian voice, a finger catching in the loop of the bowtie, yanking it into a terrible knot. Hadn't heard Sergei coming up from behind, nor was the Paisley Foundation vice president visible at that angle in the mirror. Sneaky ex-spy. But he sighed and nodded.

Mr. Smith Who Works The Front Desk by Jade Griffin

"I can help. Come." Sergei waved him closer.

He approached with reluctance and started counting in his head. The big Russian man always had ulterior motives for any sort of interaction, or so it seemed. Maybe the Paisley Foundation's vice president only behaved that way around him, always eager to unravel "the mysterious Mr. Smith".

Sergei's face remained stern with concentration as big fingers undid the knot. No words passed between them, which also didn't match the big man's usual behavior. As with all of Ms. White's coworkers, Sergei received an invitation to the wedding. Dressed in a smart black suit which strained to cover the Russian's girth, it fit better than the current mood displayed by the vice president.

Curiosity got the better of him. Convincing himself it was merely a cautionary query, he asked Sergei, "Something wrong?"

"No, Mr. Smith."

"You aren't bothering me about the device on my wrist, or where I'm from, or any of that."

"Is not a day for that." He stood, backed up the required ten feet and said, "There. Bowtie looks good on you."

He turned to the mirror. The pale blue formal decorative looked very nice indeed. Tied expertly and didn't choke him in the slightest. He turned to Sergei. "Thank you. Did you learn how to do that for spy work?"

"Eh... No. I learn for my wedding." Sergei's face shadowed over with great sorrow and longing. He turned and walked away.

Never considered that the man had no family due to them being dead. He presumed Sergei's relations were cut off after coming to America to work for the Paisley Foundation, seen as a traitor to family and country. Perhaps that really was what happened. But he learned not to engage people in conversation who had shown a propensity for digging into his own past and present circumstances, and so left it alone. Time to get downstairs and in the carriage to take them to the little chapel Mr. Paisley found for the service.

Once out on the street, three carriages awaited them. He had to ride with someone – a fact leaving him very uncomfortable, despite being reassured that the chapel was minutes away – and waited to see who he would be stuck with.

Mr. Cunningham sat in the lead carriage with Mr. Young, Mr. Midsommer as the driver. Ms. White and Mr. Paisley took off with Paisley agent Andrew Dane in the coachman's seat. That left the third carriage to he and Mr. Grummond.

The big Russian held open the carriage hatch and inclined a head to the seating within.

"I'll take the seat by the door," he informed the Paisley vice president. He started counting again in his head, hoping the prior count of four minutes thirty-seven seconds would not carry over.

Sergei climbed in without a word.

Agent Conrad Turner exited the Paisley Foundation and offered him an assist in, which he declined. Got in fine on his own, despite being small.

An attempt to settle became a jostling grab for the sides as the carriage tilted to the right, Agent Turner mounting the driver's seat. With growing unease, he asked Mr. Grummond, "It is a quick trip, correct?"

"Yes. Five minutes. I counted."

As if on cue, Agent Turner cracked the reins and the two horses took off at a jerky canter.

Regaining his balance after the jarring start, he snuck a glance Sergei's way.

The vice president eyed him similarly.

He tensed, dreading even a few minutes stuck under the prying, scrutinous queries of the Paisley Foundation's vice president.

But Sergei Grummond did not ask anything. The big man heaved a great sigh and told him, "Met beautiful young woman years after recruitment into spy work. Special division did not like me quitting program for woman, so they quit woman day of wedding. That is day I left my country. I know you read file in Repository, Mr. Smith. Such facts are not in file, because not even Mr. Paisley knows them."

He never expected Sergei to tell him something which clearly affected the man deeply. He didn't know how to respond and looked away, shuffling his feet. A great discomfort settled on him, being around a person usually full of mischief and curiosity now cowed by a reminder of a terrible past. Made him feel bad – not only for Sergei but for the fact that the man told him a personal truth not found on file at the Paisley Foundation... and he remained reluctant to respond with anything in kind. Perhaps a little could be shared... So, he eyed the big Russian and said, "Mr. Paisley also does not know everything about me. They both knew quite a bit, but not everything."

Sergei looked about to speak, hesitated, then continued with, "How did she die?"

His eyes dropped again. Hadn't been more than eight months. Why did it feel like he could talk about her death easily? Had he gotten over it that quickly? No, not that. This felt more like a time to commiserate, so he answered, "I woke up and she was dead beside me. There isn't anything else to say than that, and nothing else but that."

"You have seen much. Your eyes speak this truth. Unlike myself, you do not hide it."

"No, I don't. I want people to see. It shouldn't be hidden if I must constantly be vigilant. Hard not to be vigilant every day living with my condition. Perhaps difficult, but the only thing I can do about it is stay away from people."

"Is lonely life, Mr. Smith."

"Better than the guilt of having people's deaths on my conscience."

Sergei's head tilted briefly, an acquiescence.

Good to know the Paisley vice president finally understood his stance. Hopefully, no more trying to experiment with his condition and endanger people, unlike that incident a few months back. Yes, he forgave Mr. Grummond, but he could not afford to let his guard down. Especially now, sitting so close to the Paisley vice president and even the carriage driver with no way away and time ticking by.

The clatter of carriage wheels on cobbles filled the cabin's sudden silence, settling only when gravity pulled them per the deceleration of the conveyance. Relief settled over him. A short ride, indeed.

He rushed the cab door, flung it open, jumped down from the carriage, and strode into the small structure just off the sidewalk. The diminutive building barely looked big enough to afford the space he needed to keep everyone safe. Just inside, everyone lingered in a cluster. Scanning the place for an open area, he caught Mr. Paisley nodding to him. His

Mr. Smith Who Works The Front Desk by Jade Griffin

benefactor pointed to a corner where a seat lay waiting. Whether placed just for him or not, he sped that way and breathed a sigh of relief. Took five steps to get from the collection of nine happy, excited people to the chair. That equaled at least ten feet. The joyous group then moved to the front of the chapel -- even further away -- so he relaxed and felt it safe to take in the good feelings of the gathered. Safe to relax, if even for a short time.

His part was small. Bring the rings to the waiting couple when the priest asks, "Have you the rings?" He stayed at the ready, responded when the words were spoken, and retreated once more to the chair. Never seen the priest before but the man looked older than Mr. Paisley and didn't seem to care that the ring bearer would not stand with everyone else. The practice run concluded and everyone departed. He once more rode with Sergei but neither of them felt like talking. He wondered why Ms. White wasn't dressed special for the rehearsal but thought it likely due to the tradition of the groom not seeing the bride on her wedding day until the ceremony. Showing up for the dress rehearsal in her gown would have blown that bit.

Back at the Paisley Foundation, he lingered just at the glass front doors and watched the others trickle in. Mr. Paisley returned last, alone.

"Did the couple stay to go over other matters of preparation?" he queried his benefactor.

Mr. Paisley smiled. "It is rare in our occupation to have a day off, but rarer still for two people to find such happiness. I told them to do something fun. Perhaps Monday we will take our own holiday."

He blinked in surprise as Mr. Paisley strode past. The old man had never suggested a vacation before. Did the bountiful good feelings of the impending nuptials completely mask the horror eight months prior and Mr. Paisley was looking pleasantly at a future which the old man's wife would have no part?

The absence of Mrs. Paisley filled every inch of the sudden silence. He stared out of the big glass windows of the Paisley Foundation and tried not to let the past drag him down too much. Mrs. Paisley was to be remembered, but the present should not be forgotten over who could not be in attendance.

During the afternoon meeting, Mr. Paisley smiled wider and more often and the grand mood affected on all around him. Even Vice President Grummond. Given the big Russian's depression earlier in the day, he made it a priority to monitor Mr. Grummond for the remaining business hours. Little by little, Sergei relaxed. By the end of the meeting, the Paisley Foundation's vice president once more pestered him while he emptied the trash and tidied Ms. White's office.

"Have you married, Mr. Smith?" The question rolled out on the man's thick Russian accent, ending with a mischievous grin.

He sighed. "I don't know how you could possibly ask that of someone who looks as I do."

Mr. Grummond's chuckles thundered in the room. "Oh-ho! What matters lay inside, Mr. Smith. Still, you do not say your age, nor if you always look this way, but I have feeling you are older than me. Is possible you at one time look older. Is possible some woman found you irresistible."

Another long sigh, wherein he turned back to his work and away from the pestering vice president.

Mr. Smith Who Works The Front Desk by Jade Griffin

Mr. Grummond's smiling bulk blocked his access to the trash bin. "We see much here, Mr. Smith. Better to not take ourselves too seriously, eh?"

The Paisley Foundation's vice president left on those words, whistling cheerily to himself. That parting thought was another reminder. Like Mr. Paisley said, a holiday wouldn't be a bad idea – if he could convince himself to relax.

Nearly two years now and not once had Heebs and Jeebs stirred enough to try a transfer. He was thankful every day for Mrs. Paisley's knowledge of the arcane and skill in creating the tattoo on his back which kept him here and now. Would it, in time, fade? Or... Could he truly believe in a safe and secure life for himself?

Arriving back at the Paisley Estate held smiles and pleasant comments from Mr. Paisley. He hadn't ever seen the man so joyful. Not even when Mrs. Paisley was alive.

Mr. Paisley asked Danneby to tell Clara to have a meal ready in a few hours before heading upstairs to lay down for a late afternoon nap.

Left to his own devices, he stood in the quiet hall and listened. The muted clank of dishes and pots, the soft whisking of Danneby's dusting upstairs, Sarah humming a little tune outside while she rang out the wash. And then there was him. Hadn't any school since the last skittish teacher over a year ago, had no inclination to do sword practice, and there was no need for him to help around the estate. He could do whatever he wanted... And could think of nothing to occupy himself.

Trying to stir up an idea to idle away the time, he wandered down the hall and spent the remainder of the evening reading, but of course careful not to read the forbidden tome.

Mr. Smith Who Works The Front Desk by Jade Griffin

1893, August 27

"You're not ready? Hurry!" Mr. Young ushered him on a rapid path to the elevator.

He'd left his suit and bowtie at the Paisley Foundation, as was the initial plan, only to have a delay in arriving this morning due to a horse throwing its shoe.

Mr. Grummond, trailing behind Mr. Young, strode over to assist once more with the cloth conundrum.

"Thank you," he told Sergei.

The big Russian pulled the bowtie taut and gave him a hearty pat on the back. "Is pleasure. Must look our best for special day, yes?"

He followed Vice President Grummond – already dressed in a nice suit -- and kept his distance till the elevator opened once more.

"Getting comfortable with me?" Sergei grinned widely down at him.

Must be a comment on how quickly he hurried into the elevator. "Not a bit," he replied with a smirk.

The ceremony itself was short but not abrupt. Full of loving gazes, nervous hope, and a beaming Mr. Paisley. The whole thing went off without a hitch, aside from the two young people getting hitched. He found himself smiling at the warm feelings, sucked into the pleasant aura of harmony and, dare he think it, sweetness.

His mind idled back to when the announcement went around three weeks prior while he cleaned outside Mr. Young's area.

Mr. Smith Who Works The Front Desk by Jade Griffin

Ms. White and the typist, Mr. Cunningham, entered the Paisley Foundation president's office and shut the door. Unusual, for the typists did not venture near the Corner offices, and they rarely left their desk for more than a few minutes before the end of the day. It happened to be one single minute after closing, per the clock stationed on the wall in front of the bank of four typists. Also odd, that this particular typist carried a particular cheery mood any time Ms. White came around, so it was no surprise hearing Mr. Cunningham's opening statement.

"Mr. Young, we'd like you to be the second to know that I have formally proposed to Ms. White and she has accepted. You are hereby invited to our wedding in three weeks' time."

"Can't say that I'm surprised, Mr. Cunningham," he heard President Young reply, an audible smile riding on the words. "I'm happy for you both. I presume the first person told was Mr. Paisley?"

"Yes," Ms. White answered. "And he has happily accepted to walk me down the aisle. Invitations will be delivered tomorrow."

"Congratulations to you both and I shall leave it to you to continue to dispense the happy news."

Discreetly, he followed the couple to each of their subsequent stops, spreading word throughout the building. Vice President Grummond loudly clapped Mark Cunningham on the back. The other typists must've known or guessed, for they'd lingered to hug or shake hands with Treasurer White and their fellow typist right before they headed home for the evening. The only one who showed an ounce of surprise was Secretary Midsommer. Perhaps too busy of late to notice Mark Cunningham unable to take adoring eyes off Tricia White whenever she entered the vicinity. None could miss the lightening of her mood or the brightness of her smile in everyday things. Before, she seemed timid or overly cautious. The change to a more carefree aura followed her presently wherever she went.

The next morning, she called him into her office. He felt a spark of unbidden hope rise. All through his covert loitering the prior day, she never once announced her event to him.

"Mr. Smith, please file these in the Repository." She held out a folder.

Of course. Work as usual. He nodded dutifully, collected it, and made his way down to the third floor.

He'd just placed the final sheet of paper in the appropriate file when footsteps entered the hall.

Ms. White entered.

"Was there something more?" Though she had no papers with her in hands clasped tight to her front, she clearly had the look of coming to see him.

"Yes… Mr. Smith, you've no doubt heard that I am to be wed in the coming weeks?"

A nod.

"I… I didn't want you to feel pressured to attend, you see, given your circumstances. Mr. Cunningham and I would have asked you straightaway otherwise. We both respect you and want you to know that first and foremost."

He held up a hand to stay her. "There's no need, Ms. White. My presence is not sought for a reason, nor was an invitation expected."

She blinked at him, caught off guard by his response. "I… Mr. Smith, I came to invite you in private, so that you may decline in private, if that is your wish. We very much would love to have you in attendance, but as part of our wedding party. I've come to ask if you'd care to be our ringbearer."

His turn to stare and blink in a stunned silence.

"I'll... let you consider it. Please let me know by the end of the week, if you could." And she left.

He managed to pull himself together and present his answer before the day was done. Of course, he told her. It would be his honor, as long as his spatial requirements were met. She assured him the arrangements were already set.

"Food is good, yes?"

Pulled roughly back to the present, he tossed a look at Sergei Grummond.

The big man settled with a grunt in the seat next to him, depositing a little plate piled with every sampling of comestible available.

He looked at his own scant plate, barely touched, then back up at Mr. Grummond. Not inclined to have a conversation but started the automatic counting in his head.

"Lost in thought, deep contemplation," Sergei remarked of his visible mood. "They are not lost to us. We will see them in few days, Mr. Smith."

"I'm not concerned about that."

"Oh?" The big Russian's mouth received a whole quarter sandwich crammed into a grin.

He quirked a brow at the vice president. "There is nothing to imply, Mr. Grummond. They are obviously devoted to each other and I wish them many happy years."

Swallowing first, Vice President Grummond said, "As do I, Mr. Smith. I merely comment on facts. Happiness of married life will not steal her away from desk of Paisley Treasurer, nor he from typist pool. Strong sense of duty from both, despite Ms. White-- Eh... Mrs. Cunningham... bore witness to more horrors than even I, and she is half my age. Probably more than even you, yes?"

"Perhaps."

"Ah, many troubles hindered you from living life to fullest, eh? No matter age, Mr. Smith, I would wish same happy life for you. For now, we eat, drink, go be merry among married young people, yes?"

"Yes. Go." An indication to Mr. Grummond that time was ticking and he needed to move along.

The Paisley Foundation vice president nodded once and walked over to the happy couple, where Sergei asked newly-Mrs. Cunningham for a dance.

He watched the Corners, agents, and typists take turns on the dance floor while he sat alone. Yet he did not feel alone. Just the opposite. In the solitude at his table, he sat back and smiled, able to enjoy their joy without the pressure of being too close to do harm. Felt this before at the Paisley Estate, before Mrs. Paisley died. Perhaps a caution to not get too complacent, but he could keep that in mind and enjoy himself, could he not?

Mr. Smith Who Works The Front Desk by Jade Griffin

1893, August 28

Things proceeded business-as-usual Monday, but it was hard not to feel the absence of two people who were as much permanent fixtures as each typewriter bolted to desk and desk to floor. Curious how they may handle such a gap in typing flow, he got his answer as the elevator opened. Mr. Grummond's bulk sat hunched in Mark Cunningham's usual spot as second typist, pecking slowly away at the keys with thick fingers.

Making his way slowly around the typists and grinning at the humorous novelty of the scene, he opened his mouth to comment, only to be cut off by the Paisley vice president who did not look up from the typing.

"Ah-ah, Mr. Smith. Must concentrate. See Mr. Midsommer."

Hm. A pity. He made a mental note to come up with a good way to tease Sergei about it later and wandered across to the secretary's office.

The sandy-haired man with a goatee and mustache did not look up from the large, pink, spiky seashell being examined at the secretary's desk. "Mr. Smith. Good. I'm nearly finished."

He stood about, waiting, counting due to the inadequate space in Secretary Midsommer's office. Every office, actually. None afforded the necessary space to keep the device from activating. But he only made it to three minutes two seconds before the man looked up.

"Yes. Apologies. Would you take this down to Acquisitions? It should be placed next to the other large

Mr. Smith Who Works The Front Desk by Jade Griffin

seashell on the shelves to the left when you enter. Can't miss the spot. Wear these gloves as best you can when handling it." Removing and placing said gloves atop the desk beside the seashell, the secretary stood, started out, reconsidered something, and turned toward him to relay, "Eh... Do be careful with it. And don't handle it without the gloves. And under no circumstances should you blow into the shell. Can I count on you?"

"Of course."

"Excellent. I'm late for a meeting. Thank you. Do be careful."

"I will take care of it. Go."

Secretary Midsommer hurried out, paused, looked back at him, and then trotted to the elevator.

Given the cautions and warnings, it must be an artifact of particular import. Usually, all incoming items were handled by the Paisley treasurer. Looked as if Mr. Midsommer had taken that up during newly-Mrs. Cunningham's absence.

Taking the warnings very seriously, he slid his small hands into the large leather gloves and looked over the seashell before attempting to touch it. Spikey thing, appeared to be a normal seashell, but the size of his head. Upon closer inspection, it sported not only a reed to blow in at the modified thin end opposite the large opening, but very clear symbols spiraling all about the interior in a language he did not know. Better to simply do as instructed, so he gingerly positioned his gloved hands in between the bottom spikey bits and lifted the item from the desk. After a pause, in which nothing happened, he carried it out.

Of note on his trek to the elevator was Mr. Grummond flicking a glance his way while the big Russian maintained a slow typing pace, and that Mr. Paisley exited the vice president's office to rapidly meet him at the elevator.

"Let me get that. Don't let go with either hand," Mr. Paisley warned, pushing the button to summon the elevator.

When the mechanical ingress opened, he stepped in. So did Mr. Paisley. When it closed, he asked, "Is this thing dangerous?"

"Not quite. Mr. Midsommer didn't mention? Hm. I see. He is a bit distracted today."

"I've no doubt, as he seems to be doing his job as well as Mrs. Cunningham's."

"Er, yes. That must be the reason."

"You are helping out in Mr. Grummond's position?"

The elevator opened. He exited.

"Yes." Mr. Paisley followed and grabbed the Acquisitions door for him.

"Can I know what this thing does?" he asked, placing it beside its equally large twin on the third shelf with other strange and mundane artifacts.

"It is a conch trumpet we believe might be capable of summoning a very humungous ocean creature but, moreso, this and the other are more considered party horns. Not only are they used to herald the beginning and conclusion of war or festivities, but the sharp bits are inhabited by tiny organisms that will poke out and inject their venom. We're fairly certain we've cooked them to death in a kiln, but you can't be too careful."

"And this just sits out so that anyone not in the know could come and be killed by these things?" He did not hide his disapproving tone.

Mr. Paisley chuckled. "Oh, they won't kill you. What they inject makes you instantly inebriated for several days. Quite fun at social gatherings, with the right crowd. But I'll save such stories of my youth for another day. Time to get back to work."

He agreed and took the stairs down while the founder took the elevator up.

Immediately upon exiting the hidden stairwell, the pound of footsteps and frantic crying rushed him. Tricia Cunningham, panic-stricken, barefoot, her once-fetching pink and green dress stained and mussed, nearly collided with him. She collapsed to her knees, exhausted and sobbing.

"He's gone! They took him! They took him!"

He leaped past her and made for the front desk, snatched up the candlestick phone, and dialed the two-digit number to reach Mr. Young's office. "Tricia's here, distraught! She thinks someone kidnapped Mark!"

There was no reply, nor a click of the receiver on the other end, but he heard commotion and replaced the phone.

He wandered back to Mrs. Cunningham, not certain if he should get close enough to try and comfort her. Decided to stay back. "They're coming. Are you hurt?"

"No," she squeaked, placing her head in her hands and sobbing.

Mr. Paisley and Mr. Young flowed out of the elevator in short order. The benefactor fell beside Mrs. Cunningham and calmed her, asking, "What's happened, Tricia?"

"I-I think they took him, Mr. Paisley!" she managed through stuttering breaths. "Mark asked me to wait and went to a stall, wanting to surprise me with something. But then I saw Portia. She smiled. She wanted me to know she was there! And I waited, not wanting to lead her to him but I couldn't just disappear without warning him. Mark never came back to look for me! How did they find where we would be?! They'll kill him, or worse!"

Mr. Paisley held Tricia like a father cradling a hurting child. "There, there."

Mr. Young dashed to the phone at the front desk and made a call. "Send every agent up there to the World's Columbian Exposition. Find Mark Cunningham, who may have been abducted by Portia de Lorraine."

Oh shit... That meant the treasurer's horrible family had found her. "Is there no possibility he simply got lost?" he tried, because there was a chance it could be that... Right?

No one seemed to hear him. Not certain what he could do but stand about, feel useless, and try very hard not to yell at them to get out there and look for Mark Cunningham.

Vice President Grummond burst from the hidden stairwell, just short of trampling the people right by that entryway.

"What is this? What happen?" the burly Russian demanded.

"Mark Cunningham is missing," Mr. Young told him, wandering back to their group. "Tricia saw Portia shortly before."

Several thundering footsteps echoed down from the stairwell. Mr. Paisley coaxed Tricia to a stand and moved her before five Paisley agents streamed past and out the front doors.

"Mr. Grummond, wait here in case Mr. Midsommer returns. Mr. Young, retrieve our secretary if he is still at his prior appointment. I will take Tricia home in the hope that Mark will arrive there safely," Mr. Paisley's even tone kept complete order while holding Tricia, the poor woman racked with sobs and lamenting that her family would kill Mark.

"What can I do?" he offered as the two Corners did as the founder bid.

Mr. Paisley began walking Tricia to the front entrance. Without looking back, his benefactor told him, "Stay by the telephone. Help field any information to the appropriate Corner or agent. If anything new is discovered, telephone me at Tricia's apartment. The number is in the book in the front desk drawer."

He immediately trotted to the front desk and sat. There was no book atop its clean surface. Pulling out a drawer revealed the thin address book and flipping through its alphabetical pages had his thumb on the treasurer's number in the blink of an eye.

A deadly quiet settled in the lobby. Not even Mr. Grummond said a thing. He didn't even hear the big man breathing. A glance at the Russian told him everything he needed to know – Like the most robust of springs coiled and ready to act at the first trigger, the Paisley Foundation vice president stared straight ahead at the glass front doors. He'd never seen Mr. Grummond so… so wound up and angry. Never seen the vice president angry, ever.

It wasn't more than a handful of minutes before Mr. Midsommer's tall, sandy-haired form strolled casually along the sidewalk to the entrance.

Mr. Grummond surged forward and held them open for the bewildered secretary. More confusion lay on Midsommer's face when the Paisley vice president locked the front doors after letting the fellow Corner in.

"Panicked Tricia returned and said Mark is missing with Portia seen close by. Take Mark's seat and find him." Very little of Mr. Grummond's accent lay in the Russian man's voice during that explanation while they walked toward the elevator and stairs.

Mr. Midsommer's expression dropped from a quizzical look to shock to down to business. The lanky secretary launched at the stairs, tall form flying up them like a gangly crane.

Mr. Grummond let the hidden hatch close. The big Russian turned to him, accent returning with, "Mr. Smith, come."

"But I—"

"Mr. Midsommer will find Mark Cunningham. Then you run down and make call. Come."

Mr. Grummond pushed the elevator button and held the mechanism open while he ran over and entered the lift with the Russian vice president.

"How will he find Mr. Cunningham?"

"Psychometry is Mr. Midsommer's specialty, but can do clairvoyance as well. You will see." Mr. Grummond pressed the fifth-floor button.

Once more on Floor 5, the typists were still at their task of clacking away, but the room filled with apprehension. The three usual typing women could not keep their eyes on their work and sought any kind of explanation from the others – even him. He wanted to tell them what had happened and realized doing so could endanger the entire Paisley Foundation if the typists left their position, so he kept his mouth shut. To say one of their group may have been taken might cause a panic.

Mr. Smith Who Works The Front Desk by Jade Griffin

Avoiding their gaze and placing his attention on Mr. Midsommer, he observed the Paisley secretary sitting in the second typist's chair – Mark Cunningham's seat – with eyes closed, lips muttering silent words while searching hands felt over the typewriter keys, desk, and chair.

He'd reviewed the file of every Paisley employee and knew Mr. Midsommer was proficient in psychometry but hadn't found a definition, nor seen the man use any spells until now. Trying to reason through what incantation was being used, he spied Mr. Grummond exiting the secretary's office with a pencil and notepad, which were thrust at him.

"Take note of what he says. Psychometric clairvoyance allows feeling state of target person and often anything experienced."

Before he could ask questions, the big Russian took to the hidden stairs.

Keeping his distance would not be a problem from the four people around him. It was another jarring matter to be looked at with the frightened eyes of the three women who continued as best they could at their own typing task.

"Remain calm," he spoke to them with more ease than he felt. "The current upset is being handled by all four Corners and myself. It is best to remain here and continue your work, as this is the safest place you could be right now."

Not entirely sure, but he hoped it was true. This de Lorraine family had never entered the Paisley Foundation, nor messed with anyone in or around it, so far as he'd heard.

Without warning, Secretary Midsommer jerked in the chair, shuddered, and stammered, "Th-they have him bound, hands and feet."

He scribbled down those details as legibly as possible, ready for more.

"Bruised ribs, a blow to the head, conscious and otherwise unharmed."

To their credit, the typists did not gasp or give a start at Mr. Midsommer's jittery words, though they flicked anxious glances between he and the Paisley secretary as their busy hands few on.

"Thirsty..." Mr. Midsommer coughed. "but nothing over the mouth. I—"

The Paisley secretary cringed and ducked, dodging some unknown assailant. The psychometric clairvoyance at work must hold the caster fairly tight, for Mr. Midsommer fell right out of the chair. Writhing briefly, the lanky man's body went lax.

Should he approach? Was the man unconscious?

Mr. Midsommer looked about, frantically scanning the room through disheveled, sandy-brown hair. The man stood on shaky legs, leaned against Mark Cunningham's desk for support, and locked eyes with him. "He's being moved. Grabbed and blindfolded him, but I saw where. The decorative metal cage of the elevator, the smell of the building. They have him at The Rookery."

He was waved toward the elevator, and agreed that Mr. Midsommer did not look or sound in any condition to deliver the information himself, so he raced to the lift and shot forth once it let him out on the first floor.

Mr. Grummond awaited him there, swarming up to him, hands full with a canvas bag. "Where?" the big Russian demanded.

"The Rookery, but he's being moved." He made for the telephone at the front desk, pausing when the Paisley vice president marched to the glass entrance. "These people are supposed to be quite dangerous. You're not waiting for the others?"

"No time. I will get him." And Mr. Sergei Grummond was out the doors and hopping into a taxi carriage without another moment in between.

Refocusing his efforts, he pulled out the book once more and dialed the number Mr. Paisley directed him to.

"Has Mark returned?" Mr. Paisley's anxious voice asked.

"No. Mr. Midsommer did and located Mark Cunningham at The Rookery, but said they were moving him. Mr. Grummond is on his way there now."

"He went alone?" Even to Mr. Paisley, this came as a surprise. Not an encouraging one.

"He did. Sir, I see Mr. Young outside. I'll let him know."

"Tell him we are on a direct route of return ourselves."

He hurried toward the entrance just as Mr. Young came in.

"Didn't Mr. Grummond lock these?" the Paisley president asked.

"He did, but left just now in a rush with a canvas bag. Mr. Midsommer is back and located Mr. Cunningham at The Rookery, currently being moved from there."

Mr. Young fished in a pocket and tossed him a set of keys, which he caught easily. "Lock the doors behind me, Mr. Smith." Out the Paisley president ran, back onto the street.

Inserting the key and turning the mechanism sent a resounding *click* about the enveloping silence. He wandered to the front desk and sat with hands folded to hide his growing concern.

Over the next hour, he saw no less than ten distinct agents coming and going, as well as the return of Mr. Paisley, Mrs. Cunningham, and Mr. Young, all of whom went up to the fifth floor. Because he received no instruction other than to stay by the telephone, that is what he did.

Through his time being cast about by Heebs and Jeebs, patience was something long since mastered. Even so, he found it difficult doing so little when potentially terrible things were happening. Yet what good could he do?

After another hour, Mr. Paisley and Mr. Young emerged from the elevator. No hurry pushed their pace. It dragged, as did their fallen mood.

While Mr. Young wandered toward the front doors, Mr. Paisley came near the desk and asked, "Anything?"

"No, sir. I was thinking though… Can Mr. Midsommer use psychometry or clairvoyance again after resting sufficiently?"

The benefactor's head shook, defeated. "They're blocking any further attempts. He's tried, and also to locate Mr. Grummond, and received some sort of backlash which has rendered him unconscious. He appears fine otherwise but, after he wakes, I would prefer not to press the matter. Tricia is to call down once he regains consciousness."

"Mr. Paisley, will the wards keep them out?" he asked, masking as much concern as he could.

"It is possible they found a way through. It has been five years since last we clashed. They may have improved their methods and the use of their magic. However, so have we. Tricia is not merely sitting idle wringing worried hands. This attack has dealt her a blow but she retains her wits and her resolve to get her husband back safely."

Mr. Smith Who Works The Front Desk by Jade Griffin

The loud vibrative ring of the telephone jerked their heads toward the communication device.

Mr. Paisley nodded to him.

He picked up the receiver before it rang again.

Tricia's grainy voice told him, "Mr. Midsommer is awake and resting. If you need me, I shall be in Acquisitions and then my office."

He related the treasurer's tightly-controlled words to Mr. Paisley, who again offered a nod.

"She is gathering reagents for a spell. I will join her. Please remain by the telephone and let us know of any news."

More waiting ensued. The five-o-clock hour passed. Five thirty.

The elevator opened. Accompanied by two escorting agents, the three remaining typists exited, nodding to him as they made timidly for the front doors among surreptitious glances outside. He knew they'd stayed later than normal, the assigned agents to assure their safe travel home.

Both Victors and Dolores exited the elevator next. She set a plate down at the desk and lingered. "… I shall be going for the evening, Mr. Smith, and told not to return tomorrow… Unless you require anything else?"

He looked up at the old woman, noted deep lines mapping her face into a more aged and weary topography than last recalled. On the plate, a glass of water stood beside a sandwich. "Thank you, Dolores. This is splendid. Have a safe trip home."

"I… I live just around the block, Mr. Smith. Do have someone stop by if they've need of me, and when it's deemed safe to return."

"Thank you. I will."

She wandered out, clearly wishing to do more. He was fighting the same feeling and followed to lock up behind her.

Meandering back to the desk, he flipped the light switch off for the first floor. Better to see everything outside. He ate the sandwich in the dark and drank the water in the silence of the immense lobby, watching any passers-by, waiting for any phone call or any word from upstairs.

When no one entered or exited for several more hours, he wondered if the Corners planned to stay all night. This surely fit the need, emergency situation and all. Only the most necessary of staff stayed.

The elevator door opened. Mr. Paisley emerged, pace dragging hard with the late hour. The founder sat at the nearest couch, well outside of the required distance, and let loose a great sigh. "Nothing from Sergei, nor the agents out searching. Harold is sleeping. Vince is preparing to go out again. The de Lorraines have not tried to contact us in any way. Tricia has tried everything she knows, without success."

"And how are you holding up?" he enquired, noting the exhaustion settling on the old man. Seen it many times on other people. Not on Mr. Paisley.

The founder looked at him and managed a smile. "Just as you have been seen to, Dolores made certain to leave us nourished."

"That isn't what I asked. Everything I've ever heard of these people speaks of how dangerous they are, and powerful. Is there any hope in getting Mr. Cunningham and Mr. Grummond back?"

Mr. Paisley frowned at him. "You're asking if I feel defeated. No, Mr. Smith. There is always hope."

Mr. Smith Who Works The Front Desk by Jade Griffin

"And there is nothing in the arsenal of the Paisley Foundation that can shake these de Lorraines or get them to stop bothering Tricia and us?"

"We are working toward that, but this was not a spontaneous attack. The de Lorraine Family is often as calculating and patient as they are powerful. And so must we be. I presume you have determined that we shall be staying indefinitely?"

"Yes. Is there anything more I can do?"

"Go have a mug of coffee from the fourth floor. Perhaps a blanket from one of the guest rooms to fight any chill. I shall be sleeping here." The founder stretched out on the couch, laying back with a quiet sigh.

He took the elevator up to the second floor, grabbed a lantern there, and proceeded to Floor 4. There he found a slightly larger spread than normal in one of the conference rooms and plentiful coffee. He quickly grabbed what may be needed, including several cookies. Also snagged two throw blankets but had to wear them like a cloak to carry everything. Instead of returning downstairs, he took the elevator up.

It was eerie, the elevator opening onto a quiet fifth floor, the usual barrage of typist clacking ominously still. Two lights remained on – Treasurer Cunningham's office and President Young's office. He saw them both hunched over their respective desks as he wandered in. Mr. Young straightened, started out, and did not turn off the light but stuttered to a halt upon seeing him.

"Anything I can assist with, Mr. Young?"

"… No; aside from watching over Mr. Paisley. He is downstairs?"

"Yes." He eyed the treasurer's office with its open entrance.

"Let her be, Mr. Smith. We have our own tasks." Mr. Young continued to the elevator and pressed the button to call it.

He joined the Paisley president, who eyed him once the lift began its descent.

"You looked as though you're ready for an indoor camping trip. Brought back some memories of my youth, and a reminder that I must renew my focus, as we all want Tricia and Mark to make their own such memories."

As soon as the elevator opened, President Young strode out.

The soft snores of Mr. Paisley were not interrupted by the placement of mug and cookies, nor when he hurried after Mr. Young to work the front door lock, nor even when gently settling the second blanket over the old man.

Sipping the lukewarm coffee passed the time, as did nibbling at the cookies. Time trudged slowly none-the-less. The night's chill permeated even the Paisley Foundation's thick walls. He snuggled the blanket about his shoulders, finally resting his head atop the desk and listening to the lull of Mr. Paisley's gentle snores.

Mr. Smith Who Works The Front Desk by Jade Griffin

1893, August 29

A hand upon his shoulder had him jerking up in an instant. Whipping about, Mrs. Cunningham's sleep-deprived face filled his view. Mr. Midsommer knelt near Mr. Paisley, waking the founder as well.

"Something has changed," Mr. Midsommer told them while Mrs. Cunningham moved a safe distance away.

Rubbing his eyes, he took a look around the many windows of the first floor. Darkness lingered. A glance at the wall clock behind him indicated 4:11 AM.

"They are no longer blocking me from locating Mr. Cunningham," the secretary continued. "I can't get anything definitive but have narrowed it down. He is being held at some sort of food establishment. Smells like... Italian spices, olive oil, excessive fresh garlic, tomato sauce, fried meats, and some kind of old machine grease smell."

Mr. Paisley sat up slowly. Not due to age but in correlating this new information.

He wasn't the only one who saw hesitant recognition on the old man's face. Mr. Midsommer beat him to the query.

"You know where he is?"

"...I do." Mr. Paisley set aside the blanket, rose, and straightened an unrumpled suit. "That restaurant was chosen specifically, and you were meant to describe it to me, which means they mean for me to pay them a visit."

"But you can't!" Treasurer Cunningham protested.

"I most assuredly can, and I shall. It is you who cannot go, my dear. You are the one they want back, and I shall not have it nor tolerate their bullying. But I am not reckless. I'll be using their patience against them and await the return of Mr. Young and Mr. Grummond. Mr. Midsommer, if you will join me upstairs?"

Tricia Cunningham started to follow them. "But, Mr. Paisley—"

"It is imperative that you do **not** leave the building." The founder stood before the elevator, blocking her. "Therefore, you will not be told where I am going."

The elevator closed. Her shoulders sagged. "Why can't he see I cannot sit idle while others suffer because of me?"

She asked it of no one, but he felt she deserved a response. "He sees, but you're worth more to him."

"It isn't right," she argued.

"No, nor is it fair, but you also can't give your family what they want. Won't they just keep doing as they please?"

Her jaw tightened, anger held within. "I would very much like a part in ending them."

Her vehemence came as a surprise. No one ever spoke of the de Lorraines favorably, but Tricia Cunningham's vocal venom indicated she would prefer permanent eradication. He couldn't think of anyone he hated as much as he saw on the treasurer's face. Well, maybe Heebs and Jeebs. They definitely deserved their current prison. Given how her family likely treated her, and their current cruel actions, he guessed her feelings were warranted. Trauma had a tremendous effect on people. But then her expression changed to hope, eyes latching onto something distant.

He looked for what pulled her attention.

At the glass front doors of the Paisley Foundation, in the dark predawn drizzle, stood the unmistakable bulk of Vice President Grummond.

Mr. Smith Who Works The Front Desk by Jade Griffin

He couldn't help a grin of relief and snatched up the key atop the desk amid a flash of lightning.

Thunder crashed and Treasurer Cunningham was at his side in a blink, her nails digging into his shoulder and pressing him back to his seat.

"Mr. Smith..." she whispered, her breath full of dread. When had her face fallen from hopeful to fearful? Her eyes always on the entryway, he strained to see, to understand what compelled her.

Tricia's sudden inhale shuddered. She pushed him downward, pulling the telephone closer to her in the same move. She managed to get out, "Mr. Grummond is not alone. Stay hidden."

Dropping below the desktop, he peeked out under the four-inch gap between desk and floor, trying to see past the rain. Another flash of lightning, and a glimpse of a small figure in the dark just behind Mr. Grummond.

"Come right away." Her tremulous voice betrayed every ounce of effort to hold back tears.

She replaced the receiver with a click and moved away from him, but only just far enough. He saw her feet remained facing the entrance so very far away, and yet not far enough from whatever lingered without.

A bang made he and the treasurer jump. Another bang, and another. The ruckus came from the front doors where Sergei repeatedly walked into the glass as if drunk. For what reason? Bound hands? Lost key?

Mr. Midsommer burst from the hidden stairwell. Well-polished shoes skidded to a halt as the secretary faced whatever held Tricia very still. "Is the person behind Sergei...?"

Mr. Smith Who Works The Front Desk by Jade Griffin

"Portia."

All motion in the lobby ceased. Rain pounded soundless outside. No one breathed. He followed their lead. If Tricia didn't want this Portia person to see him, he would listen. Even so, he tried to get more of a look at the goings-on from the miniscule four inches of space between floor and desk. It was simply too dark, dawn too far away. He did spy the long barrel of a shotgun pointed lax toward the floor, held in Mr. Midsommer's hands.

Sergei walked bodily into the glass, banging it once more. The elevator opened.

Must be Mr. Paisley, who flicked on the lights during another bang upon the doors.

He could not view the founder's face but, by the position of feet, saw the old man turn toward the other two, then proceed toward the entrance of the Paisley Foundation.

Tricia did not follow, though he heard her muttering a spell.

Mr. Midsommer's shotgun rose out of sight. The Paisley Foundation secretary followed after Mr. Paisley.

Both secretary and founder moved into his view as they neared the front doors, Mr. Paisley ready with the key and Mr. Midsommer aiming the gun.

The key slid in, was turned. Mr. Paisley grasped the handle and pulled it toward him slowly, using the glass as a partial shield.

Sergei took one step. The first-floor lights illuminated a face not only devoid of emotion but also color. Hard to make out but it looked as though the big Russian's eyes were clouded over and a great ragged scar encircled what was visible of the neck. One more step and the Paisley

Mr. Smith Who Works The Front Desk by Jade Griffin

Foundation vice president passed the wards about the threshold. The sigils crackled, fighting the negative energy of a foreign spell. Sergei jerked as if electrocuted and all animation left the lifeless body. It collapsed to the ground with a great thump. The poorly-attached head came loose and rolled halfway across the distance toward him. Mouth agape, dead eyes stared at nothing, stared at everything, stared at him. It was the vicious truth of the situation which bore into him: Sergei Grummond, dead.

No one moved except Mr. Midsommer, who trained the shotgun on the raven-haired person stepping in past the wards as if they weren't there, over the body of Sergei Grummond, and stood deceptively aloof while staring expectantly and slightly up at Mr. Paisley.

Drips of rain fell from the young woman. The patter in the lobby sounded like bombs in the stunned silence, matching the frown on Portia's face. "So you're the pain in the ass I've heard about. Not much to look at, but as you can see, looks can be deceiving."

"Leave," Mr. Paisley commanded with great severity.

"I will, and before little Tricia can finish her spell, but I was sent to deliver a message. Evan de Lorraine wants you and your group to stay out of family squabbles from now on, old man. You are to deliver Tricia personally to him at Lonzo's. He wanted to make sure you remember the place."

Concealed rage spilled into Mr. Paisley's reply. "I do."

"Good. You have until tomorrow at 4 PM to make your final arrangements; a courtesy he grants because of your time together. If you do not, we will take my white sheep of a cousin presently and bring down your entire building."

Mr. Smith Who Works The Front Desk by Jade Griffin

She threw a snide grin at Tricia, then swiveled about and shot into the rain as if she flew. Perhaps she did. He had no idea, nor if it were safe to come out. Not until Tricia's sobs echoed in the silence and Mr. Paisley quickly locked the door.

By the time he scrambled up from the floor, founder and secretary were hefting their vice president's decapitated body.

He approached, averted his eyes as he walked past Sergei's head, and joined the men. They said nothing, nor could he help them as they moved the body to the elevator.

He stayed on the first floor to be near weeping Tricia, covered Sergei's head with a blanket, struggled with indecision on whether to move it and how to start cleaning up the sudden fetid blood and fluids which leaked onto the floor amid pools of rainwater and began smelling terribly, tried very hard not to let any grief hit him. Not now. Not when there were things very much in need of doing.

His feet decided, dashing to the water closet. He grabbed the basin of water and the pitcher as well as the wash rag, juggled them to the detritus on the tile floor, and set about mopping up the fluids. It stank so much more up close. Had reanimating the body with magic made it rot so quickly? He gagged, glad for a strong constitution to hold in what remained of coffee and cookies.

The elevator opened. Mr. Paisley strode out and made for the front doors. The founder did not seem keen on stopping, so he asked, "Where are you going?"

Mr. Paisley replied, "The de Lorraines do not make idle threats. At the very least, they are capable of doing what they say and won't hesitate to try if their instructions are not followed. But, if they have given us until tomorrow evening, they will stay to their word and I will be using every second I can."

"But, Mr. Paisley—"

"They won't act against their word unless we do not comply." The founder's words came out snappish. Mr. Paisley paused, took a breath, sighed, and replied in a kinder fashion, "It is imperative that Tricia not leave this building until I see this through. You either, Mr. Smith. Do I have your word?"

The old man's gaze burrowed into the Paisley treasurer until she looked up and offered a defeated nod. He did the same.

"I am off to get Evan a gift." Mr. Paisley hurried out the glass entrance of the Paisley Foundation, into rain and puddle and uncertainty.

The entrance locked once more, he returned to scrubbing.

Not ten minutes later came pounding feet on the street.

Looked up in time to see Mr. Young leading two Paisley agents up to the door.

Numb as to what should be said, he chose silence and let them in.

Mr. Young and the agents took one look around, saw their treasurer brushing tears from red eyes, the smeared blood on the tile, the covered round object yards away, and paused.

"Portia," Mrs. Cunningham told them, her voice hoarse with caged grief.

He cleared his throat and added, "Mr. Midsommer is upstairs, Mr. Paisley is out, …Mr. Grummond is dead." His eyes wandered to the vice president's head.

No one spoke after that devastating news.

As he locked the entryway once more, the Paisley agents collected Sergei Grummond's head, keeping it wrapped up. Mr. Young collected Tricia and they went up in the elevator.

He scrounged a bar of soap and bleach from the first-floor water closet and returned to his task.

By sheer force of will, the job was done and his work left the impression that nothing whatsoever had occurred. No streaks stained tile or railings, no smear on the hidden door panel, nor the smell, except what lingered on him and a poor regard for his attire. Even washing up in the water closet, he smelled like rotting blood and fat, his hands and clothes saturated.

He again used the stairs to poke around Acquisitions until a long shirt and the smallest pants available were found, both of which he could wade in if they were a pool. Snatched up a belt off the rack in the clothes section of Acquisitions and made his way up to the fourth floor. Thought he'd seen a shower in one of the rooms. Sure enough, the water closet near the last guest room also had a hanging tank full of cold water built into a recess – an old-style shower. He undressed, threw the stained clothes under the head of the shower, and stood on top of them. Just stood and cried. Cried a lot.

It wasn't the same kind of grief he felt upon waking to dead Mrs. Paisley. This hit different. It felt like… unfairness, regret, and of course loss but no guilt. The strongest thing felt was anger. And when the tears were spent, he pulled the cord and sucked in great gasps at the chilly deluge hitting his bare body. Scrubbing fast and hard, the water soon ran clear. He dried, dressed as best he could by rolling sleeves and looping the belt twice so he could cinch it about his tiny waist. The wet clothes he hung to dry on the metal bedframe.

Mr. Smith Who Works The Front Desk by Jade Griffin

Needing more to occupy himself, he gathered his cleaning supplies and returned to the first floor. Mr. Young came from the stairs and found him polishing the final smudges off the glass on the outside of the entryway, just after sunset.

He turned at the man's approach.

"Please join us upstairs, Mr. Smith."

Locking up, he took the supplies and followed Mr. Young into the elevator.

They reconvened in Conference Room 1, as it looked like a meeting had started prior to his entrance. Perhaps more of a grieving session. Mrs. Cunningham sat quiet, her head bowed, but her eyes remained red and puffy from recent tears. Mr. Midsommer's eyes held additional moisture as well.

"No word on when Mr. Paisley will return?" he asked while moving a chair against the back wall to sit as far from them as possible.

Mr. Young answered, "Not yet, and the ward Mr. Paisley carries prevents anyone from tracking him."

"I see. And where has Mr. Grummond been taken?"

"There is a mortician we use. Saved his life once, so he doesn't ask questions when we bring him people to hold for us ... Mr. Smith, you say you are an average person in non-average circumstances, but we've been dealt a tremendous blow. How are you?"

The reminder was a surprise, but necessary. Not everyone found it easy to compartmentalize – a skill he became quite good at due to Heebs and Jeebs. He forgot that these were also normal people in non-normal circumstances and some grace was due. With compassion, he replied, "Thank you for your concern, Mr. Young, but my sorrow will keep for the time being."

The Paisley president gave a nod. "Despite the weight of our grief, we similarly must place things aside. As such, it has been mentioned that, whatever the nature of your circumstances, the de Lorraines would find you a most valuable prize if they learned of you. Perhaps it is best for you to return to Mr. Paisley's estate for the foreseeable future—"

"I will not. Mr. Paisley made me promise to remain here, just as Mrs. Cunningham also promised. Such being the course, if there is anything I can do to help here, I'd like to do so presently."

"Very well. We shall move forward. Mr. Midsommer, have you located the place the de Lorraines want Mr. Paisley to meet them at?"

"Yes. Lonzo's is an Italian restaurant seven blocks away."

"If we send anyone aside from myself and Mr. Paisley, they'll kill Mark," Treasurer Cunningham protested.

"We won't, and avoiding or postponing your arrival would be best if possible. None of our tomes contain a spell to disguise a person to look like you?"

"No. Even if we had such a thing, or gained one from Miskatonic's library, it may not fool my family."

"Portia threatened to bring the building down," he asked. "Is there a way to prevent that, if they're capable of doing it?"

Treasurer Cunningham answered, "She has no skill in magic and falls fairly low in their chain of command. Sending her to deliver the message meant she was expendable if we chose to retaliate then. She couldn't have done… that… to Sergei." Tricia paused but the grief won out and she fell silent.

"Unlike ourselves, the de Lorraines avoid any public image and won't go guns blazing at us for that very reason," President Young explained. "They may, however, send underlings to do so. I have several agents posted around the building so that no one can set any explosives, and to alert us of any potential fire fights, but the threat is real. If they can find a way to end us or harm us as quietly as publicly possible, they will, which is why we must make a stand. They've killed our vice president, are holding another of our employees, and that will not go unpunished. Is there anything more you know that we can use?"

The question posed to Treasurer Cunningham, she gave a resolute nod and answered, "My uncle is the current head of the House and is as old as Mr. Paisley, but he won't look it. The chief weaknesses of all de Lorraines are their arrogance and desire for power. They are most vulnerable when they believe they have won, just as they are most dangerous when they feel their power is threatened. They will expect us to sneak reinforcements in, or have agents waiting, and look for any excuse to kill you all. I'm sure the restaurant they picked has some sort of meaning but I don't know what. It isn't on any ley lines, unlike most of their estates, located in Chicago, Boston, Salem, and London if you're looking for somewhere to strike while their leader is away. I would not advice doing so at this time. Evan won't be alone but he's the most arrogant of the lot. He'll want to do everything himself so he can parade the fact that he reacquired me himself and therefore no other family will be in attendance. Just hired muscle. If we can—"

"Making plans without me?" Mr. Paisley's annoyed voice preceded their view of the founder right before the old man entered the conference room.

Relief flooded the room, himself included, for he'd begun to worry something had happened to his benefactor.

Mr. Midsommer spoke up first. "Sir, we had no idea where you'd gone, when you'd come back. If you'd—"

The founder waved such reasoning aside. "The only way to come at the de Lorraines is to be craftier and do something unprecedented. Am I to assume your current plans involve attacking their estates? We might get a few of them but it will initiate a true war between us."

"Sir, we can't just give in to their demands."

"And I have no intention to, Mr. Young," Mr. Paisley's raised voice silenced any further talk in the room. "What I intend is to give Evan de Lorraine a present he cannot resist; something which is powerful enough to end any further desire to come after dear Tricia ever again; something that will end very badly for the Head of House de Lorraine."

"You're... You're not taking me with you." Treasurer Cunningham's baffled statement voiced the confusion and brewing hope they all felt.

"Tricia, dear, you cannot go anywhere near your family or you will be lost to them once more. What you had to endure prior... I **shall not** have it, do you hear?" Again, the founder's volume rose to shake the glass set into the door.

"Tell us your plan," Mr. Young encouraged.

"Not this time, Vince. It is imperative that none of you are aware of this plan's intent."

"Mr. Paisley, this is not the time for secrets," he argued.

Mr. Smith Who Works The Front Desk by Jade Griffin

"It is the **best** time for secrets, Mr. Smith. There must be no discernable way for the de Lorraines to know or predict what is coming and I aim to keep it that way. To ensure that, I cannot let any others know."

A strange strength emanated from Mr. Paisley's words. Like… the founder sat incredibly sure that the plan would work, and all of it kept tightly concealed by an all-enveloping vehemence and sorrow prompting the founder's current actions.

Mr. Midsommer blinked several times, mouth falling open, and it was clear the secretary saw the same inevitable. The sandy-haired man composed the following words carefully. "Sir… They're going to kill you. You must know that's why they asked for you as well."

"They may try. However, my goal is to deny them any such attempt and dislodge their interest from Tricia Cunningham, returning her new husband to her. Mr. Young, make certain the agents maintain the perimeter. It is imperative that no one get through to harm this building or the people in it. Mr. Midsommer, contact Miskatonic University's library and call in as many favors as needed to secure a spell which will make an object irresistible to such a power-hungry man as Evan de Lorraine. Mrs. Cunningham, you are to scour my old journals to look for anything further we can use against him. I've placed them on your desk for easy access. Off with you."

Quickly, the three scuttled away, eager to be put to task, to help fight what was coming.

He did not get up. He waited, listened for the sound of the elevator, the silence in the hall, his eyes always on Mr. Paisley.

The old man had been waiting for the same thing. Closing the conference room door, a heavy sigh settled the founder back in the head chair.

"Is there still hope?" he queried, not to be mean but to actually gain an answer. "Or did you send them off to do busy work?"

"Yes, there is more than hope. No, it isn't busy work. It is possible they will find something I have missed. It is not always easy working through fresh grief, Mr. Smith. I've given them hope, as well as a chance to do something about a terrible situation."

"But is there more to it than that? To me, it appeared you planned that whole dialogue."

"More? Oh yes, Mr. Smith. But it is something they, for variable reasons, may not approve of."

"And I will?"

"I can hope. I want every single de Lorraine to pay. I want them all to die." Like a rollercoaster, his benefactor's mood shifted from vehement rage to calm. "You see, I have a plan, as I said, but it requires something very special I am afraid to part with and am feeling my own mental failings are preventing the risk of it. A show of great strength is necessary to put the de Lorraines in their place, to prove we are not to be trifled with. I understand that many may view what I would do as unfair in many regards, but the de Lorraines do **not** fight fair, and they will **not** stop until they are beaten back or until they have Tricia and leave us decimated. If we are to survive, no fair option is left to us."

"And will you tell me your plan?" he tried, believing there must be some reason they were still talking and not acting.

Mr. Paisley gave him a smile. "In part. I have purchased a very special box; a magic box. It was once made to hold very bad things and will appeal greatly to Evan, especially when I put something I value inside it."

"And you have something in mind already to put in this box?"

"As I said, I am weighing the risks."

Must be something difficult to give up, despite the circumstances. "Is there anything I can do to help, Mr. Paisley?"

A pained smile from his host. "You have already done more than anyone should in these trying days. Your resilience is bolstering, my boy, however a cup of coffee and some cookies from the other conference room would be well-received."

He slipped from the chair and trotted out to fetch them, keeping an eye on the conference room while hurrying back. Mr. Paisley's manner alluded to more hidden than what was revealed. Didn't want to return only to discover the errand let the old man slip away. On the contrary, Mr. Paisley sat sagged in the chair, chest rising and falling with calm breaths.

Placing the plate of cookies and cup of coffee without a sound onto the conference tabletop, he sat there for a time in the calm. It was nice, and a luxury it became harder to ignore as one none of them could afford. None but Mr. Paisley, who clearly needed the rest.

Tiptoeing out, he ventured up to the fifth floor and found Mr. Young and Mr. Midsommer typing away. Their faces drawn and movements sluggish, he stopped himself just short of yelling at them for willingly draining their energy when they were so essential. With the remaining typists safely at home, the usual power source for the wards must be dwindling. As the wards prohibited de Lorraine magic, they could not afford to let that power fade.

Mrs. Cunningham stepped out of her office, caught his tense scrutiny of the scene, and approached her fellow Corners. "That is enough. You're both exhausted. We'll take over." She looked right at him and pointed to the furthest typist chair.

When Mr. Young and Mr. Midsommer vacated their seats and plodded to the elevator – hopefully going for a lie-down on the fourth floor – Mrs. Cunningham sat at Mark's assigned seat. She turned and told him, "Just type. The glyphs do everything else. Two hours should prove sufficient, and then we will rest."

He started, and tried to ignore the subtle but tangible wearying as magical energy was sucked out of him. What the typewriter glyphs pulled from people would replenish quickly, as evidenced by the 9 to 5 pace kept up by the employed typists. He trusted that, as he trusted this felt absolutely nothing like the soul-crippling drain of leaching a person's potential.

Mr. Smith Who Works The Front Desk by Jade Griffin

1893, August 30

He blinked, waking with a start. His head shot up from previously resting upon the typewriter, eyes scanning the whole area. The windows all around let in predawn light, the entire fifth floor empty of people.

Confusion and panic grabbed him but he forced them down. Just change clothes. Everything is fine.

On the fourth floor, he passed the two nearest guest rooms and could hear at least one Corner snoring away. Not sure which. In Conference Room 1, Mr. Paisley's head lay in folded arms, calm breaths whistling past the white mustache.

Hm. Opening the last guest room door to change his clothes could wake them, and they really should sleep. Another day in his attire wouldn't harm anyone. Utilizing the hidden stairwell, he decided the first floor was a better choice and a possible avenue for new information.

Descending with growing reluctance, he found himself staring in the dark at the crack of light lasering in from the first floor on the opposite side of the aperture. He got all of the scent and stains out, so why did he still smell death and rot and sorrow?

Swallowing hard, he pushed through out into fresh daylight filling the giant lobby. The passage was shut quickly and he breathed a sigh of relief, for no fetid scent remained. Only the memory. Must've been what hit him in the stairwell. The memory of what happened. One thing definitely stood out as different, however. Two agents held their places at the front of the building – one near the front entrance and one on the west corner. It was a comfort that he knew them by name,

Mr. Smith Who Works The Front Desk by Jade Griffin

but also brewed a little fear that something bad may befall other faces now familiar.

Having not much to do but wait and see if there may be need of him, he sat at the front desk.

Half an hour later, the slip of the hidden door opening startled him.

Treasurer Cunningham exited, though her step slowed upon seeing him. The reason presented itself easily, the bulge of a gun protruding with other cumbersome objects in her handbag as she made for the glance entrance.

He bolted forward, beat her in a race to the egress, and spread his little arms across the glass and metal. They bumped back behind him, unlocked. Understandable if the Paisley Foundation wanted to keep a public image and show nothing was wrong, despite everything being wrong. Especially wrong if anyone saw him blocking the entryway. Hoping to make as little scene as possible, he spoke with as commanding a voice as his seven-year-old physique allowed. "You **cannot** go out. You promised."

"And what of my promise to Mark, to be there for each other? We have each seen horrors in our lives, Mr. Smith. How often have you wished you could've done something? How many nights lying awake, looking back?"

He'd known such torment, truly, but it was not enough to force him away. Sleep deprivation engraved deep lines under her determined expression. She'd likely not slept in the last three days. "You're not thinking straight. We all agreed you've got to stay here."

The telephone rang at the front desk.

The treasurer's eyes narrowed and, in that instance, she almost resembled Portia. "You should answer that."

He planted a firmer stance, pressing himself against the glass and metal doors. "Fair certain it's for you."

Would she charge him, or would she back off? She was too close.

Time ticked by, echoed from the clock at the far back of the lobby.

The telephone stopped ringing.

A shadow fell over him.

He tilted his head back to see Agent Dane staring the treasurer down from the other side of the glass.

Tricia Cunningham's shoulders slumped.

The elevator opened.

As the treasurer moved away and sat stiffly at the nearest couch, he relaxed and awaited Mr. Paisley's approach.

The founder took time and care in confronting Mrs. Cunningham, but applied a face scrunched up with hurt while staring down at her stubborn, straight-ahead stare. "I did not save you to have you sacrificed at another time, Tricia. Have you so little faith in me?"

Her eyes remained straight ahead, fighting tears, fighting to maintain her composure and not be consumed by anger and defeat and so much more. "I looked through your journals and found nothing helpful."

"Not even my letter to you?"

Her eyes flit to those of the old man. "Calling me your chosen daughter only makes me want to fight for you and Mark more."

A smile of pride wreathed Mr. Paisley's face. "Know that I have a method at my disposal to attack your uncle when he is most vulnerable, that it is a very good plan with the least casualties possible, and that it **will not work** if you leave this building. We both know they will kill Mark as soon as they have what they want, which is the both of us. My plan grants the most chance of success, **if** you remain."

"If it is such a good plan, tell me what it is," she demanded, bits of that plying de Lorraine tone leaking into voice and expression.

"I can't. It relies on your trust. Do you trust me?" Mr. Paisley enunciated the last four words slowly and clearly.

She knew what it meant to agree; that to continue fighting against her allies played into what her family wanted, but would mean her fight for now was over. She fought it as long as she could before leaning her head into the old man's nearby leg, seeking comfort.

Mr. Paisley lay a hand atop her auburn hair. "Let us return upstairs and have a cup of tea, hm?"

She went with the founder, who collected her stuffed handbag and carried it for her.

A great sigh of relief escaped him. He had **not** wanted to face off against Treasurer Cunningham, nor run out of time for her or Dane, nor disobey Mr. Paisley. He happened to agree with his benefactor. She couldn't be allowed to leave or the de Lorraines would win.

As soon as he took a step away from the door, the rattle of carriage wheels and horse hoof clomps at his back forced him about.

A carriage pulled up in front of the Paisley Foundation. The driver – a stout man about forty years – hopped down and smiled at the nearest agent guarding the entrance, tipping a cap and issuing a presumably friendly greeting, muffled by the glass but audible as such. The rest lay unintelligible until Dane, still at the doors, pushed them open and looked to him.

"Says he has a delivery for Mr. Paisley, purchased yesterday morning from a shop downtown. Can you verify?"

"Is it a box?"

The cheery driver grinned upon hearing the question and peeked in at him, nodding with an answer of, "It is. A box in a box. Want me to bring it in?"

He issued a single nod and stood far back as Dane followed the driver to the rear of the carriage, watched the unloading of a large item, and held the partition while the guy hefted the crate inside. Dane followed the driver in as well.

"Where d'ya want it?" the man asked.

"By the desk is fine. Thank you."

Eyeing him, the driver asked, "Say, what d'ya do here?"

"The Paisley Foundation is a philanthropic business which works to ensure the security of the public and private sectors, both politically and socially."

"Like security, or charity?"

"Yes."

The driver placed the large crate down gently, straightened, and eyed him again, snorting a laugh. "Well, the place is big enough. You're all set. Boy, I've never heard a kid talk like you before. The name's George Arthur Ames, by the way, but people call me Artie."

"Thank you. Mr. Dane will see you out."

"Oh, uh... Sure thing."

Once the driver was escorted out, that left him free to examine the crate. Nailed shut, he went in search of a hammer.

A cursory inspection of Acquisitions did not reveal a single hammer or crowbar. He didn't want to be away from the box long, because Mr. Paisley must've ordered it for whatever conceived plan, so he returned to the first floor.

As he emerged from the elevator, Mr. Paisley sat on the crate watching for him, a hammer held loose in his benefactor's right hand.

"Care to help an old man?" he was asked, the founder's eyes burrowing into him.

The intensity of Mr. Paisley's gaze halted him briefly but he shook it off. None of them were at their best at present. Looking for some way to help in the present situation, he took the hammer and waited for Mr. Paisley to take a seat well away at one of the nearby couches before attempting to pry the crate open.

"You know that I am a man driven not by ambition but by the desire to help others," the founder told him when the first side came free.

He flicked a look at Mr. Paisley, unsure what provoked that start.

"You do not know that I was not so in my youth. Arrogant, hungry for the unknown, I found a fellow of similar desires in Evan de Lorraine. However, it took less than three months of witnessing his depravity to open my eyes to what becomes of a man who stays such a course without reservation. After I left his company, I met Maisey and my life was shown a new and glorious direction with a moderated passion of discovery. As things changed, I changed with them, always aiming for the better. We were reminded of that when you appeared and I have cherished each new change save one."

His work paused – not just because the crate was proving very tough – and glared at his benefactor. "Are you telling me this because you plan to sacrifice yourself?"

Mr. Smith Who Works The Front Desk by Jade Griffin

"No, Mr. Smith. I am no martyr. My plan is one of revenge." Mr. Paisley stood and approached, reaching for the hammer.

He passed it along and moved away, watching his benefactor rip the crate apart with aggressive force.

Pushing the pieces and panels of wood aside, Mr. Paisley revealed a plain box made from honey-colored wood, sanded and lacquered with intricate carvings all around it. Looked very old.

"Do you trust that I am – if anyone can say so of themselves – a good person with the intentions of others at the forefront of my decisions?"

His eyes went again to his benefactor. "I do, despite that you do things which unintentionally hurt yourself or others."

"Even if my intent is to hurt Evan de Lorraine in every way possible?"

A pause before he replied, "If he is behind all of this and whatever happened to Mrs. Cunningham in the past, I'd say he is deserving of your wrath. You plan to put a bullet in him?"

"A bullet did not stop him last time. Blowing him up is too difficult to conceal and would harm others grievously. No, something far more potent and precise is needed to end Evan and, unfortunately, I have run out of time and options." Mr. Paisley took in a breath, let it out, eyed the meandering people on the paths outside and in their carriages going about their daily lives, oblivious to anything but their own mindset. "You asked what I will place in the box to destroy Evan de Lorraine?"

And waited rather patiently for an answer, he refrained from saying aloud.

"In order to succeed against our foe, I must be willing to sacrifice not only my life but the regard of those I care about the most." Mr. Paisley's eyes bore into him once more. "I plan to use **you** to end Evan de Lorraine, Mr. Smith."

He stared, unblinking, reheard it several times in his head, and found himself unable to think of a reply.

"More precisely, my plan is to have you get in the box and deliver it along with myself at the appointed hour. With some skill and a fair bit of luck, Evan will be dead in fifteen minutes."

"I… I don't think I can condone that," tumbled haltingly from his mouth.

"Why not?" The buried anger stirred like the waking fury of a dragon. "On the grounds of morals? Evan de Lorraine tramples our morals and we are left burying our fellow. I will not **sit** for another day nor another hour and **allow** the desecration of all that I hold dear! They have Tricia's husband and I possess **no** safer way of retrieving him, nor stopping House de Lorraine from terrorizing us further. I shall not force you to do this thing, Mr. Smith, but we may all die if you do not. Either way, I am leaving in two hours."

Mr. Paisley placed the hammer atop the desk and strode calmly to the elevator, once more composed.

He stood still and quiet for some time, exactly as he'd been when Mr. Paisley left the first floor. Doubt, shock, and incredulity froze him. Then, secondly, indecision. Could he even consider using the device on his wrist to purposefully kill anyone? Yes, he understood Mr. Paisley's motivations. Look at what the de Lorraines had done in just two day's time? To Sergei… To Tricia – their own flesh and blood! It was no way to treat family. Family, to him, meant so much more than anything heard or witnessed from these de Lorraines. He felt very strongly about family, having been ripped from his own and then unable to establish any connection with people for so long. Not until he wound up here, now, with the Paisleys... They saved him, and Mrs. Paisley thought of him as family. With Mr. Paisley's warning that they all may die if he did not do his part against Evan de Lorraine, he felt the fear of losing everyone grow like looming figures, clawing over his shoulder and from within each shadow. But, even with fellows and acquaintances threatened, was it enough to sentence a bad man to death?

A glance at the clock showed him the hour of 2:39 PM. Fear squeezed his chest. How had inner contemplation sucked time away so quickly?

The elevator doors opened. Mr. Paisley exited and approached.

Cold fell over him, because he knew the founder would ask again, and he wasn't ready, didn't have an answer.

The kind man must've read it all over his face, for Mr. Paisley told him, "I understand. Such a decision is not meant to be easy, not even for people of our experiences. Very well, Mr. Smith. We shall make do with what we have."

When the old man turned away, a different fright prodded him onward. "Mr. Paisley, sir..."

Their eyes met and he saw the founder felt the indecision and unfairness just as much as he.

"While I have no doubt that Evan de Lorraine is a bad man, and we may deserve retribution for his harm to the people here, **is** it our only option? Truly? Not just the easiest or best, but the **only** viable option?"

Mr. Paisley faced him, folded hands neatly in front of clothes once well-pressed and now slept in and two days old but still maintaining their shape, their composure, just as his benefactor did when faced with such a question. "I have exhausted all that I know and am exhausted. If there are other ways which do not involve the de Lorraines simply turning about and attacking this foundation after the meeting due in one hour, I suppose I am not meant to know. Perhaps my emotions blind me. Perhaps I am not as clever as I think I am. I can only answer, Mr. Smith, that I do not know, and that I have done the best that I can. I know that, if you would go with me as I meet with this perilous person, you offer a far less biased view of him, despite the danger of you being in the fray. And I know, Mr. Smith, that in the event Evan de Lorraine is not stopped, his next matter of import is to raze this entire foundation. It is not merely on anger and grief which I act, but an instinct of survival."

He stared long at the large, blondewood box beside him. He didn't want all of these acquaintances... these fellows... harmed. Mr. Paisley was right to point out the lack of time. Sometimes one simply had to do what one could, even if the doing must be an unwelcome act. Perhaps he could even sway it so that this Evan de Lorraine would not die and perhaps be taught a lesson?

"What exactly does the box do?"

Trying to hide the start of hope, the founder bent down quickly, pulled a scrap of paper from a coat pocket, and read the foreign words. Latin? Italian? Uncertain, but the effect was clear, as the wooden box unfolded like a mechanical flower until it lay flat, save for a small, raised cushion to sit upon.

Mr. Smith Who Works The Front Desk by Jade Griffin

"I've been told that whatever is inside cannot see past the solid walls of the box. The contents also cannot be heard or scryed from the outside and thus remain a mystery. There should appear a lever to let yourself out, have you a great need, but it would be in all our interests to keep knowledge of you away from any de Lorraines."

"And yet you'd use the effect of the device against them," he argued. "I don't like it. But, as you said, the decision should not be easy. If it were, we would be too much like them. As it stands, I don't know if I can justify inaction, given that we would be attacked here later. The element of surprise, the allure of the unknown… These are your best weapons and cast even better odds if I'm in this box. So, I will do it… but if I feel my condition is being abused or those around me should not be affected, I'm getting out of it and away from all of you."

Mr. Paisley offered a smile of gratitude flavored with sympathy, knowing what was being asked went against other promises made to him. "Do you need to use the lavatory?"

Not certain how long he might be in the box, given they'd just over an hour until the meeting, he did so. Finishing up and wiping the remaining moisture from his hands on his oversized clothes, he approached the flat structure, then flicked a look at his benefactor. "And… I just sit there?"

"Yes."

Once he'd settled on the cushion, Mr. Paisley took up the paper in hand to read more foreign words.

The box curled up about him mechanically, encasing him, and he felt as if a djinni in a bottle. He did not sit in the dark, as expected, for the wood walls around him glowed as if warmed gold. More translucent, like honeycomb, somehow allowing partial ambient light to filter in. And in front of him, a lever appeared to sprout right from the wood. Everything in order so far, he took in a breath, let it out, and noted the air did not feel close or warm. Magical ventilation, like the light being allowed in?

"Doing well in there?"

Mr. Paisley's voice came across very clear – as if he were not in a box made of wood. "Yes, sir. Can you hear me?"

"If you're responding, Mr. Smith, I can't hear you but thought a test in order. Now for the next one."

He frowned, wary of the noun used.

Heard Mr. Paisley walk away. Could even hear the front doors open, footsteps approach, stop right next to the box. Too close! Why would Mr. Paisley do this? And then he knew. This was a magic box. Would the device on his wrist be able to penetrate the magic and still activate and drain Evan de Lorraine?

He held his breath, waited. Had to wait quite a while, and so took many more breaths, always counting in his head. When the nineth minute ended, he felt it activate, pulling the potential from the person beside him standing next to the box!

He scooted from the cushion to the lever and pulled to let himself out.

Nothing happened.

He tried flipping the lever, pushing it, twisting it.

Three more levers appeared.

He tried them as well.

Five more levers grew on the roof of the box.

Another minute swallowed up.

Mr. Smith Who Works The Front Desk by Jade Griffin

It wasn't working! The device continued to drain whoever stood near!

Placing hands on either side of the confines, he shifted his weight back and forth, rocking the wooden prison, trying to get away.

"That will do, Mr. Dane. Thank you," he heard Mr. Paisley say from not too far away. "Go get some comestibles. I'll maintain your post until you return."

"Thank you, Mr. Paisley. I... Sorry. Felt a little light-headed."

"It's been quite a few days. Off with you."

He calmed his mind and breathing, heard the elevator's mechanical door open and close, heard shoed feet approaching.

"My apologies, Mr. Smith. I had to make certain the effect would take. And, additionally, the lever is proving more difficult than I alluded to? There is a way for you to get out of the box, Mr. Smith. That, I was assured. What I do not know is the location of the lever needed to open the box. Good thing we still have the magic words."

He glared up at the voice, unseen, feeling all at once used. Mr. Paisley knew it would be difficult for the occupant to get out. And he, the idiot, did not recall that this used to be a box to imprison evil things. Should have asked for more details. So, Mr. Paisley essentially trapped him with trust and just enough information. Just enough, and his own willingness to take part in whatever was to transpire. He couldn't be too mad at the clever old man. He'd agreed to get in the box and do this.

So, he sat back down on the cushion and kept his ears sharp, trying to be ready for whatever came next.

Happened to be Mr. Paisley lifting the receiver of the telephone and making a call.

"Mr. Midsommer, I've sent Mr. Dane up for refreshments. As Mr. Smith is currently occupied, when you have a moment, let Mr. Dane know I'm calling a brief meeting in the first-floor lobby with Mr. Young and Agent Turner in fifteen minutes, then leaving to settle this matter once and for all."

A pause wherein he could hear garbled, tinny sound – whatever Mr. Midsommer replied.

"You are to remain here and make absolutely certain that Tricia does **not** leave. Do I have your word? Good lad. I shall return in less than three hours. If I do not, fear the worst and act accordingly."

The receiver clicked back onto its rest.

The wooden front desk chair creaked under the weight of a person resting back.

"So I am occupied, am I?" he complained, banging on the side of the box three times, hard.

"Whatever your disagreement, we are proceeding as planned. Please settle, as I will not be elaborating on the contents of the box to anyone no matter what provocation you try."

He crossed his arms and glared about the box. Kicked one of the levers with his shoed foot just to see if anything would happen.

Ten more levers sprouted up in various spots, on every side of the box, including its bottom.

Mr. Paisley's shoed feet scuffed away, toward the entrance. He heard them open, close, and open again moments later, followed by at least three pairs of shoed feet.

Mr. Smith Who Works The Front Desk by Jade Griffin

That matched in time with the elevator door opening and they were joined by one more set of footsteps. At least none sounded close enough to activate the device.

"Perfect, Mr. Dane. Now then, I am due for my meeting with Evan de Lorraine presently. You and Mr. Young will assist in loading this box onto the carriage and ride with me to unload it once we reach our destination. Mr. Turner will drive the carriage and depart with you both after delivering the box and myself. There is no time for questions, nor need for further debate, so I would appreciate some haste, gentlemen."

A pause settled amid whomever lay gathered. Then the sound of stretching pants cloth as two persons bent down, presumably to—

He was thrown to one side and into three levers as the box tilted.

"Be very careful with the box, Mr. Young."

He felt Agent Dane and Mr. Young walking more carefully with the box, giving him time between their jostling steps to set himself back on the cushion and brace with arms and legs for when it was placed down.

"What is it?" Dane asked.

The founder replied, "Something to be very careful with. Keep it upright and as flat as you can."

He grew increasingly uncomfortable with the thought of Dane remaining near to aid in transporting him, knowing the Paisley agent had not been away from him long enough to reset the device. He had no idea how long the ride would be, or if—

Bumped once more, he could not fault that they tried to make the lowering of the box gentle. What became clear was that they'd placed him inside the carriage and not in the rear as if baggage. He knew because of the closeness of feet stepping and scraping close by. So very close... The squeak of wood under seat cushions, the tilt of the carriage to one side as not one but two individuals entered the carriage cab, their shadows descending his box into a darker confine.

"Mr. Young, you are not trading places with Mr. Dane," he heard Mr. Paisley's adamant protest.

"Apologies, sir, but I am. You are absolutely not attending this alone."

"I cannot predict what they will do if you come."

"Neither can I, but, as an added measure to keep our treasurer in place, I promised Mrs. Cunningham that I would go in her stead, to look out for the both of you. I also feel my presence will be a favorable aid."

The carriage jerked forward, pushing him into the back of the box where an inconvenient lever appeared to jab him in the spine.

"Unless Evan kills you on sight."

"... True."

"You have always been a bit impetuous, Vince."

"And have used it many times to my advantage. However, sir, if we are to walk into a very dangerous situation, should I not know the plan, or at least the contents of this box?"

"No. You should not. And leave your manipulations at the door. Evan de Lorraine will be insulted at such a trick."

Silence.

"Are you still desiring to go? I can ask Mr. Turner to stop."

"... A promise is a promise."

"Indeed. And, if you mind what further I shall impart, perhaps we may all return whole."

"I'll do my best, but why are you not taking any spells or artifacts with you?" President Young asked.

"I have all that shall be effective against Evan de Lorraine."

"You mean the box? It's integral to your plan?"

"You have precisely five minutes by this pocket watch to stop your manipulations – on me or anyone else. Evan is a man of great ambition and low patience. If you speak to him out of turn and have nothing to truly catch his interest, he will kill you simply for impertinence."

Pause, then a sigh from Mr. Young.

"Very good. Keep in mind it is only my history with him which grants me an audience. I bested him a time or two and now he wishes to torment me in person. You have earned neither his notice nor respect, if he even knows who you are, and he will have no qualms over squashing anyone not fitting those categories. I hope you remain an unknown to him. Silence will be your weapon. Use it well. The less he knows of you, the better off you'll be."

"That extends to attempting any spells against him?"

"Indubitably. He is far more fluent in his use of magic than you or I combined. Moreso than our dear treasurer or secretary. As such, any hint of the start of incantations and he will attack. I should think practicing silence now would be your best line of defense."

So reminded, no talking followed. Only the squeak of the carriage, the clop of hooves, and ambient sounds outside on the street.

He grew anxious as his count passed eight minutes. Relief overtook him briefly when the pull of gravity indicated the halt of the carriage.

"Remember, Mr. Young. Disclude yourself from all conversation whenever possible," Mr. Paisley told the foundation president, then grunted to a stand. "And do take care with the box, both of you. The contents are fragile."

Two pairs of feet shuffling, carriage rocking. Without warning, he was forced against one of the sides, the box yanked one direction.

"Hey!" he yelled, then banged on his little prison in protest.

All motion and sound paused.

"Did you hear that?" he heard Agent Turner ask on a low tone.

President Young replied using the same subdued volume. "Be careful and be quiet."

"Come along," Mr. Paisley could be heard some span away.

Both Paisley Foundation employees heeded the need of silence and the founder's call, hefting his box with gentler hands. They must've entered into a structure of some kind, for the walls about him darkened to a dim glow.

"You will leave, Mr. Turner," Mr. Paisley said, hushed. "Mr. Young, can you take the box alone? Good. Quickly now!"

He was transferred with minor jostling. Slower pace, more rocking.

Footsteps retreated. The carriage reins cracked. Horse hooves cantered off.

A brief silence settled as Mr. Paisley and Mr. Young walked carefully forward. Very carefully, as even the slightest jostling sent the box this way and that. Felt like he was being shook, despite bracing himself. He felt Mr. Young

Mr. Smith Who Works The Front Desk by Jade Griffin

straining under the weight of holding him as they walked a short way. Placed on the ground, some feet backed away. More feet approached. Couldn't tell who moved away and who hadn't; just that more persons were near to him. This complicated things, as he began a secondary count in his head.

The outgoing voice of a young man startled him with, "Arthur! And underling. Unexpected, but my own have been itching for a fight. Perhaps they shall have one after all? However, I do not see my niece. Where have you stashed her?"

"She may be brought along presently, if I feel the time is right."

A pause, and then a grin in the voice. "You test me after I sent your Russian underling back to you in walking pieces?"

"I propose a trade." Mr. Paisley speaking, a chair was pulled back and then filled by most likely his benefactor.

"A trade and not a gift? Brazen of you, as you have not met my demands. I admit it is a curious-looking thing. What have you brought?"

"An item of great value to me, and one of great power."

"Ah, and you mean to trade this to me for…?"

"You are to return my employee and remove all de Lorraine presence from Chicago henceforth. You are similarly not to make ripples elsewhere or the Paisley Foundation will be forced to attack you at every possible opportunity and unleash a powerful force the likes of which you have neither seen nor can you counter."

Laughter, clear and full of delight, followed Mr. Paisley's calm words.

"Oh, Arthur! You wield a threat built on nothing. We were explorers under a different banner decades ago. Tenacity, yearning for knowledge, made of hardier stuff than this. I chose this restaurant because it was my only true win against you. Remember how you pined after that poor young thing and she chose me instead? Ah, you do remember. The day the fight left your eyes and that yearning spirit was doused. Look at you now. Old, tired, boring."

A fight over a girl? Hadn't expected that, but even such a reveal did not distract him from the time ticking by. Though Mr. Young's ten minutes had since passed and the device did not activate – indicating the Paisley president had thankfully moved far enough away – the others were still ticking away, including Mr. Paisley's. His benefactor sounded very close.

"Time changes a man."

"Not when you can ignore its march across your mortal form. And you come before me with, what, mere words? When you know who I am, what I am capable of, and still deny me what is mine?" The ring of a single hand clap broke the silence. "Very well. To honor your utter gall and also the times we ventured together, I'll give you a chance to show your hand."

A pause. Nervous sweat itched his pits. Not sure what Mr. Paisley planned to do or how long this would take, if he would be revealed or locked in the damned box forever.

"Still no?" Evan de Lorraine asked. A measure of respect flavored the query.

"The power I wield is not to be wantonly displayed. It is locked away for a reason."

"All the best ones are." When silence followed Evan's smiley words, the head of House de Lorraine continued with,

Mr. Smith Who Works The Front Desk by Jade Griffin

"So be it, but know that inaction is just as deadly as hasty action – a fact you have clearly forgotten, and so I must show my hand."

Silence but for the creak of a person turning in their chair, some shuffling feet. A door creaked open. Someone grunted, shoved, ushered forward with awkward steps. Perhaps with bound feet? The shuffling stopped abruptly, on the de Lorraine side of the conversation. Two quick steps behind him, from Mr. Paisley's side, halted by Evan de Lorraine's, "Ah-ah." as well as some rough hands against bodies wishing to move.

"As I see things," the head of the de Lorraines continued. "I'm sitting across from an old bag of hot gas who stupidly brought the president of his company to accompany him when he knew he was going to die. You claim to have an item of great power yet refuse to display it. I call for the return of my niece and you bring threats. You show no teeth. Time has softened you, Arthur. Even more than I feared. It will be a mercy for you, putting you down like a tired dog, but not before you learn once and for all not to deny me what is mine."

There fell a short pause before Evan's voice changed to the guttural monotone of chanting.

Mr. Paisley's chair stuttered back.

The person held on the de Lorraine side gasped for air in a most hideous way.

"Stop it! Release him!"

Evan did not cease spellcasting at Mr. Paisley's shouts.

One person's squeaky-oiled shoes rushed only three steps before opposing feet-pounds from others and an "Oof!" slammed the one person audibly into a wall. Other shoed feet pounded toward Mr. Paisley. The old man's grunts and struggles fell very close when his box was suddenly shoved forward. Felt like by a foot, he thought, rubbing at his head. Hadn't time to brace before it banged on the box's interior.

The device on his wrist activated amid the ruckus. His panic kicked in. He tried rushing himself against the side of the container but there was too little space. He only managed a slight shimmy. From inside the miniature prison, there wasn't anything he could do but listen to the punching, struggling, chanting, and gasping.

The gasps turned desperate, then devolved to wheezes. In moments, the choking sputters faded, drowned under the spell's hammering words. A body-sized thud landed right next to him, rattling the whole box, startling him. The chanting ceased. The Paisley men's efforts to get at Evan settled in quiet defeat. The room bowed to silence, and to Evan de Lorraine.

"I never fear letting my power show as needed, Arthur. Or do I need to kill your president as well before you hand over my niece?"

Mr. Paisley's labored breathing – the only response – held a mix of grief and fury.

His box was pulled this time, closer to Evan de Lorraine, whose voice loomed. "Let's see what present you've brought. Hm. A puzzle to open, eh? Bring Mr. Young over. Perhaps he knows how to crack it? And if not…"

Forced footsteps – Mr. Young being muscled near – were interrupted by Mr. Paisley saying, "Only I know how to open it. Let him go and I will show you." The old man's voice still bore strain but managed a more even and angry arc.

"No. Show me and I may let him go."

Mr. Smith Who Works The Front Desk by Jade Griffin

"He needs to leave in order to bring Tricia here. She will not come with anyone but Mr. Young."

A brief pause fell, as if Evan were trying to decide if Mr. Paisley were lying. Honestly, he had no idea, but Mr. Paisley was too close! Everyone was too close! The device hungrily drew in the potential of not only Evan de Lorraine but Mr. Paisley and the two people holding them. At least Mr. Young hadn't started being drained… yet. He felt each of the others, each distinct, and nothing being drawn from the poor soul on the floor.

He tried yanking another handful of random levers to find the one to open the box, but only succeeded in provoking more to appear. It infuriated him so much, he picked up the cushion, used it as padding, and slammed himself against a random side, which gained Evan's notice.

"Whatever is inside is quite eager to get out, don't you think?"

"It senses power," Mr. Paisley said in a dangerous tone.

"Off with you then. Bring me my niece."

Three pairs of shoed feet moved away. Far away. The device pulled only from the three people nearby. From their two voices, he knew Mr. Paisley and Evan were closest. He felt the energy being drawn from them escalate in flow. Flipping as many levers as quickly as possible resulted in yet more levers. Was it a combination? Were there two needing to be flipped at the same time? If he didn't get away soon, they'd be drained completely in minutes!

Abandoning the levers, he braced with arms and legs, then thrust his scant weight back and forth, trying to rock the box enough to walk it away.

"Ah-ah-ah." His efforts were halted by strong hands, the box was lifted. "Quite weighted. Are the contents alive?"

His only warning before the box shook violently.

"Yes. Please, be careful."

The shaking ceased. "So, it is something you truly value. Excellent. Worth my time."

Still braced inside the box, he similarly did not miss Mr. Paisley's sincerely worried tone. Glad Evan stopped shaking him, but it felt unsteady where he ended up. Was he resting on the arrogant man's lap? Shouldn't move, but he still felt the device drawing from three people. He swallowed hard, thinking it'd be worth his own injury to try and get himself further away from Mr. Paisley. He couldn't let the old man die! Not like what happened to his wife!

"Tell me how to open it. Now."

Definitely on a lap. The commanding tone was punctuated by synchronous jostling.

"Here," Mr. Paisley replied. The old man's voice sounded very close – too close! – and hollow. "Only a person with sufficient magical ability may open the box. And whomever speaks the words on the paper becomes the box's only controller. Place it on the table."

The coarse slide of a paper across a flat, wood surface. Mr. Paisley's chair creaked back, the sound of being filled by a weary person. Still too close! Then the box shifted, moved, and settled onto a firm, flat surface.

"This is Greek. Is this a *koutí tou kakoú*?"

Clear, unbridled excitement seasoned Evan de Lorraine's tone and he knew it would be impossible to dissuade the man's desire, even if he could get out of this fucking box! Why were they still talking? **Why** wouldn't Mr. Paisley move away? He knew no one could hear him but wanted so badly to yell and holler as their discourse continued.

"A special type, yes. Repurposed to be not a 'box of bad' but to contain something else."

A short pause, then Evan recited the same words heard not two hours prior.

From inside, the top unfurled first, like the petals of a flower or a magician's trick. The room above him revealed darkness, lit only by lanterns hung near red velvet curtains. Then the sides of the box came down and he sat in its remains facing a handsome, young man with dark hair and eyes hungrily scanning his small form.

Evan de Lorraine's smile turned from greedy to humored. "What is this?"

"What I prize the most in this world, Evan."

He froze, because he didn't know what to do! Yes, get away from the both of them, but Evan de Lorraine would grab him if he tried to run. And he couldn't remember what Mr. Paisley said to Mr. Young about the best weapon against the head of House de Lorraine, and... and Mr. Paisley sounded so sad, and did the man really value him more than anything else?

He turned, dared to look at his benefactor, whose visage appeared much older and more tired than ever before, held in place by the hands of some goon no doubt hired by the de Lorraine family. He knew equally that, if he remained around them much longer, the device would drain everyone completely, and, given Mr. Paisley's sad expression, that was entirely his benefactor's plan from the start.

A steely grip latched onto his right wrist.

He jerked reflexively and swiveled toward his grabber, but there was no pulling away from the Head of House de Lorraine. The man reeked of evil intent, more than anyone he'd ever encountered. This bad man delighted in the torment of gaining something so precious to Mr. Paisley, who never acknowledged the lackey holding the old man firmly in a chair, and who held no reservation minutes earlier when killing the innocent man laying just a kick away.

He didn't know; not for sure. He'd hoped... And yet that hope turned to heavy stones in his gut, for the person dead on the ground was Mark Cunningham. The poor typist's eyes bulged from suffocation, face purple and neck red from being clawed at, fingernails bloody with the effort of trying to scratch a hole to gain air... He looked at Evan de Lorraine's glee and all emotion and struggle left his small form.

The man laughed at his young face, feeling a win, of besting an enemy, relishing every second of it... And then stopped. The smug smile fell like a rock. The man stared as wrinkles formed on once-young hands – aging right in front of everyone.

Evan de Lorraine released him hard, spinning him away.

He fell against the edges of the flattened box, the surfaces now smooth and unlevered. He got back up.

Evan abandoned the seat and took a step to the rear.

He stepped down into Evan's vacated chair.

"What are you?!" the confused man demanded.

"Didn't you hear? Or are you **deaf** to the words of others?" he sneered, pushing every last bit of distaste for the man into his seven-year-old voice as he hopped down from the chair and edged farther from his benefactor, closer to Evan de Lorraine. "I'm what Mr. Paisley prizes most in this world."

For once in his life, he dared to will the device to drain the bad man faster and end this. It didn't work by his command or wishes, however the pace increased as it always did, pulling more of the potential of all of the people nearest him. He ran behind Evan de Lorraine, not to jump the man but to put the most distance between himself and Mr. Paisley.

Evan took it as an attack and lunged at him with a knife pulled from a boot. Missed, but he made sure to keep a solid five feet away from the man's reach. Just enough space to let the damned device do its job. More potential was drawn from Evan, whose hair grayed and skin spotted at a faster rate. Not just visible. The drain was something people could feel if around him long enough. Given the panic displayed, Evan de Lorraine felt every last drop rushing out like a torrent.

"Stop it! Stop or I'll kill him!" Evan shrieked at him, pointing to Mr. Paisley.

"I don't care about him," he lied with the Devil's own grin and tossed out a phrase Mr. Paisley had used. "I care about power. Your power."

Evan must've seen through the lie, or perhaps weighed it worth the risk, for the de Lorraine leader started hand motions to go along with whatever spell the evil man began to utter.

He cast a glance back at Mr. Paisley, held firmly in the seat by the de Lorraine mook. His benefactor looked truly afraid for him, but he similarly held his ground and threw himself at Evan, wrapping his little arms around the evil man's leg.

The spell sent hot pinpricks all over his body, then squeezed his bones. He had no idea what the spell was or would do but matched the pain and squashing with all the force he could muster and held on for dear life, eyes clamped shut, hoping that, whatever happened, Mr. Paisley would be spared and Evan de Lorraine would not.

The evil man's voice strained to get through the recitation of the spell. He felt the flow of potential trickle to nothing and knew the device on his wrist had taken everything from Evan just as he heard the evil man's final utterance crescendo into a scream violently ripped and engulfed by a high cosmic whistle, a tear in space itself.

There was all at once nothing in his grasp but cloth. He fell to the ground amid an eerie hush.

Cautiously, he cracked open an eye. Stillness. The room smelled of charcoal and burnt metal.

He scrambled up, eyes darting about.

No sign of the bad man... Only clothes.

He lifted the abandoned suit.

From the shirt once worn by Evan de Lorraine, a perfectly-formed sphere of polished, compact black rock rolled out and across the floor.

"Mr. de Lorraine?" muttered the terrified and confused lackey, who stumbled over to stare at the sphere. The big man reached down to touch it.

"Don't! Or the same'll happen to you!" he warned. Presumably, Evan's spell backfired and did... that... so it was a lie to the lackey. However, he similarly didn't want the goon to make off with... whatever Evan de Lorraine had been reduced to. Definitely dead, as the device now only pulled from the nearby mook.

Mr. Smith Who Works The Front Desk by Jade Griffin

His words were enough to send the goon running for dear life, out of the restaurant and into late afternoon sunlight.

"Mr. Smith…"

He turned to his benefactor, who was struggling to stand and had no strength to do so. He similarly could not help the man, except to move farther away. The device lay dormant, given he stood more than ten feet back with no more living people in range to draw from, but the damage was done. Deep, permanent lines traced Mr. Paisley's wearied face.

He swallowed hard, tried to hold himself together. Tears forced their way through.

"Clark, go." Mr. Paisley tried a feeble shooing gesture.

"But…" What could he say? His benefactor wasn't actively dying… probably… but he knew how much potential had been taken from the old man. Not everything, but a lot. Too much. He feared what would happen if he left, and what would happen if he stayed.

"Talk later. Go."

He turned and ran for the door, only to just miss colliding with a limping President Young, gun drawn, who rushed back inside.

Immediately pausing at the sight of his familiar form, Mr. Young's shocked face tracked him until he slipped well out of sight.

He didn't stop running after rounding the first block. Dodging person, cart, carriage, and animal, he ran until his legs went to jelly. Not back to the Paisley Foundation. No, he couldn't go back there and answer the questions which would most definitely be put upon him. He didn't want to be around anyone or anything, and the only place he could imagine might be acceptable for solitude was the Paisley Estate.

It took several hours of travel, but his determination held fast – to arrive at his location and to stay away from everyone. Legs burning, his throat similarly parched, the sight of the large swaths of tall amber grass held more comfort than he felt he deserved. Plodding up to the golden sea, he fell amongst the dry plant-ocean, exhausted, hurting, and cried his eyes out.

Time meant nothing, nor the turn of the planet into darkness or the chill in the air. It wasn't until the crashing roll of a fast-approaching carriage intruded on his solitude that he sat up and opened eyes to full dark. He peeped through the grasses as the carriage thundered by. It came to a skidding halt in the gravel of the estate's courtyard under a vast sea of stars. Couldn't make out who exited the carriage, but he heard the faint calling of his name in Mr. Paisley's frantic, distant tone.

Picking himself up and jogging to the open front doors where light poured out to greet him, he called inside, "I'm here!"

Mr. Paisley rounded the corner of the foyer.

What relief he felt seeing his benefactor up and about!

Even bearing a great deal of weight on a cane, the old man made haste to scan his small form from a barely adequate distance. With a sigh unburdening a world of stress and sorrow, Mr. Paisley sank into the velvet settee nearby. His host's eyes shut and every ounce of composure drained away.

"I thought they might've found you," he breathed, dragging in wheezy breaths through a voice further strained with an effort not to shed tears. That fell away in a breath and the old man's sobbing began. "I'm sorry, Mr. Smith. I am so sorry it came to that. And poor Mark…"

He shut the front doors and kept a solid twelve feet away. He could not offer physical comfort, despite Mr. Paisley's obvious need of it, and wondered where the staff were. No one came. Wished someone would come, because he hadn't anything to say.

When the man's sobs became too much, he dashed past, up the stairs, and shut out the world.

He sat upon the bed in the dark, staring out at the night sky and the dim light of the Chicago skyline. Everything felt numb, so overcome with what had happened.

Not that he hadn't harmed anyone before, nor seen dead people. It was that – out of everything done in his expanded life – he never once wished such harm on another… until today. Still felt Evan de Lorraine got what he deserved. Especially for killing Mark Cunningham. He didn't regret what he did, and that was a problem. Would he become no better than Heebs and Jeebs, or Evan de Lorraine, flaunting his power because he could? Such thoughts haunted him and he gained little rest.

Mr. Smith Who Works The Front Desk by Jade Griffin

1893, August 31

He woke to sunshine and birdsong. Strange. No one roused him and no sounds filtered up from downstairs.

Dressing quickly, he descended in a rush. Expecting to see Danneby, his step faltered upon seeing the cook, Clara, standing in the foyer wearing her hat and coat. By her face, something terrible had happened. He braced for the worst news.

"Mornin', young sir. I... I'm sorry to be the bearer of bad tidings but poor Miss Sarah died early this mornin' from a snake bite she got yesterday. Mr. Paisley was there for her at least, then went directly over to the Paisley Foundation to sort out all of that business. When I arrived early this morn, I couldn't find Mr. Danneby, but he's there, still in his room under the stairs. Seemed he succumbed to his bad heart, probably last night. I took the liberty of sendin' for a mortician, as Mr. Paisley told me you were still on the grounds. The mortician'll be here presently to collect Mr. Danneby... Young sir, I already told Mr. Paisley but I'm afraid I can't work here any longer. Sorry." The plump cook attempted a nervous curtsy before hurrying out the entryway, not bothering to witness any response from him.

He felt nothing and could do nothing.

The quiet swallowed him. The estate, once filled with warmth and industry, felt like a graveyard as he stood on the last step. Lonely and cold. Sometimes death didn't happen right away when a person had their potential stolen away. Sometimes it was slow, agonizing, and cruel. Other people around them were often affected. Like now.

Mr. Smith Who Works The Front Desk by Jade Griffin

The mortician arrived an unknown time later. He pointed out the butler's room under the stairs when asked on the location of the deceased. Wandering back upstairs, he felt in no mood to witness them taking Danneby or have his damning presence around anyone.

He remained alone with his grief all day and honored poor Danneby and Sarah with fond memories. Sarah, always reserved, always professional. Danneby, a devoted and ardent servant whose respect for the Paisleys shadowed all others. The loneliness grew when, upon waking the following day, the house lay still as a grave. A search of the house and grounds confirmed that he was alone.

Mr. Paisley's absence persisted into the next day. Up well before the sun, he similarly received no request, invitation, or horse to take him to the Paisley Foundation. His benefactor had a change of heart, avoiding him? No. Such thoughts were selfish. Vast change in so short a time must make it difficult to reorient, especially as his benefactor maintained leadership of an important business also rocked by loss. Given that he still felt responsible for most of those changes, more or less, it seemed wrong to want to be around them. Perhaps best if he never returned.

He debated yet again on simply picking up and leaving the estate, the entire state of Illinois, just running from everything, but that yielded no solution. Running was all he did in the past. He had a fair thing going here and should pick up the pieces of it to make it better than fair once more, to fight to keep what he'd gained… as long as they could forgive him, and he forgave himself.

It was during a particularly long stare out the second-floor window on the second morning of solitude, waiting anxiously for the sun to rise and any sign of people, that he decided he'd had enough. Drinking a fair amount of water, he took the keys from the bin, locked up the house, and started out for the city shortly after dawn.

Arriving at the Paisley Foundation's front doors several hours later, he found them to be unlocked and so he walked in. An unusual amount of activity greeted him in the lobby, where people in overalls hauled wood and other construction supplies behind a covered area where the front desk once sat but had since been moved to the middle of the lobby, and where the sound of industry and building carried from the opposite side of the canvas cover. Agent Turner, standing near the entrance, nodded to him.

"Is Mr. Paisley upstairs?" he enquired.

"No. He's overseeing the progress." The agent gestured the direction of the workers.

As he approached, Mr. Paisley emerged from behind the canvas, bearing quite a bit of weight on a silver-handled cane, yet lifted by a smile. That smile dropped upon seeing him.

The founder came near and told him, "We'll talk in the conference room."

Following Mr. Paisley to the elevator, he tried not to read too much into his benefactor's altered mood as the mechanical door closed for the short ride.

"You were told about Sarah and Danneby?"

A nod.

"And you walked the whole way?"

A nod.

"A pitcher of lemonade waits in the conference room. See to your thirst and then we'll talk."

That is precisely what he did, taking the cool, refreshing cup to the furthest seat from the organization's founder. He observed Mr. Paisley easing slowly into the head chair, and that the founder took note of his observation.

"I wanted to be the one to inform you of the passing of Miss Dolores," the founder opened.

He choked on the sour drink.

Mr. Paisley waited until the sputters and coughs died down before continuing. "She did not arrive as expected yesterday. An agent went to her home, only to find her in bed. Died in her sleep."

The news brought pain and anger. Didn't know what he wanted to say and kept his mouth shut.

"I know you had a great rapport with Dolores and understand you may feel a need to sequester yourself away from everyone, but it is better for all if you did not return to the estate."

"I have no interest in being left with no word on the future or the current state of things, unless you feel rightly that I am to blame for how things turned out?" Couldn't help the accusatory tone. Mixed well with guilt and sadness in this case.

Mr. Paisley let loose a long, weary sigh. "It would delight me to say there are other factors contributing to the bad luck of those around me, but you and I are in a unique position to condemn ourselves. However, there is no seeing the light if we only look for darkness. I've some tasks for you."

"So it is back to business as usual?" he spat out.

After a pause, Mr. Paisley's rational voice replied, "Your acid is not appreciated. And, no. It has been anything but business as usual. I have planned and attended two funerals and now must do so for Sarah, Danneby, and Dolores. I witnessed Mark's death first-hand, the desecration of my vice president by magic, and all in a span of four days. The head of the de Lorraines at least is dead, and they have been sufficiently cowed that I doubt they will try anything against Tricia – at least not in the foreseeable future – but at the cost of three highly-valued employees and my entire house staff, two of whom are dead. I know not when House de Lorraine may try to exact revenge but am certain it will come. The Paisley Foundation is down staff and hobbled beneath its grief, but I refuse to let my work go to ruin simply because my influence and… well, my luck, if you will… have all but run dry. The situation is distasteful and unfair, and I am more responsible for the fate I have put in my path and the paths of others close to me than **any** action of your own choosing. I have lived many decades, Mr. Smith. Not all of them good. No matter how long you suffered in the Hell you came from, you have been as freed from it as I can provide. Perhaps others in the future may answer more on your condition. In the meantime, we must make do with what we have, and create what we have not."

He didn't have anything to say to that, despite the old man being right.

Mr. Paisley pulled from under a shirt a large necklace very uncharacteristic of the man's usual attire. Brought it out just for him to see.

"What is that?"

"Just a bit of luck to ensure I am around long enough to see my immediate plans complete." The founder tucked it back under his clothes. "Your arrival today is a bit premature, as the work isn't to be finished until tomorrow, but with the loss of my staff, you shall be moved here presently."

"Moved? You want me to live here?"

"Yes. Best we can make of present circumstances."

"And those are?"

His challenge to state the reason was met with a piercing stare. No words exchanged, he knew his benefactor felt the end drawing near. Whatever the medallion's magic, it would not be enough to hold back death.

His jaw ground. Not enough, he blurted out, "You want me to stay here, to spare me more grief? It won't matter, so I will not be leaving you alone," he protested.

"You can and you shall. I will be fine on my own, Mr. Smith."

"But—"

"I am most likely dying, yes, but that will happen on my own terms, I assure you. And I will not be completely alone."

While he puzzled over that statement, Mr. Paisley continued.

"Mr. Smith, I need you to stay away from the estate in the coming days. Building you your own room here is for your own good. I will not have you sequestering yourself in that empty, old house. You need to hold fast to your purpose, son. This is where I believe you should be."

Despite making the most sense, it was proving difficult to be as rational as the dead-set Mr. Paisley – no pun intended. He tried, asking, "Can I at least know whose company you will be keeping which requires my continued and permanent absence? Have you hired new staff?"

"Not precisely. Call it a very specific type of recruitment."

"Recruitment. As in an employee?" The first heard of since meeting his benefactor.

"Yes, of a specific type. I must see if they pass muster, if they can hold their own, and then proceed accordingly."

He blinked at Mr. Paisley as another possibility came to him. "But this ... recruit... is joining you at the house? Is it an employee for the Paisley Foundation or are you recruiting someone to manage the estate?"

"Yes."

The quickness and finality of the reply left nothing further to be discussed or known. He stared long on the old man's face, fighting to accept the fact that his benefactor would not be around for much longer.

"As previously stated, I have attended and must attend more funerals, plus the time needed to orient the recruit and determine if they are a viable option for the position I have in mind. I apologize for my absence of late – especially as you are aware my time is short – but, as you can imagine, things here have been... busy."

Too busy to collect him to attend any of the funerals? He didn't say it. No point. Wasn't prudent for him to attend the services and be questioned by any not in the know wondering who the kid at the funeral was, or be forced close to any people.

"I understand that you have not had proper time to mourn, nor anyone to share your grief with, and for that I apologize. If you wish to mourn alone at the estate today, or if you desire to get to work here until close of business, I will make sure there is a fresh horse for you at the stables. Which shall it be?"

Mr. Smith Who Works The Front Desk by Jade Griffin

"... I'll stay." Best to return to work, as this might be the last day spent near his endearing benefactor, even if it meant dodging queries on what really happened at the restaurant. It hurt to even consider that there would soon be no more time with Mr. Paisley. He knew venturing down that path would eat up precious time, so he decided on an easier topic to distract them both. "How is Mrs. Cunningham?"

"Sad, angry, and hiding it all under business as usual. Good to see you attempting the same."

Could say the same of Mr. Paisley. The old man clearly didn't feel the need to grieve at present either. So be it. "Does she know I was there?"

"No. Only that Evan de Lorraine has been dealt with. Mr. Young saw you leave but has nothing to say, nor to note in his report, on that account. A bit quiet lately, but this is the first he's dealt with the de Lorraines and the first real blow dealt to him as president."

"How can I help?"

That smile first seen this morning on Mr. Paisley's face returned with his offer. No, not the same one. That one, he recognized, was for show. This one conveyed genuine hope and good feelings and all of it for him.

Everyone stayed too busy to ask him anything beyond work, nor did he bring up anything at all. His time gobbled up on various errand runs, he found himself sent out for meals due to the loss of Dolores inciting the Victors to take a vacation, or out to collect paperwork from other agencies, and filing three times the usual amount into the Repository. Didn't care for going out on the street, as it got him too close to people for too long, but the others needed him to. Each time slipping away as soon as he could, he managed to deny the device any chance of activating.

Set himself up a workstation of bins at the desk on the first floor, sorting and filing the excess of piled up paperwork. The construction crew relocated the front desk just before leaving at a prompt 5 PM. Everyone else worked on. He only realized the time when first Mr. Young and then the typists dragged as they made their way out past 6 PM. When Mr. Midsommer and Mrs. Cunningham exited the elevator, he kept his eyes on work while attempting to not look like he avoided conversation. Didn't matter. The pair walked past him and left without a single look his way.

Almost directly after they turned a corner and left his view, the elevator opened once more.

Mr. Paisley offered a small smile at first sight of him, though he struggled with walking and leaned heavily against the front desk.

"I'll get one of the agents to bring a carriage," he offered.

At the front doors of the Paisley Foundation, one of the horse-drawn conveyances pulled up, driven by Agent Dane.

"Mr. Midsommer has it in hand, Mr. Smith. Will you be along presently?"

He looked on the work at the desk.

"It can wait, my boy. I know you don't have much in the way of belongings, as a habit, but you must prepare for your move here. Put it away for now. Come along. Tomorrow shall be your last day at my residence."

It felt too soon. With a sigh, he stacked the papers neatly and placed them in a square basket atop the desk. Yes, some things could keep, as others were soon to expire. Best to

Mr. Smith Who Works The Front Desk by Jade Griffin

measure his time accordingly and spend it with one who would soon be gone, and also to pack.

1893, September 3

His last hour in the Paisley Estate left him anxious. Not eager to leave, he would miss this place. Felt almost like home, in a way. More than any place since being stolen from his actual home. Found himself wandering the halls and eventually wound up at the workroom. Mrs. Paisley had taken to measuring his height on the wood frame of the space. For the year since he'd lived with them up until her death, she would check his growth every month. All of the marks clumped together and only one stood a fraction higher than the others.

Curious, he took off his shoes, placed his feet against the doorframe, aligned against it, and positioned his left hand atop his head. Careful to keep it still, he ducked and turned. His fingers held position a notable space above the old marks.

He'd grown, and a whole inch at that! It was a sign of change. No. Progress. Proof that, despite every change in his life, he overcame or accepted and moved on. Finding light instead of darkness.

With a resolute sigh, he took the keys, locked the estate, and mounted the same horse that brought him here yesterday evening.

After stabling the horse at the livery around the corner, he lengthened his stride. Almost 5 PM.

At the Paisley Foundation, Mr. Paisley awaited him. The old man smiled and dangled a set of keys while resting at the front desk seat.

"To the front doors here, in exchange for those to my home front doors."

He smirked and passed over the keys to his benefactor's estate. Accepting those to the Paisley Foundation, he eyed the founder with concern.

"Oh, don't give me such a face, Mr. Smith. Your room is complete and I shall bring your things presently in the morning. Packed up and in the foyer as I requested?"

"Yes, sir."

"Very good." Mr. Paisley paused, looked him over. "We haven't the time to do a great many things I'd hoped to do, but I will be arranging a private meal at one of the best restaurants in town, just for you and I, once everything is settled."

He nodded, trying to believe what he did not feel. Was it placation? Just something to make both of them feel better? And... Would Mr. Paisley last long enough for everything to settle?

"I will see you on the morrow, my boy. Enjoy your new room, such as it is until your things arrive. The bed is made and dressed in fresh linens bought just this morning."

"Thank you, sir. Have a good evening."

A smile, a nod, and Mr. Paisley was away.

He locked the entrance to the Paisley Foundation, watched the founder get assistance into the carriage, and the carriage drive off.

He returned to the front desk, then turned and stared at the wall and its hidden panel to access his new room. Fresh paint, fresh wood, a fresh start.

He promptly dashed away from it and for the hidden stairs, bounding up to the fourth floor and reaching the landing out of breath. Didn't feel like running away anymore. Outrunning his sorrow? Yeah.

Mr. Smith Who Works The Front Desk by Jade Griffin

1893, September 4

Didn't sleep well in the guest room, or for very long. It was anxiety. Same reason he didn't feel like sleeping in his new room. Too much change going on, having recently gotten used to the everyday. So, he went somewhere more familiar. Not hungry, he showered and put his old clothes back on, then went down to the first floor. Unlocked the doors, sat at the front desk, and waited for everyone to arrive.

At 7 AM, the Victors arrived first, their vacation concluded. Senior issued a curt nod and Junior eyed him in confusion. Both carried an armload of supplies and continued to the elevator.

The Treasurer and Secretary arrived more or less at the same time just before 8 AM, followed by the three typists. He received nods and greetings but no conversation. Did the Corners know this would be his new place of residence? Did any of the employees?

President Young pushed through the glass entrance next and made straight for the front desk. "When Mr. Turner comes in, please send him up to my office."

A nod.

Mr. Young started away, paused, looked back at him, debated saying something, but pressed on to the elevator.

Agent Turner wandered in half an hour later. He delivered the message, noting Mr. Turner did not appear surprised by the summons. Instead, a hint of excitement in the Paisley agent's eyes.

When Mr. Paisley finally arrived, it was after 9 AM. The coachman helped the founder out of the carriage, grabbed a familiar box, and carried it into the Paisley Foundation behind Mr. Paisley. The old man walked slow and stiff. Concern choked him the closer his benefactor got, for it threw in his face how little time remained.

"Place it there, on the desk."

After following Mr. Paisley's instructions, the worn top hat was tipped in respect before the coachman proceeded out.

Mr. Paisley ignored the safety of distance and walked right up to him. "Before you fret, over something missing…" From behind, the founder pulled his long *katana* and set it with great respect atop the box before moving away and sitting at the nearest couch.

"Thank you. Wasn't sure if I should bring it myself. At my current size, it is difficult to conceal and draws too much attention." It certainly made Mr. Paisley walk funny, which had been disguised as old age hobbling.

"Indeed." The old man stood with a grunt. "Apologies, but this is when my absence starts in earnest. If there is nothing else before I go?"

He shook his head.

Mr. Paisley turned to go.

And reconsidered. "Sir?"

The founder paused.

"Be careful. Please. However much luck that amulet grants you, don't do anything risky."

Mr. Paisley chuckled. "I shall do my best. I do plan on having a nice meal with you, Mr. Smith, when this business has concluded."

When his benefactor exited, he sat for a moment, not willing to carry on as normal. One thing sat very clear, however. The *katana* could not very well be left out. Most people wouldn't even know what it was and might mess with it. They'd surely have questions – none of which he felt like answering or prompting.

He struggled the whole box of belongings to the floor and shoved it under the desk, then went to Acquisitions and found it lacking of the supplies he sought. To the Corners, he went. Avoided Treasurer Cunningham in favor of Secretary Midsommer, of whom he asked, "I'm in need of a hammer and nails. Might you know where they are?"

"Mrs. Cunningham has those in her office."

He gave a nod, hiding any reluctance, and went there. He avoided most interaction with her over the last few days, because of her great loss and because he still felt partially responsible.

At first sight of her, she looked tired but perfectly fit for work and eyed him inquisitively when he stood just outside her doorway.

"I'm looking for nails and a hammer."

With a soft smile, she pulled open a desk drawer and held out the hammer in one hand and a handful of nails in the other. "Mr. Paisley tasked you with a carpentry project alongside the other on the first floor?" she enquired.

He stared too long. Didn't know what to say. Just took the supplies, gave a nod, and left.

She didn't know. Didn't know that Mr. Paisley's life would soon come to an end. Might not even know the construction was to build a room for him to live in when the old man passed on. And she couldn't know. Until it could be announced in a meeting, there remained no way to explain his knowledge without mentioning how he knew her rescuer was going to die. He couldn't do that. Couldn't have her view him with regret, sadness, or even hatred.

Once back at the desk, he used the tools and a few scraps of leather found in Acquisitions to form a series of little straps and slid the *katana* gently in. Didn't wanna go in his new room. Didn't wanna have questions about his weapon. This was the best solution.

As for the other meager belongings, he had nothing of true value and didn't feel like doing anything with the remaining items. Mostly clothes. One photograph – of Mr. and Mrs. Paisley. He had no idea if the old man knew he took it. If so, hadn't cared to mention it. Perhaps he should move the items, at least into the room. And yet, the Paisley Foundation first floor got very little foot traffic in the way of people off the street. The agents weren't likely to touch the box. Tucked under the desk, most people wouldn't even see it.

The elevator opened during his internal debate. He swiveled about to see Mr. Young exit.

"Could you join me on the fourth floor, if you're available?"

A nod and he followed the Paisley president into the vertical conveyance.

Upon entering the first conference room, there lay a suit of nice clothes upon the large table. A suit his size, he noted while moving to the back of the room. When Mr. Young sat, so did he, at a sufficient distance away.

"It has been brought to my attention that you haven't an official position here at the Paisley Foundation. While you have filled whatever we've tossed your way, it's time to offer you a legitimate posting within our establishment. And, while there hasn't appeared to be much need in the past,

Mr. Smith Who Works The Front Desk by Jade Griffin

times are changing. Our reputation has grown, and we've printed some new pamphlets for the first floor." Mr. Young pulled one from an inner coat pocket. With an expert shove, the paper skittered across the table his way.

Picking it up, the leaflet's front displayed a photo of the Paisley Foundation building, and the back contained photos of each Corner. In the spot of Vice President was Agent Turner's dutiful face, so the man presumably received a promotion as well. The interior held the mission statement, brief history, and purpose of the Paisley Foundation but it was the inner fold with its photo of Mr. Paisley which caught his eye. Below the photograph lay the dates 1820-1893.

He pinned Mr. Young with a glare. Printing the old man's year of death before—

"I know what you must think of me, but I know what is coming. I won't speak of it again once we leave this room but, clearly, you are also aware, as I suspected. No need to ask how, and no need to judge each other on our actions. The matter brought to the table is that of your place here. You **do** have one, and are a valued member of this foundation. What I am more interested in is whether you will choose to remain here for the foreseeable future once our founder has… moved on. I am not asking what Mr. Paisley wants. I need to know if **you** are still willing to work with us and within our rules as long as your own are met. If so, there is an unclaimed desk on the first floor and a tailor-made suit here. Can't have our front desk employee wearing old attire, now, can we?"

On Mr. Young's approach, he had variable opinions. On his state of clothing, he could not argue. Not since before Mrs. Paisley died had he received new clothes.

Mr. Young continued, "If you accept, go change and a stack of paperwork will be waiting for you. If you decline, you know where the front doors are… but we would prefer a good-bye if you are so inclined. Know that this job – this lifestyle – isn't for everyone, Mr. Smith. There is no shame in knowing your limits. I will leave you to your decision."

He watched Mr. Young leave, watched the Paisley president look only ahead.

It was what he should be doing.

He stared at the suit made of very nice fabric in a shade of green so dark, it was almost black.

Did he want to work in this place once Mr. Paisley died? Where else would he go? He held no wants or desires for anything other than what he had, and those around him were trying to make it as stable as they could before even more change unsteadied his world. No, dammit, he did **not** want to pick up and start fresh in a new place!

So, he gathered up the clothes and made for the last guest room, shucked his old ones, and adorned his small form in the gifted wear.

Must've used the same tailor Mrs. Paisley patronized for his first set half a year ago, as the clothes fit very well. More than that, they felt right. This decision felt right. With a sigh that unburdened shoulders wound tight over the last several days, he made his way down to the front desk to see what sort of paperwork awaited.

It took only a few days to settle into the new routine. Rise early, dress, make the bed, brush teeth, leave the fourth floor room, sit at the front desk, ignore the new room at his back, greet all of the employees when they entered, attend to his front desk duties like answering the phone the two times it rang, sorting and filing paperwork, cleaning garbage bins, and then retire to the fourth floor guest room at the end of the hall each evening. All the while, the box stayed under the front desk and the secret room made just for him remained untouched by him and anyone else.

After nearly a week of routine, he broke the monotony by taking a book from Acquisitions to read in the evening. Read carefully, as the meticulously accurate Repository labeled it as a tome filled with knowledge of outer beings. Reaching a section describing an alien people he'd encountered on one of Heebs and Jeebs' weirder castings, he determined such knowledge was not likely to drive him insane and read the whole thing. Gave him terrible dreams. Refreshed memories, the sensation of tumbling through nothing, he woke with a scream caught in his throat and the blanket twisted about his legs. He stayed awake and returned the book before even the Victors arrived in the morning.

It was during an unstoppable yawn just past ten in the morning where he blinked and found Mr. Paisley opening the front doors.

Smiling, he stood and jogged over to join the slowed founder. Greatly slowed, it seemed.

"Good morning, Mr. Smith!" At least the old man's tone rang cheery. Happy even.

"And how has the recruit turned out?" he enquired with a bright smile. It really was nice to see Mr. Paisley again, despite how worrisomely slow his benefactor's cane-dependent plod toward the elevator became.

"Fair, I shall say," the founder replied in a sturdy voice. Sturdy and confident.

"Shall I let them know you are on your way up?"

Mr. Paisley paused and grinned, looked him up and down. "Fitting in well here, I see. Yes. Give them a ring, and feel free to join us. I'm sure there's quite a bit to catch up on."

He trotted over to the front desk and dialed Mr. Midsommer's number, told the secretary that Mr. Paisley had arrived, and hurried to catch the elevator to join the old man.

"I'm glad you decided to stay, my boy."

"I am as well. I like it here."

Mr. Paisley's beaming smile lasted even after the elevator door opened onto the fifth floor.

He watched the typists, saw them look away from their work briefly, catch sight of who arrived, and their posture straightened and smiles adorned their faces. Even the newest lady who started working only three days ago, taking Mark Cunningham's old desk. He realized Mr. Paisley's arrival to the fifth floor was for their benefit when the old man stayed near the elevator, smiling away, waiting for the Corners to join them and head down to the fourth floor to discuss current matters.

During the meeting, his attention remained divided between basking in the commonplace comfort of having the founder returned and marveling at such attentiveness to those employed at the Paisley Foundation. Mr. Paisley knew his importance to these people and assured such presence to bolster those brought low so recently.

It was the sudden silence which reoriented him to the here and now, then a moment of discomfiture as he realized the four Corners and Mr. Paisley were staring at him.

"Hm?" he enquired.

"Congratulations," Mr. Paisley prompted. "Mr. Young just informed me that you accepted the front desk posting."

"Uh... Yes. Thank you."

"Did you have a matter to bring to our attention, Mr. Smith? Something overly-distracting?" newly-appointed Vice President Turner enquired. The man was only trying to give him a chance to speak up, and perhaps give a good showing at the ex-Agent's first Corner meeting in front of Mr. Paisley.

"No, Mr. Turner. Except to extend my own congratulations. I'm sure you are filling the role of vice president nicely." He allowed them to see his mood shadow over once more, let them think the changing of the guards brought about a distant gaze. Honestly, it did. Too much change. Too many close people lost in such a short time, and one more to come. But they didn't know that. And they couldn't. He redoubled his efforts to focus on the matter at table; something about a suspicious theater performance in the area.

Halfway through determining which agents should be sent to investigate, the pen Mr. Paisley was holding slipped from a weakened grasp and rolled under the table.

"I'll get it," Mr. Midsommer told the founder before bending way down in his seat to collect the writing utensil. On the way back up, while Mr. Young reached for the glass of water nearest, Mr. Midsommer's head banged on the underside of the table. This startled Mr. Young, who bumped the glass, which fell to the floor and shattered.

He tensed, shot Mr. Paisley a look.

"I'm feeling rather tired and will leave this in your capable hands," the founder said, rising with effort and moving to the door.

He pushed up from his chair and squeezed by the confused faces of the others to meet his benefactor in the hallway. Not to stop the old man, but to walk with. To the elevator, too. However, the elevator would not open.

Mr. Paisley ignored the inconvenience and opened the panel to the hidden stairs. Thus began a slow descent with grunts of effort, wherein the founder told him, "That was no coincidence, as I am sure you are aware. Damnedest things have been happening all week."

"So, you feel it." A statement, not a question. In his experience, more sensitive folk could feel the creep of bad luck and death coming for them. That, or just put the facts together.

"I do. Perhaps it was not the best idea to make an appearance here."

"I disagree. They needed to see you, sir."

"As did you. I am aware. But they must learn to live without me. As must you. I will not be in to see them again, Mr. Smith. Can't jeopardize everything I've built here by spreading my bad luck."

"Sir, I think—"

"If they ask, make up any excuse you like, but I shall not jeopardize any others. You are an exception, and most likely immune to my misfortune, so I shall be honoring the promise of supper... As soon as an establishment will take my reservation."

He could not come up with anything reasonable to keep Mr. Paisley in the building, knew the founder's absence was for the best, and followed the old man to the entrance. Watched to make sure no carriage ran the old man down, cringed each time a person bumped into his benefactor on the crowded walkway, and hoped there'd be no issue wherever Mr. Paisley intended to go for the day.

The elevator door opened, working perfectly.

He turned for a look, saw Treasurer Cunningham exit with a pensive step.

On his way back to the front desk, she asked him, "You also feel something is wrong, Mr. Smith?"

He nodded, took his seat.

She sat at the nearest couch. "I asked the Corners their opinion, and if perhaps Mr. Midsommer might look into what may be going on. Mr. Young is disinclined to pursue such a method at this time and Mr. Midsommer agreed, but I'm worried. Did he say anything to you, before he left?"

"Concerned about the future, content so far with the progress of a new recruit he's personally reviewing, and doing his best not to worry anyone with his concerns. He isn't a young man. The stress and loss have visibly taken a toll. All of us can see that. He doesn't want us to worry about him." All of it true, and yet the real reason and truth remained hidden, thundering toward them like an unstoppable train.

Mrs. Cunningham gave a nod, concern shadowing her face. She returned to the elevator and left him be, his response perfectly acceptable.

In the quiet of the front desk, he sat and stared at his hands, the desktop, out the windows at the bustle of people, losing count of how many times he sighed his worry to the empty air. Emptiness pressed on him, and it lingered like the most consuming of unwanted guests.

Closing time happened promptly at 5 PM, but it could not come fast enough. He locked up after the last employees departed for the day. He retired to the room on the fourth floor, lay in bed, unable to sleep, to conjure any distraction away from the inevitable.

Mr. Smith Who Works The Front Desk by Jade Griffin

1893, September 11-12

A knock at the door jerked him awake. Confused, he waited, listened.

"Mr. Smith? Are you in there? It's past noon."

Shit! He scrambled up, grabbed his clothes, and threw them on quickly. "Just a moment!"

In under five minutes, he was out.

To the elevator they went together, so he felt it right to address the matter.

"I apologize. I haven't been sleeping well. Have I missed anything important?" he asked, entering the elevator when it opened.

"... No. We were concerned, as we hadn't seen you anywhere." The Paisley secretary followed beside him. "If you're feeling up to it, there are several files on your desk needing some attention, and one of our agents is bringing in a suspicious item within the hour which Mrs. Cunningham is waiting for."

"I shall get right to work. Has Mr. Paisley sent any word?"

"That he is resting and knows the place is well in hand. He asked about you. It's why I came looking. I apologize for waking you."

"I'm glad you did. I should not be lax in my duties here. How else are you to depend on me?"

"... Yes, but... Mr. Smith, don't forget that you must take care of yourself as well. Do you...? What I mean to say is... Are you in need of anything?"

He looked at Midsommer and blinked. Yes, he knew the Corners saw him as an equal, as was Mr. Paisley's plan from the start. Still, the every-now-and-again reminder that they cared about his well-being surprised him. It really shouldn't, because he felt he knew them. Just something else to get used to – that these people remained invested in his mental and physical health.

"Thank you, Mr. Midsommer. I appreciate the reminder but haven't any needs at this time. What about yourself?" Only right to return the query.

"I... I am concerned, and confused, about a great many things in the last week, to be honest. I've never had any doubts about Mr. Paisley, and yet... Something happened during the meeting with Evan de Lorraine. Something other than Mark Cunningham's death. Something worse. Treasurer Cunningham has asked me to attempt clairvoyance or psychometry to look into the matter, despite President Young telling us to leave it be. She won't let it rest, because she believes it will help Mr. Paisley. There was a single item that returned with him – the carbon sphere. If it really is all that remains of Evan de Lorraine, it'd be unwise to use psychometry on it. The mental backlash of experiencing a person's final moments can be detrimental. Given this, and that you've spent a fair amount of time with him, has he spoken to you about what happened there?"

He sighed, shook his head. "No. He never spoke of it. I don't expect him to. Mr. Midsommer, this will have to fall under one of the main tenets of the Paisley Foundation; that this will remain a thing unknown. While there isn't a problem in questioning things of this nature, Mr. Paisley deems it unsuitable for passing on. I trust him and his judgment on the matter. It sounds like President Young also trusts Mr. Paisley." And he stared at the secretary with querying eyes.

Mr. Smith Who Works The Front Desk by Jade Griffin

"No. You're right. Of course, Mr. Smith."

When the elevator opened, Midsommer stayed while he exited. He went to his desk, heard only the elevator close and take the secretary with it.

He sighed. Another one sufficiently mollified. He wondered if Agent—if Vice President Turner would come at him next.

No one did, and it remained a fair quiet day. What little there was left of it, having slept almost half of it away. Careless. None of the guest rooms were big enough to accommodate his need for space. He must consider that…

He turned and looked at the wall at his back. Someone else may have already considered that. Could the hidden door be locked from the other side?

The glass entrance to the Paisley Foundation opened. A courier breezed in on a purposeful stride which took the young man right to his desk.

"Telegram for a Mr. Smith Who Works The Front Desk?"

He held out his hand.

The courier handed the missive over without batting an eye, swiveled on smart heels, and left.

He opened the telegram.

W45H1NT 259
CHICAGO ILLS SEPT 11
MR SMITH WHO WORKS THE FRONT DESK
     CARE PAISLEY FOUNDATION   CHICAGO ILLS
PLEASE JOIN MR PAISLEY AT THE RENNAISSANCE FOR A BLACK TIE DINING EVENT 11PM SEPT 11 WEAR ANYTHING BUT BLACK
                     MR ARTHUR PAISLEY
3129AP

Formal event, eh? And don't wear black? He grinned at the invite, appreciative of his benefactor's attempt to resist social standards, having never seen this side of the old man. Not normally one to go against the norm himself. Also, it just wouldn't fit timewise to get a whole new suit his size in such a short time, so the almost-black green suit would have to do. Perhaps a different tie could be acquired. Would there be one in Acquisitions?

Finished with daily work, he headed up to the second floor to look for a tie. Found several that would do but opted for the gold one. Looked better than the red, burgundy, or chartreuse ones he located, plus it had tiny paisley patterns on it. Not enchanted ones. Just normal paisley, but it complimented his suit well, he thought.

While the invitation listed a time quite late in the evening, he surmised the purpose was so he and Mr. Paisley could have a quiet time perhaps free of onlookers. Perhaps his benefactor even paid for a private table or room to accommodate his particular need for space.

After 5 PM, he wished every exiting Corner a good evening. Vice President Turner, last to leave, cast a glance back at him but did not start any conversation. Perhaps wondering what the person at the front desk was doing so late and showing no sign of finishing for the day. He decided to ask sometime soon just how much Mr. Turner knew.

Locking up for the evening, he collected a map from Acquisitions and determined the best route to get to The Renaissance Hotel. Next, he gathered his suit and borrowed tie, cleaned his shoes to a nice shine, made certain his hair was as combed as he could get the slight curl in the front, tied the tie while fighting back the instant reminder of the

Mr. Smith Who Works The Front Desk by Jade Griffin

loss of Sergei Grummond, and sat patiently at the front desk. He looked up behind him at the clock. 6:49 PM. Not tired but needing something to do, he wandered up to the Repository to read about the copper bowl brought in earlier which Mrs. Cunningham catalogued into Acquisitions. That distracted him for another hour. Poking around Secretary Midsommer's office, he located something new: a romance novel. Bit of a surprise, but not quite to his tastes. Still, it was a distraction… until glancing at the clock showed him the hour of 10:40 PM!

Racing downstairs as fast as he could, it did not slip his mind to relock the Paisley Foundation. Speeding along the sidewalks, he happily noted very few people out so late. No need to get close to anyone. But, upon crossing the third street on the way, the high tweet of a police whistle pierced the pleasant night air. He turned and saw a policeman jogging toward him. No doubt a truancy officer thinking some kid running around out late and up to no good.

Though he carried the telegram, he had no proof he was the missive's recipient, nor any identifiers linking him as an employee of the Paisley Foundation, so he ran like the Devil chased him.

Despite the disadvantage of looking young, his diminutive size afforded him a better chance of hiding and the speed and agility to outrun even a police officer. Luck held with him there, but vanished the closer he got to The Renaissance, for he tripped and fell into a puddle, ripping the pants and skinning both knees.

Cursing under his breath, he wondered if Mr. Paisley was wrong about the bad luck not affecting the creator of it.

Proceeding to The Renaissance's front doors, two men in hotel uniforms moved to block his path.

"Where d'ya think yer goin', squirt?"

Eyeing him with suspicion, he knew there would be no darting past them, so he displayed the telegram and replied with a calm, "I have a message for Mr. Paisley who is dining in the restaurant."

The left one with the mustache said, "Little young for courier work, and out a bit late, dontcha think?"

"My brother's sick and I wanna prove I can do the job just as good as him. We all gotta make bread, right?" He put on a determined expression to fit the lie.

"Oh? And what's he sick with?"

"Honestly, Mister? Love-sick. Out with some bird instead of doin' his job. Well, I want his job and I'm out here proving I got what it takes." Bit over the top but his inspiration came from the romance novel Secretary Midsommer kept in the office.

The two front doorsmen shared a look. Mustache smirked and held the double doors open for him. "Alright, little man. In ya get. And, if you're real professional, you'll find Lettie in the back might let you take something from the pie counter. Tell 'er Ritchie says hi."

Thank God his charm was still intact. With a nod and a grin, he dashed inside and in an elevator in two breaths.

He let out a big sigh when the elevator let him out onto a floor dominated by a large foyer thick with cigar smoke. Coughing, he waded toward the lit restaurant sign visible through the heady cloud. Not enough cover to slip by the head waiter whom he thought looked distracted enough examining a seating chart at the thin podium.

Mr. Smith Who Works The Front Desk by Jade Griffin

The pencil-thin man with slicked-back hair slid in his path and asked, "Can I help you?"

"Yes. Mr. Paisley is expecting me this evening. I'm Mr. Smith." He held up the telegram, hoping a direct, confident approach would work.

The head waiter spun toward the restaurant. "This way, sir."

He followed into what was indeed a fancy place with pristine, white tablecloths, wood panels and wallpapered scenes of earlier Chicago days, candlelight at each table and in wall sconces, and quite a few people lingered in the place. He worried briefly on being too close to other patrons, but the head waiter led him all the way to a private room, the door of which held open for him, the waiter bowing him in.

Unused to such treatment, he paused until Mr. Paisley's hearty chuckles issued from within the room.

"Laughing at my expense so early?" he asked, striding in.

The partition clicking shut behind him, he smiled at first sight of his benefactor, dressed in a tweed charcoal-hued suit and red tie, seated at one end of a long table, the place lit cheerily by electric lights instead of candles. The one nearest to Mr. Paisley flickered.

"Good of you to make it... eventually," was the old man's reply amid more chuckles.

He sat at the far end of the table, at least ten feet away, and settled on a smirk. "There were a few snags. Not easy for a kid to get around late at night these days."

"Indeed, but I did tell them to expect a very young person as my guest and that he would call himself Mr. Smith."

"Oh, the waiter wasn't the issue. A truancy officer and front doorsmen were a little tricky, as was a pesky puddle."

"All of which no doubt worked up an appetite. I have a bit of a reputation here, so they don't mind staying open a bit late for me. Order what you like, Mr. Smith." The old man indicated the menu positioned at that end of the table.

He selected three things in as many seconds and placed the menu flat. Blocked his view previously and he didn't care to stare at it. "Care to give details on this recruit, or the purpose behind such an elaborate means of hiring someone?"

"I sought someone to both manage my estate and fill the position of night watchman, as it were."

"Night watchman of your estate?"

"Of the Paisley Foundation. As you currently reside there, I needed someone with integrity, discretion, strength, and fortitude."

"And you believe you've found such a person in less than fourteen days?"

"Twelve, and at the expense of more than I'd have cared to give up, but yes. We shall see. As of now, my distance from the recruit is necessary."

The light behind Mr. Paisley executed a brief flash, muted pop, and went dark.

"The real test is if the recruit decides to apply to the Paisley Foundation. That is still up for debate, but I will not have my lack of potential swaying anyone important to the future of what I have built."

A knock preceded the head waiter's entrance. The man took their orders and promptly left.

Mr. Paisley regarded him a moment before asking, "You don't wish to have something more elegant than coffee, bread, and tomato soup?"

Mr. Smith Who Works The Front Desk by Jade Griffin

Compared to his benefactor's order of turtle soup, quail with asparagus, claret, and three types of fruity gelatin, it appeared quite meager. He shrugged. "You said order whatever I'd like. I find that I like simple things."

Mr. Paisley's grin spread even further, if that were even possible.

While they sat alone, he thought to bring up all manner of things to the table during their wait, starting with, "Why do you have a front desk if it isn't anyone's job to sit there?"

His benefactor fell quiet, straightened a relaxed posture, and they locked eyes. "It isn't in the Paisley Foundation records, but Maisey would sit there. She delighted in greeting people, despite that we don't often receive clients."

"I'm sorry to bring her up, if it is painful."

"It isn't painful, my boy. Not for me. I was concerned that it might upset you."

A second light – the one nearest Mr. Paisley – popped and the room grew a bit dimmer.

"I appreciate your concern, but this is an open forum, I take it? Not just for myself but for you as well. Anything you want to get off your chest?"

"Actually, yes."

But the head waiter and two other servers arrived with their meal and conversation came to a halt.

As the staff moved about the table depositing the soups, claret, and his water, the table was bumped hard enough that Mr. Paisley's cane rolled to the side and tripped one of the waiters, causing them to spill the hot soup on his host's pants. The room erupted into shouts from the head waiter, a yell from Mr. Paisley at the instant burn, profuse apologies as the other waitstaff attempted to aid him, and one of them falling backward into the tray, flipping it into the air, and caught at the last second by the quick head waiter. Mr. Paisley's glass of claret, however, did not survive and wound up shattered on the floor.

Waffling between fuming at the staff and bowing out profuse apologies to Mr. Paisley, the head waiter ushered the offenders away. Backing out of the room in a great bow, the head waiter told each patron, "I will personally bring your selections and everything will be free of charge. So very sorry, Mr. Paisley. I will move you to a new table right away."

"Not necessary, Mr. Garrett."

"But... the glass!"

"Accidents happen, Mr. Garrett. It shall remain on the floor for now, and the charge shall remain on my account. Don't be too hard on your staff."

"Thank you, Mr. Paisley. You are too gracious." Bowing two more times, the head waiter left and the door shut with barely a sound.

"Are you alright?" he asked.

"Minor burns. Nothing to be overly-concerned about, though I don't favor smelling of turtle soup. Despite the misfortune, I do intend to enjoy this meal... or as much as I can."

The accidents, bad luck, and dying lightbulbs put him on edge. "Perhaps we should move to another room."

Mr. Paisley's left brow rose. "Do you believe it will matter?"

"I... I don't know."

"We both know what is happening. I for one find it fascinating."

"Fascinating?" Anger bubbled up. He clenched his jaw to contain it.

"Yes." Mr. Paisley's voiced opinion stood confident.

Any further talk was interrupted by the head waiter knocking, then opening the door quickly and wringing distressed hands. "I beg your pardon, sir… We… we seem to be out of asparagus, and the quail has burned. I sincerely apologize, Mr. Paisley. This has never happened before. I…"

His benefactor sighed wistfully. "Perhaps it is best if we depart. Mr. Garrett, it is no fault of your own, but bad luck is following me today. Mr. Smith, shall we go for a walk?"

He got up from his seat but asked, "Is that wise?"

Mr. Paisley flashed a smile. "I do believe it is."

Ignoring the head waiter's cascade of sputtering apologies and self-mortifications, they left the restaurant.

"I couldn't bear for the place to catch on fire because of me, or any further mishaps to the staff. It is a pity I couldn't let you sample their fare. Here, take this and purchase us something from that cart." Mr. Paisley pointed out the direction and started passing him a few coins. They slipped from the old man's grasp and rolled down into a nearby drain. "Drat."

Having rather enough, he ran in front of his benefactor, who started walking again, and held up both hands. "Mr. Paisley, I must caution you against any action at all. Anything you plan to do could end your life."

With a patient sigh, the old man approached very close. "I am currently enjoying these final hours watching how many ways the universe tries to end me. While I don't encourage my death and will step aside any time something tries to fall on me, we both know that this is inevitable."

Fear prompted him, and he knew it, but he asked anyway, because he didn't want this to be so. "Sir? Is there nothing you can do?"

Hands settling into pants pockets, his benefactor replied, "I believe I've done enough, don't you? Built a foundation bearing my name and ideals, filled it with people who believe the same to carry on my lineage, and have lived an adventurous and caring life for most of my seventy-two years. If you mean is there anything I can do to stop the creep of death? Nothing I would care to try. Anything attempted would either rip me horribly to shreds or harm those around me. I shall not avoid this, as I endeavor to leave peacefully. *Amor fati*, my boy. I embrace my fate. And, with that, I have another choice spot to finish our evening, if you'll oblige."

He felt like rebelling against the old man's attitude, knew it was selfish to deny Mr. Paisley whatever the founder wanted in his last days or hours, and gave a resolute sigh. Wondered how late it could be. Thought on asking Mr. Paisley to consult the pocket watch poking up from the charcoal suit and decided it didn't matter. Time was short enough. So, he gave the old man a smile and nod. "Stay here. I've got some money on me."

Dashing across the street, he flashed his coins and told the vendor of the red and white-canopied cart, "Two of whatever you've got left."

The man, who had been leaning over trying to pull at some internal area of what looked like a glass-encased popcorn popper, straightened and looked him over. Speaking with a German accent, the vendor replied, "That is exactly it, young man. I have quite a bit left and cannot get the confounded confection out."

He dared to approach and have a look, and then the smell hit him. His shoulders sagged, a nostalgic smile blossomed, and he leaned in eagerly to behold a glorious mass of popcorn and peanuts all stuck together with molasses.

"I have tried keeping it warmed but it is too sticky and keeps clumping up."

"Well, um, I'm sure you'll get it right soon. I'd love to have some if you'd care to chip me off some? It smells just like, um… Smells real good!" Couldn't help his mouth watering, especially as supper was out the window. On top of that, this smelled **exactly** how he remembered!

The man obliged his request, mentioned something about taking the cart to the World's Columbian Exposition, and handed him two paper bags of the stuff. Oh, the scent of molasses over the peanuts and popcorn wafting from the packages kept him grinning all the way back to Mr. Paisley.

His benefactor shared in his joy and the snack as they stood about on the street, especially at his sigh of absolute pleasure at the first bite.

"Had this before?" Mr. Paisley asked.

A nod.

"You've had this where you're from. I know a reminiscent look when I see one," the Paisley Foundation founder pressed.

Another nod. "Almost tastes the same."

"Shall we? Where I have in mind is not far."

He followed an acceptable distance behind Mr. Paisley as the old man started off.

"We were interrupted in the restaurant, Mr. Smith, but I'd like to continue," his benefactor said upon very carefully looking both ways and starting across the street.

It wasn't the easiest to hear the old man so he jogged closer, knowing he could stay within five feet for at least a short time. Plus, he wanted to keep an eye out for anything coming at Mr. Paisley, despite the streets being practically empty. He started counting in his head.

"Maisey told me it bothers you a great deal that you do not know how old you are and that is why you don't care to state your birthday. It occurs to me in my seventy-two years of wisdom that you cannot possibly be more than half my age, Mr. Smith. Possibly no more than two decades old. No matter your perception, you do not carry yourself like an immortal being. I should know, having encountered a few. Many things still surprise you, and you care about your fellow man. You care a great deal. I hope that settles your mind that you are not someone of indescribable age."

"Thank you." He meant it, too. "It does weigh on me at times, but I'll choose to believe in your reasoning and experience."

Mr. Paisley beamed. "Good lad! Makes me feel better calling you that, though I daresay I'd call anyone younger than me a lad."

As his benefactor crossed from W. Lake onto N. Franklin St, he spoke up. "You're going back to the Paisley Foundation."

"Yes. No one is there, and I have measures to ensure nothing untoward occurs."

Given the confident way the old man tapped the amulet under the white dress shirt, he also put his trust there and reluctantly followed, but with the required distance between them.

Mr. Paisley waved him ahead when they came to the front doors, which he opened. He locked them promptly while Mr. Paisley leaned heavily on the silver-handled cane and started a plod to the elevator.

He trotted after but advised, pointing out the vertical conveyance, "I don't think that is the best choice right now."

"I don't think I can make it all the way without it," Mr. Paisley admitted feebly, leaning against the wall until the elevator opened.

When the founder entered and reached for the switch to select a floor, he made his choice and got in, too. He started his count.

As soon as the mechanical door closed, he knew it was a mistake. Felt it even before the entire elevator carriage jerked to a halt. The one lightbulb in the metal box flickered. Panic hit him.

"Sir, if you boost me up, I can get out at that hatch there and perhaps climb to another floor."

"No, Mr. Smith. Just wait a moment and have a little faith."

"Faith in what?" he demanded. "Faith in God? In any higher power?"

Mr. Paisley replied, "Faith in me. That I will spare you any blame, that I have orchestrated these remaining moments with great purpose and am using my bad luck to full advantage. So far, it appears to be going as planned."

He stared at the founder in disbelief. "You wanted to be trapped in here with me? How could this possibly spare me any blame? I have less than eight minutes to get away or—"

"Or you'll kill me? No. You will not. May we continue our chat while we wait?"

"Chat? Sir, I can't just stand here and—"

"What do you know about them, the two entities in that device?"

"I... Not very much. Please, sir!" He couldn't go through this again. He **wouldn't**! Eyes darting about the secure metal cage, he saw no way out but up and that meant climbing on Mr. Paisley to reach it. Dammit!

"You should know they aren't the only things which eat potential or sway luck." Looking over a shoulder, the founder eyed empty air with wariness. "Sometimes I believe I feel it; one of those things, lingering, drawing out what little I have. No substantial evidence, but it is as if I feel it in my bones."

"Mr. Paisley... Arthur... Just give me a boost, okay?" He tried a lighter tone, trying to disguise his rising panic.

The founder took two steps, stood right in front of him, placed both hands on his slim shoulders. "Mr. Smith, stop. Let it happen."

"I can't! I—"

The old man pulled him into a strong hug. "You can, son. Just stay right here with me."

He wanted to beat at Mr. Paisley's sides, force the old man to let him go, but ended up crying into the comforting embrace instead. Why? Why did Mr. Paisley have to go, too?

Five minutes. Six. Seven. The light flickered rapidly and blinked out, showering them in darkness. The trickle of tears gave way to a gasp. The elevator creaked under the strain of its luckless passenger. His grip on the old man tightened.

"There, there. I've got you."

But the founder let go with one hand! He didn't know what was going on, what to do!

"Just wait, and have some faith," he heard calm in the dark as the other wrinkled hand let him go.

He felt like a child, terrified in the dark, terrified of losing the person closest to him, terrified of causing that loss yet again. He held Mr. Paisley with every bit of will and strength he possessed.

The elevator lightbulb blinked back on.

How...? Daring to hope, he looked up.

Mr. Paisley held the luck amulet in both hands, admiring the glint of the large, faceted garnet in the elevator's illumination. "Like me, this pretty talisman is no more than an empty container. Eh... Not entirely empty yet."

Mr. Paisley unscrewed a top to the amulet and knocked back what was most likely a shot of alcohol. Strong alcohol, given the face his benefactor made.

Mr. Paisley winced, "Not the most pleasant stuff, but I supposed it isn't meant to be."

"I've never seen you drink before," he said, baffled by the act.

Mr. Paisley's brows rose. "Oh, this? I suppose there is a poison for every occasion, my boy."

He never thought alcohol would make a difference, except to dull the senses, so how in the world did a drink – or, more accurately, holding the amulet with the pure intent of drinking the contents – reverse the run of bad luck? "Was that... Did you drink a potion?"

"Of a sort."

"But you said... Sir, if there was a way all this time to reverse what I did—"

"I'll have you know I did this all to myself," the old man stated with a measure of pride.

The metal carriage began its ascent, but the founder stepped over to it and manually halted their journey.

He continued to stare, dumbfounded.

Mr. Paisley chuckled, in a mood even more carefree after the rejuvenating draught. "Such a face! Further proof that you are nowhere near my age. I have learned to embrace change instead of fighting it. At the very least, I have learned to use change to my advantage and that is saying something. But, now, I am very curious about what new adventures await beyond. Have you ever considered an afterlife, Mr. Smith?"

He had no response. Only a growing need to move away. Nine minutes. Could he possibly trick Mr. Paisley in that time, get to the controls?

"I have." The founder reclined against the elevator's control panel, blocking it completely. "Given that ghosts do in fact exist, souls undoubtedly persist. Seen them chained to objects. Released one or two of them, off to wherever souls go when their way becomes clear. I have every hope of seeing my dear Maisey again."

As the last seconds slipped away, all effort and care left him. He gave in to the inevitable and, in the far private of his mind, safe from bringing up his own fears and sorrows, agreed that it was a nice hope to have.

More seconds ticked past.

Silence filled the elevator. Silence... and nothing more. He stared at his left arm, yanked the sleeve back, saw the damn thing still attached, and yet...

"The device... It isn't activating!"

Mr. Smith Who Works The Front Desk by Jade Griffin

"I should expect not, as I have no remaining potential, my boy." Mr. Paisley turned to the elevator controls and set them to the fifth floor. As it took them up, the founder continued with, "You see, I have taken the liberty of poisoning myself and will soon be dead. I was quite serious when I stated I would go on my own terms and these are the terms I have chosen. I do have a final request – that you sit beside this old man in his final hours? Would you do me the honor, son?"

"The drink... was..."

"Poison. Yes. Bought from a very reputable apothecary."

The elevator opened. Mr. Paisley stepped out and looked back at him.

He couldn't help staring. At the audacity, and the generosity. Mr. Paisley, no longer affected by the potential-draining device, had taken complete control of the end. The founder walked and talked with more strength and surety, holding the cane instead of relying on it. Whatever the poison, it seemed to grant a little boon in this precious time together.

The elevator door started closing.

He leaped out before they shut the moment away and found himself inches from the man who took him in.

Mr. Paisley grinned down at him, placed a hand on his shoulder. "This way, Mr. Smith."

To the hidden egress the founder led. Once inside the secret stairwell, a second previously-unseen hatch was revealed. He followed the old man up a new staircase which led to a door. Opening it, a soft, chilly breeze greeted him like a long-lost friend. Fresh air, open space, and the closeness of a person he cared about left him standing speechless on the roof of the Paisley Foundation. From this height, the little blips of streetlamp light dotted pathways crisscrossing the entire city. Some buildings – hulking shadows against the starry sky – held lights of their own as whomever inside worked very early. The World's Columbian Exposition he'd heard so much about and was not likely to attend stood out in the distance, lit with electric lights and shining like a white city all its own, one giant ferris wheel similarly lit and standing as a beacon to the people, to him. He didn't know when day might break but he felt oddly confident they would both bear witness.

Mr. Paisley chuckled. "Good to see you appreciating the view, my boy. There. Let us sit there."

The founder pointed out an area where a blanket lay, held in place by two small baskets, the scene lit by a dim lantern hanging to the right of the roof access. When the old man eased down on a groan, he followed.

"Seems ages since last I came up here," Mr. Paisley reminisced. "I proposed to Maisey on a rooftop. She loved heights."

Wading through the shock of the poisoning and the fragile relief that the device would not be taking anything from his benefactor, he latched onto the old man's wrinkled hand.

Mr. Paisley looked down at him with sympathy. "My poor Mr. Smith… How long it has been since you've allowed yourself to be close to someone."

"Two decades," he muttered, a smile leaking out. Despite everything, or due to everything, tossing the elusive timeframe back at the founder seemed rather funny in the moment. Sad and funny at the same time, humor won out.

Mr. Smith Who Works The Front Desk by Jade Griffin

Mr. Paisley thought so as well, for chuckles bubbled up and ended in a pleasant sigh. "Do help yourself to the snacks. I surmised my bad luck would not grant me an evening meal and would likely ruin yours, so I had Mr. Midsommer leave some things up here. Just some simple things."

He thought he caught his benefactor wink at him before he opened the nearest basket. Inside were some of his favorites, and all of them simple – an orange, a buttery roll, a container of water, a paring knife, a fork, and one surprise – a small cake. He pulled it out to show Mr. Paisley and found the old man displaying one as well.

The founder beamed and told him, "Happy birthday, for all of the missed birthdays. And happy death day to me. I plan to celebrate, Mr. Smith. This is a triumph, after all. I have built so much and even managed to cheat that impossible device you're currently stuck with. Ha! Not even the great Evan de Lorraine could counter the confounded contraption, and yet I did."

Mr. Paisley's smug expression did not last long, given that the impending death reminder brought his own mood low. To cheer him, the founder said, "Have hope for the future, my boy. Someone – and I hope soon – will find a way to remove it. To us!" And, silly old man, used the cake like a glass and offered it high like cheering a toast.

He did the same.

"It is quite lovely. The bakery down the street makes wonderful cakes."

He nodded.

Mr. Paisley set the plate aside and turned toward him. "Now, I only have an estimation on the effective timing of this poison. I feel as though my time is growing ever short. Is there anything you'd like to get off your chest? Anything you'd like to know? Anything in the world?"

It didn't take long for something to pop into his head. "Why me?"

Mr. Paisley blinked at him. "Why did the universe plop you into my field? I haven't the slightest idea. Why did we take you in? Anyone could see you were in need. You were also fascinating. Still are! And you are, above all, a good person who deserves good people around you. People you can trust. I do hope you see I am leaving you in trusted company."

Another nod. "But why do you look on me as your most prized person? I haven't been here nearly as long as Mr. Midsommer, or even Mrs. Cunningham."

"My relationship with Tricia Cunningham has never been as close as we'd have preferred, Maisey and I. True, we saved her, but she has her own legacy to break from in order to truly find herself. You, on the other hand... You really are who I prize most in this world, Mr. Smith. I would hate to see this foundation go to ruin but you... It would devastate me if anything happened to you. Maisey felt the same way. If only briefly, it has been a pleasure and a delight being in your company and taking you in as if the son we always wanted."

Conflicting emotions hit him. Anger that the old man saw him as a son and treated him so but never had the balls to say it to his face before drinking poison, and such profound sorrow that the man before him would soon be dead. He couldn't think of anything to ask or that he wanted to know. He just wanted Mr. Paisley to not die and knew that was impossible.

Mr. Smith Who Works The Front Desk by Jade Griffin

No words were needed. The old man scooted closer and pulled him near to lean against. He appreciated it, needing the hug. Same for Mr. Paisley, who conveyed in that one act the depth of love felt. Out of everyone in the world, Mr. Paisley chose him to spend a final day with.

"How have you enjoyed the room I had built for you?" his benefactor broke through the silence.

He truly thought of lying, but the pause grew and revealed the truth.

Mr. Paisley's inquisitive face fell. "I see. You haven't been in to see it at all?"

He shook his head.

"My poor son, I do hope you will."

When Mr. Paisley spoke nothing further, he frowned in concern, for the man stared off toward the creeping dawn. Where had time gone?

"If you could do one thing for me, son?" the old man started, voice thin, drifting. "Just live. Try your best to live life to its fullest. You are still very young. Yes, you have been whisked around to places and times exotic and vast, but you've not had a chance yet to truly live and enjoy life."

"I'll... try."

"Try hard. Our time is so brief when one looks back. Try very hard."

He and Mr. Paisley fell to silence wherein they both watched the color of dawn. The chill started to get to him, too, and he leaned a bit into Mr. Paisley's side. It wasn't enough, and time slipped fast and rare, so he wrapped his arms around the old man, squeezed good, and showed just how much it all meant. Squeezed him until Mr. Paisley started to let go.

Mr. Smith Who Works The Front Desk by Jade Griffin

"I planned this all, you know... Sunrise." The old man's face wrinkled further with a bit of a smile, eyes pulled away to somewhere beside them. "We were always such night owls... Weren't we, Maisey..."

A strange sound – an odd exhale – and Mr. Paisley slumped away from him, onto the blanket.

He didn't let panic ruin these last moments. He lay down beside the old man, took one cool hand in his, and wrapped his other arm around the lax body. Not a hug but a hold. Holding on. He held Mr. Paisley until the pulse slowed to nothing, the skin grew cold, and the sun burned his eyes with a flood of morning light when it crested nearby taller buildings.

Not since Sergei Grummond – not since Mrs. Paisley. No, even long before that. How had it been so long since he'd a proper chance to grieve? So much sorrow... He felt so punched by the aloneness, it poured from him in an unstoppable torrent. He barely took note when Mr. Midsommer knelt beside him, urged him to come inside. Didn't ask how the Paisley secretary knew where to find them. Didn't say a word to anyone. Wanted to run, to hide, but that part of his life – the running – was over. Mr. Paisley wanted him to enjoy life. And he would try. Just not today.

Where he ended up finding a modicum of comfort, ended up being the most unlikely of places. The other Corners must have searched the entire building before discovering him shedding grief in the office of the Paisley Foundation president. He knew Mr. Paisley sat here for a time and perhaps that is what drew him to such a station.

Upon finding him in the seat, Mr. Young and the others backed out and left him be. Didn't ask him to leave or if he needed anything, knowing this was a time for emotional space as well as his usual physical requirement. They obliged it beautifully, his quiet sobs uninterrupted.

Mr. Smith Who Works The Front Desk by Jade Griffin

1893, September 16

A date had been set. Two more weeks until the funeral. Needed time to invite anyone of note, to prepare the press, send telegrams and notices, keep an eye out for the elusive recruit who'd only spoken to Mr. Young so far, and a million other things before interring the founder's ashes beside the wife's. He played an important role in such communication, and the decision on what to do with the carbon sphere which was once Evan de Lorraine. Mr. Midsommer said it should go to Mrs. Cunningham, but she wanted nothing to do with it. He suggested it sit as a reminder in Mr. Young's office. A reminder of power and knowledge backfiring.

Such a busy time, the last few days. More people than he'd ever seen or spoken with in this time stopped by to confirm if the rumor held truth and to offer condolences. Many asked for more details and he readily referred each one to President Young, Vice President Turner, or Secretary Midsommer. He secured travel to the mausoleum, not only for the remains but for the Corners, agents, typists, and the Victors… but not himself. Just tried not to think about it. Press on. Just get through the day and on to the next. It wasn't living, but…

Wasn't living.

Mr. Paisley wanted him to really live and enjoy life and here he sat staring at the old man's last gift to him. Like an unopened present when you knew your parents were never coming home…

No. He promised he'd try and this wasn't trying.

Mr. Smith Who Works The Front Desk by Jade Griffin

In the end, he admitted to himself the reason: purposeful avoidance, because of the reminder of permanency. Enough. It was time.

Just after dawn, he made his way to the wall behind his desk. And stared at it. There it waited for him, because Mr. Paisley built it for him… Reluctance unjustified, he grabbed the hidden pull and opened the secret room.

The scent of freshly painted wood hit him. Inside, he found not a small space but one the size of three rooms, complete with ample ceiling space. Located a switch for electric lights and flipped it on. There on the side wall sat an open door leading to a private water closet. Further in, near the center, Mr. Paisley had the same practice pole set up for him to continue his personal training with the *katana*. Also, a bed, a bureau with mirror, and nothing else. Almost nothing else. He spied a small book atop the bed. On the cover, written by hand in black ink:

Life Lessons for Mr. Smith

Surveying the gift amid the bare accommodations, the emptiness and unbustliness of the area – an area made especially for him to do with as he saw fit – and couldn't help a tightening throat. This wasn't the Paisley Estate, and it wasn't like anyplace he'd ever been in his life. The people here put out effort to make him feel welcome and to create a private space for him. At the Paisley Estate, he always felt like a guest. Here, it was different.

Such thoughts brought on melancholy, but he shoved them aside. One thing became especially important in that moment.

He turned around and left the hidden room, went to the new and very large front desk, pulled out the pair of scissors from the desk drawer, and returned to the portal of his own space. Another glance at the Spartan area before placing himself snug against the doorframe. The scissors came up and struck just above his head. Turning about, he carved a bit more depth to the divot made in the inner entryway. Just like how he planned to carve his own niche further into this foundation. Now it felt more permanent, more like home.

He'd just shut the hidden passage when movement at the front of the building caught his eye.

A nervous man lingered there with darting eyes and reluctant steps. No hat despite the rain. Dark-haired head soaked by the light drizzle, it indicated a longer time out in the weather. Not only did this person need some kind of special assistance with an obvious problem, but it might also be a very interesting problem.

The man swiveled around and pressed against the glass to peer inside.

Curious what problem the man might bring them, he jogged to the front doors and unlocked them, holding them open to encourage entry.

"Is… Is this the Paisley Foundation?" Reluctant, but another glance about and the guy hurried in. A slight accent leaked through. Italian?

"It is." He started counting in his head but smiled while leading the man to the back of the lobby. "I'm Mr. Smith Who Works The Front Desk. How can we help you?"

END

NOTE:

For those curious what Mr. Paisley did in those last days absent from the Paisley Foundation, pick up a copy of *A Lone Collection*:
https://www.drivethrurpg.com/product/451500/A-Lone-Collection?affiliate_id=3161774

Coming Soon!

Amor Fati: Embraced Fate (Call of Cthulhu tabletop roleplaying campaign)
Amor Fati #5: Hound Of Fate (Call of Cthulhu tabletop roleplaying game)
A Lone Recruit (solo tabletop roleplaying game)
Touch Of Paisley – an NPC anthology (collection of short stories)

Mr. Smith Who Works The Front Desk by Jade Griffin

Bibliography

The Tsuba the Katana and the Samurai Soul part 3 - The Ethnic Home
https://www.theethnichome.com/the-tsuba-the-katana-and-the-samurai-soul-part3/

Ellis Island history
https://en.wikipedia.org/wiki/Ellis_Island

Kenjutsu vs Kendo
https://www.youtube.com/watch?v=mY3t1TnMYHI

Brief history of Chicago trash
https://news.wttw.com/2020/05/28/ask-geoffrey-brief-history-chicago-trash

Cracker Jack history
https://en.wikipedia.org/wiki/Cracker_Jack

Mr. Smith Who Works The Front Desk by Jade Griffin

About the Author

Though her usual genre is sci-fi and fantasy, discovering the tabletop roleplaying game *Call of Cthulhu©* Chaosium has lit Jade Griffin's imagination down a darker path of Lovecraftian horror. She has published the six adventures so far in a series of *Call of Cthulhu©* ttrpgs, starting with Taken For Granite on http://drivethrurpg.com with the campaign due out December 2024.

Her debut into horror began with *The Journals of Lacy Anderson Moore: Monster Hunter of the 1800s* on Amazon Kindle, with more NPC novels on the horizon. The *Lacy Moore* books are companion novels to her *Call of Cthulhu* rpg series and therefore both player handouts and a minor mythos tomes.

Jade Griffin lives in the high desert of northern Nevada with her family and an array of pets from several Phylum of Animalia.

You can find more of Jade Griffin's work, current projects, and appearances at:

http://jadegriffinauthor.com